IN SEARCH

of

WALKER WELLS

A Novel
By
Culpepper Webb

Culpepper Webb

**Copyright 2016 by Culpepper Webb, All Rights Reserved
Library of Congress 2016904379**

Preface

In Search of Walker Wells is the fourth rewrite of a book I began over fifteen years ago. Aside from a few scenes, the book has little resemblance to the original. Walker Wells is a man in search of himself and God, this search triggered by traumatic events in his life. It is my thought that humans confront themselves and their relationship with the Creator at times of tragedy or reflection; or in the case of Walker, both. My belief is that humans are the only creatures that possess the capacity for this pursuit. As we seek this relationship, or choose to ignore or deny it, it determines our life-path: our thoughts, our actions, as well as our inactions. Our response could even determine our life in the hereafter. It is my hope that this book will cause you to seek answers or to reaffirm them.

    I thank Ronda, my wife, for immeasurable patience in allowing me to write. John Floyd, Ralph Smith, and Robert Hitt Neill were quite helpful with this book. Finally, I thank each of you who read *Lifted from the Waters* and encouraged me to keep writing. You furnished rays of light in moments of darkness.

    The characters in the book are imaginary; many of the locations are not. Leland, Madison, and Natchez are cities in Mississippi. Monmouth Plantation and Tripod's grave are real. There is a memorial to two fallen policemen on the same lawn as Tripod's grave. I honor them by mentioning this fact here. When in Natchez take a carriage ride and enjoy it. I also hope you will enjoy your ride through the life of Walker Wells. Culpepper Webb

Culpepper Webb

March 5, 1962

Leland, Mississippi

    Shrill sounds of the voices of fourth, fifth, and sixth graders come from all directions. Camille Adams skips rope counting every jump. Charlie Capicci yells "touchdown" as his paper football stops on the line that separates the squares of concrete on the sidewalk. Henry David Nobles calls out, "I got you, and now you're it" as he tags someone I can't recognize from behind. All this happens as I wait my place in line to challenge Bobby Fortenberry, who towers six inches above me, in a game of tetherball. Bobby's in the sixth grade and I'm in the fourth, and he's gone undefeated, downing every opponent in short order ever since I got in line ten minutes ago. We're playing on the concrete area between the school buildings, the ground too wet for play. It's March, and it's been raining since the start of the year; just mud and puddles of water everywhere. Besides, Mr. Sandiford told us not to set foot on anything that wasn't concrete. "We'll have no mud in the halls," he said, and he's got a big wooden paddle.

    The bell better not ring before I get my shot at Bobby. It seems like I've been waiting in line forever, and I'm freezing 'cause I forgot to bring my jacket to school; second time this week. Good. Bobby just served, and the ball whirls well above Horace Thompson. It looks like that picture in our science book of a planet orbiting the sun, and Horace just watches the ball.

    "Hey Horace, where's the ball?" "Need a stepladder?" "Bet you wonder what the ball feels like. Sure would be nice to touch once, wouldn't it?" Everybody throws in their two cents and the ball circles the pole, the rope getting shorter and shorter until "game over." Horace never touched the ball.

"Walker, I'm gonna be nice and let you serve, partly 'cause you're just a measly little fourth- grader, but mainly 'cause my fist is gettin' sore. Might not be up to playing tomorrow," Bobby says.

Not going to say anything back to him. Might rub him the wrong way, and he's big enough to beat me up with one hand behind his back. I step up and place the white ball in my left hand and view it closely, small square indentions covering the ball, the word "Voit" on it. Man, this ball is full of air, hard as a rock. I bet Bobby's fist is getting sore. Now, how am I gonna do this? Unlike Horace I've at least got a chance. I get to hit the ball once.

"Hurry up, Walker!" "Hey, I want my shot too." "Not fair! The bell's gonna ring."

Gotta block those guys out and breathe deep. I grit my back teeth. I can feel my jaw jutting out. I'm holding the ball in my left hand, making my right fist tight as I can, raring my arm back, and now I'm going forward with all my might as I whack the ball. Hey it's circling high above Bobby, once, twice, a third time, his eyes circling with the ball. Those eyes look weird! Matter of fact, Bobby is weird. Although he's a sixth-grader, I think he's older than that.

"Good hit Walker!" "Yea!" "Look at it go!"

Uh oh…I don't think the ball's going to make it around a fourth time. Bobby's eyes have stopped circling and he's got an "I'm angry" look in them. He just tightened his fist and is raring back to hit the ball. I better back up. Look how far he moved his arm back, far as it can go. Now he's coming forward full force and he…he …missed the ball. He missed the ball!

"Wow!" "Look at that!" "What's he gonna do?"

I tighten my fist and hit it hard as I can. Wow, that ball is flying around the pole, Bobby's eyes circling fast as ever. Looks like they might spin out!

"Look at Walker go!" "Get him, Walker," I hear Larry Edson, then Henry David Nobles yell.

What now? He's gonna get one more chance, maybe. He's gone to the front on his side. What if I can tip the ball first, right over his outstretched arms? I'll give it a go. Hey, I did it! The rope is disappearing until it's all gone, the ball touching the pole, and now it's slowly unwinding.

"I won! I won!" I scream.

"Way to go, Walker!" "Walker's the new champ!" "It's my turn to take on Walker!"

They're all clapping and cheering. This has never happened to me before. Wait, Bobby's not saying a word. He's got that "angry look" on his face again. I'll just look away and not think about him right now. This is the best moment of my life; the very best.

"Walker. Walker Wells."

That's Mrs. Maston's voice. Where is it coming from?

"Walker, over here," she says as I see her from the corner of my eye and I turn to face her. She's signaling me with her hand.

"I've got to defend my title," I say.

"You need to come with me right now," she says with no smile on her face, which is not unusual. She doesn't smile much.

"But," I start to plead as she stops me before the next word.

"Walker, come with me right now."

I walk away from the tetherball pole towards Mrs. Maston who is looking at me through her wire-rim glasses, their arms lodged within her gray bun. She's staring at me.

"Have I done something wrong?" I ask, not knowing of anything I've done that might get me in trouble.

"No, but I do need you to come with me," she says with that serious look of hers as she turns and heads toward the back entrance of the school never doubting I will follow, as I do.

For some strange reason, and I don't know why, I look up into the sky. The day is neither sunny nor overcast. The sun is struggling to come through the gray, but it's not quite able to get there. I've seen this same sky, or at least one similar to it, many times. I am, after all, nine years old and in four days I'll be ten. That sounds grown up to me. I take one more look at the sky, as if I am trying to remember it, before entering the school building as Mrs. Maston holds open the door. The heavy metal door makes the loudest noise as it shuts behind us.

Except for Mrs. Maston and me the hall is empty. I hear the sound of my leather soles each time they hit the shiny tile floor. Mrs. Maston's shoes tap each time the point of one of her high heels hits tile. I smell the wax on the floor, its odor one of a kind. Mr. Zambroskie always keeps them waxed and can spot a speck of dust from the end of the hall. Hey, we're passing my classroom.

"Where are we going?" I ask. Mrs. Maston offers no reply. We turn right at the end of the hall, and I know we are headed to Mr. Sandiford's office, but I don't know why. I'm confused.

Mrs. Maston stops, allowing me to enter the room of Mr. Sandiford's secretary. She always sits like a guard in front of Mr. Sandiford's office.

"He's here," the lady says.

Mr. Sandiford walks out to see me, and he, unlike the secretary and Mrs. Maston has a kind look on his face, not what I expected. I've never been to his office before, and from what I've heard, that is a good thing.

"Come on in, Walker," he says, signaling me to go first as he closes the door behind us. "Have a seat," he says next, motioning with his hand to one of the two chairs in front of his desk as he rounds it to seat himself in a big leather chair on the other side. My heart is pounding, my stomach filled with air, just as it did when I jumped off the high diving board. Why am I here?

Culpepper Webb

The chair is higher than my desk in the classroom, my feet not quite reaching the floor. I take a look around searching for the wooden paddle. It is not to be found, and I am glad. All I see is a pot with a plant in it by the window, a couple of framed pieces of paper on the wall, and a fancy pen holder with a pen in it amongst papers on his desk. Mr. Sandiford is leaning back in his big chair, his elbows resting on the arms of it, his hands cupped just below his chin. He releases his hands and leans forward, now sitting upright and looking at me. He's a big man who used to play college football, and this is as close to him as I've ever been. I've always been afraid of him, but I am not right now.

"Walker, your mother ought to be along any minute now," he says, pausing for a moment before asking, "what do you enjoy doing?"

I guess he expects me to say studying, but that wouldn't be the truth because I really don't. "Tetherball, I like playing it this time of year. I like football and baseball, and I like going fishin'. Daddy takes me fishin' for crappie every year at this time, right around my birthday. I turn ten in four days and he's gonna take me Saturday. Last year I caught a three pounder and everybody was looking at it when…"

There's a tap on the door before it opens, the secretary from behind me saying, "Mrs. Wells is here."

"Bring her in," Mr. Sandiford says as he stands to greet Mom. "Come on in, Ida." He rounds the desk and slides the other chair back to seat Mom, just like Daddy does for her when we go out to eat.

Mom's got a Kleenex in her hand. She's been crying. "Thank you," she says to Mr. Sandiford as he circles the desk to sit in his chair. For a moment everybody is quiet before Mom turns toward me and extends her hand to hold mine. Her hand is shaking but it steadies once it reaches mine. She holds my hand tight and is looking straight at me. Tears pour down both cheeks, and she's trying to put on a smile. In a flash I think of rain coming down while the sun is shining. She tightens her hold on my hand and says, "Your daddy had a heart attack at his office this morning," pausing for a moment, then saying, "it was quite sudden, unexpected," before she pauses again, tightening her grip on my hand until it almost hurts. The room's all quiet again, Mom just squeezing my hand, the tears getting bigger and pouring faster right down her cheeks and dropping from her chin as I wait for what comes next. Mom is not one to cry. "They rushed him to the hospital and the doctor was there waiting on him. But…Walker, your father died."

    What is Mom saying? She releases her hand from mine and begins to wipe the tears with the Kleenex.

    "Do you need some more tissue, Ida?" Mr. Sandiford asks.

    Mom nods her reply, and Mr. Sandiford reaches in a desk drawer and hands Mom a package of Kleenex. She removes a couple and wipes her eyes and cheeks with them. For a moment I look away from Mom at Mr. Sandiford who is looking at me. His look is kind.

    I don't understand. I just can't figure this all out. Daddy and I won't be going fishin' Saturday. No wait… Daddy and I won't be going fishin' *ever*. Now I understand; but I don't understand. All I know right now is that I have a deep pain down inside me and it hurts.

Culpepper Webb

***

The long, black Cadillac makes the turn off the paved road to the gravel one that is lined both sides with leafless trees that must have been here forever. They are huge. I'm in the back seat of the biggest car I've ever seen, and I can hear the crunch of the tires on the gravel as we ride. Mom sits next to me, staring out the window. She's done a lot of staring for the past two days, ever since Daddy died.

The car slows, then stops. A man in a black suit with a white shirt and a thin black tie opens my door and another opens Mom's. She rounds the car and meets me placing her hand out for me to hold as we walk toward the green tent with chairs under it. We've held hands more the past two days than we have in my whole life. Oh it's cold! I'm cold even with my jacket on over my suit. The wind whistles and howls. People nod as we walk. The church was packed. Daddy ran the factory that makes upholstery for chairs and couches. He didn't own it; he just ran it. It shut down for part of the day so some of the workers could come to the funeral. The Negroes weren't there. From what I can tell the folks at the factory respected Daddy, as did a lot of folks around town, so much so there were people standing at the church.

"We're to sit here," Mom motions to two specially marked folding chairs in the front row. My mind is drifting. I don't even remember the walk from the car. I've done this a lot the past two days, my thoughts mainly of Daddy, things we did like going fishin' last year, or him sitting in his chair reading the newspaper with the television going. He'll never sit in that chair again, and he'll never see me catch another fish like that big crappie I caught last year. In a little while they'll put Daddy in that hole in the ground just beyond the tent, and I'll never see him again; and it will be up to me to remember him in that chair or the smile on his face when I pulled that big crappie out of the water. I hope I don't ever get too old to remember the look on his face when that fish came out of the water. He was proud of me. I was always proud of him. I try to listen to Reverend Dixon who's already started talking. I don't remember a word he said back at the church. My mind was on Daddy and Mom.

"So we look with assured hope beyond these surroundings and our current circumstances, which on a day such as today can be so bleak..."

What does bleak mean? Another word I don't understand like the ones he used back at the church. That's when my mind started wandering. People brought more food yesterday than I've ever seen in my life: cakes, pies, casseroles, fried chicken and more fried chicken. I ate drumsticks 'cause that's the piece I like. Somebody brought a whole wooden case of Cokes in the little bottles, the way I like them. And just like the drumsticks I didn't count how many I drank. But that's OK 'cause there's still a bunch of them left. The drumsticks and the Cokes took my mind off Daddy. Ouch! I feel a pain in my chest when I think about him.

"Oh death where is thy sting..."

Sting? Last summer I got stung by three wasps that built a nest in the screen door by the back steps. Built that nest right up near the top of the door where the screen enters the wood, and they got me when I opened it. Daddy knocked that nest down with a broom handle and lit it with a match while Mom went and got baking soda to rub on the stings on my hand and arm. It didn't take the pain away. The wasp made me hurt on my hand and arm, and Daddy's dying makes me hurt in my chest.

"Our hope is based..."

Look at Mom, right next to me, her eyes wet with tears, not pouring down her cheeks like the other day, just moist. She's listening to Reverend Dixon, I think, although her eyes look like they're looking at something in the far distance and she's thinking about what she's seeing. She's done a bunch of staring in the distance the last two days every time things get quiet. She must have been doing a lot of thinking. So have I.

Culpepper Webb

I've had plenty of time doing nothing since I didn't go to school yesterday or today. I'll go back tomorrow Mom says.

"As we look out beyond leafless trees to the empty fields cast against gray sky, the cold wind blowing hard against us, the *bleakness* of this present moment could lead us to despondency. Yet, through faith and hope..."

Reverend Dixon is again using words I don't understand. Ouch, Mom is nudging me with her elbow to get me to close my eyes. We're fixing to pray so I better shut my 'em tight. But first I can't help but look at her, her eyes closed now, and it looks like she's thinking real hard beneath that black hat she's wearing. Her skin is white, real white, and the bottom of her ears point just below the gold earrings that cover her ears just above the points, her dark-brown hair covering the tops of her ears. Although I can't see her eyes, I know they are brown. I need to remember what she looks like, her eyes, ears, face, and all. I hope I get to see Daddy one more time so I can do the same.

"And we ask that You grant comfort and strength to Ida and young Walker, the comfort and strength that You alone provide. We ask these things in Jesus name. Amen."

People stir, and are beginning to talk. But Mom continues to sit just looking at the casket, so I keep my seat. I look through the trees to the open field. A lone dead cotton stalk bends with the wind.

"Ida, we'll be thinking of you and Walker," says Mrs. Hemphill, as Mom and I continue to sit. Mrs. Hemphill is old, nothing but gray hair on her head and wrinkles on her face. She looks real serious.

"Thank you," Mom says, her brown eyes set straight on at Mrs. Hemphill.

Mom can be strong when she needs to be. Now that it's just the two of us I need to be strong too. The crowd is gone now. A man in a black suit walks up.

"Mrs. Wells, you had asked for one more look. I think about everybody's gone so..."

"Yes, I'd appreciate that," Mom says as she stands, motioning me to rise with her as I do, the two of us following the man to the casket where another man in a black suit stands. They lift the top and move to the side as Mom and I walk to the front of the casket and I look down. I need to remember Daddy, set him straight in my mind and hold on to it. I look at him just as hard as I did Mom during the prayer, and maybe harder. He's wearing that dark gray suit with pinstripes, his favorite one that he liked to wear to church this time of year. Looks like they trimmed his hair, every one of them in place. His hair is brown, lighter than Mom's, and I see one, two, three gray ones in with the brown. He just turned forty. There're a couple of creases in his skin. He looks a little older than I remember him. He has a smile on his face. Not like the one when I caught the crappie, just a small one; a pleasant one. I close my eyes and concentrate so I can remember.

Sunday, March 4, 2012

Leland, Mississippi

"We're here," I say as I open the back door to Mom's home. I let Laura enter first as I start to lay the chicken casserole on the kitchen counter before noticing the oven set at low temp. I slide it in the oven.

"I've been home from church for twenty minutes. Thought you'd be waiting for me," Mom says.

"The casserole took longer than I thought," Laura says, covering for my tardiness.

"Come give me a hug," Mom says to me as I cross the den to where she sits in her easy chair which angles for her to view the backyard through a huge window. Her hug is tighter than usual. She doesn't want to let go.

"Go pour us some iced tea; it's on the kitchen counter. Then come back and sit down so we can visit."

Mom drinks iced tea every day, even if it snows. "Thought you might be hungry," I say before Mom cuts me off.

"Don't pull this eat and run routine on me. I haven't seen you and Laura since Christmas."

I lay the iced tea glasses on napkins on the table between Mom's easy chair and mine. She wants a napkin under her glass even if it's on asphalt. I take a seat.

"So how was church?" Laura says.

"We spent about eight minutes on the Sunday school lesson and the rest of time talking about the goings-on about town. None of us gets out that much anymore, so we mainly visit. The preacher talked about Noah. I've heard that story before."

Mom doesn't want small talk. "How'd you sleep last night?" I ask my question earnestly.

"Not well. I've been awake since three. Harold's death has been on my mind for this entire past week. Last night I woke up dreaming about it. Although he died on the fifth, I think you coming today advanced things."

Mom slept longer than I did. I didn't dream about it. I woke up reliving it right down to watching a tetherball go around a pole. Later my feet were not touching the floor in that chair in Mr. Sandiford's office. I went out about four and ran five miles in a cold mist. I tried to "run it off." It didn't work. Mom's looking out the window. I think she might spend more time looking out that window than watching television. My, it is drab out this time of year, the grass dead-brown, the trees without leaves. Her eyes are on the sparrows in the bird feeder, their beaks pecking on the seeds. "Mom…Mom."

"Yes."

"I was thinking earlier this morning about that witch, Mrs. Maston, escorting me to Mr. Sandiford's office."

"Walker, don't speak that way about the deceased. I didn't bring you up that way."

"You noticed that I spoke no ill of Mr. Sandiford. Until that day I pictured him as a man who slept with a paddle. When I was in the first grade the second graders told us that he had an electric paddle with nails in it. I was too scared to misbehave. After Daddy died I viewed him in a different light. He was always kind to me. I shared an experience with him I will never forget, and I regret that I didn't attend his funeral. As for Mrs. Maston."

"Walker, don't get started…"

"I can't help it, Mom. To this day the knuckles of my right hand still hurt from the strikes of her ruler. She didn't ever cut me slack after Daddy died. It's a miracle I can still type and write."

"She was in poor health."

"Couldn't have been that poor. She died last year and she was closer to a hundred than ninety. I *don't* regret missing her funeral. My knuckles are hurting right now just thinking about her."

"Walker!"

"Yes, Mom."

"I don't know how in the world we began talking about Mrs. Maston, but let's move on. What kind of flowers did you bring for your father's grave?"

"Daffodils; I picked them this morning. We've got a backyard full of them and it's the most cheerful flower I know of."

"They warm things on a cold day," Laura says.

She told me on the drive up she would try to stay in the background as much as possible today. I can tell she is trying to stay quiet. That's not easy.

Mom's expression is wistful. "I'm not going to tell you anything you probably don't already know, but I feel like talking."

I'll stay quiet.

"So much has gone through my mind this past week: childhood, marriage, rearing you, my years alone, straight on to age eighty-five. In between each memory I kept coming back to thoughts of the day Harold died and the months there following. I felt so alone at night. I would wake up in bed and reach for Harold and there was not even an indention on his pillow. Nothing. I can't explain it. Unless you've lived it, you just don't know. Although we were only married thirteen years those years have impacted every day since. Our marriage gave me you. There's not a day that goes by that I don't think about you, Walker. I carried you nine months; spent eight years with just the two of us in this house after Harold died. You are my one and only, my son forever. If someday I lose my sense of the present, I'll be thinking of you."

And I haven't been to see Mom for over two months, only two hours away. Busy, busy, busy. No; guilty, guilty, guilty. "I need to come see you more often. I've let time slip. Laura and I are heading to Natchez for my sixtieth Friday. Maybe Saturday week."

"Maybe?"

She's giving me that look. "We'll go eat lunch," I say without consulting Laura. From across the room I catch Laura's nodding approval. Mom's smiling a deep smile.

"Never got close to remarrying," Mom says, the smile vacating her face.

She's told me this more than once, much more. But she wants to tell me again. It's on her mind.

"Never even dated. Didn't want men around when I was rearing you, at least the ones who were available in this small town. By the time you were grown I was well into my forties, and by that stage those who had tossed wife-one under the bus were looking closer to the cradle. You also have to remember that back then people didn't move around as much in marriage as today. Besides, I learned that the good Lord and I could get along quite well without assistance. All things being said, your father, Harold, was the love of my life, and I think it best that it has stayed that way. Thoughts of him still bring a smile to my face."

She's got that deep smile again.

"Walker."

"Yes Mom."

"I'm gonna see him again someday. I believe that with all of my heart, mind, and soul. Don't know what he and I will look like, but it will happen. We will both be in the presence of God."

I can't say the same. When I die, I believe I'll be dead; and that's all there is. There's certainly no point in getting into a discussion with Mom about this today. My lack of Christian belief disturbs her to no end, as it does Laura. Their concerns for me are without measure. I'm not an atheist, I'm truly not. I believe in a creator, an uninvolved one who built the universe and has been sitting on the sideline since. I've been entrenched in that belief or disbelief, whatever one might call it, for almost four decades. I ...

"Walker. Walker Wells."

"Yes."

"You get that distant look when you get something on your mind. You can't fool your mama. Anything you want to talk about?"

"Not really."

"Aren't y'all hungry? It's almost one o'clock. Why don't I get the casserole," Laura says.

"That's fine with me," says Mom. "We've done some of our best visiting ever in the dining room."

***

I make a left turn into the cemetery. It's an oasis of oak trees in the middle of a vacant field about a mile from town. Everything around this town is close, convenient one might say. These oaks are massive. As I recall, they were tall fifty years ago. But then again everything seems large at that age. I edge to the side of the gravel path halfway down and park the Explorer. Daddy's grave is out a ways to the left. No one has said a word for over a mile.

"I'll get the door for you," I say to Mom who is seated next to me.

She nods.

Mom has slowed. Her mind is quick as ever, but not her body. I steady her as we walk, the ground mush, but no water standing. Laura walks behind, the arrangement of daffodils in her hand. We come to the grave.

"Did you know I come out here every couple of weeks?" Mom says.

"You need to be careful. You might trip and fall."

"I usually bring somebody with me. Most of my friends, and that number is thinning, don't play bridge *every* day. Their husbands are here too. Although our numbers are shrinking, there are a lot more little old ladies than there are little old men."

She's right.

"Laura, let me see that arrangement. Oh my, those daffodils are bright. March is the bleakest month of the year in the Mississippi Delta. I bet the sun won't shine five days before I turn the calendar to April."

"I'll place them right here," Laura says to Mom as she starts to place the flowers on the ground a foot or so in front of the gravestone. The arrangement is quite tasteful. She put the stems in whatever that stuff is that keeps the flowers in place inside the vase.

"Laura, if you don't mind, lean the flowers against the gravestone," Mom says just before Laura lays the arrangement on the ground. "The wind always blows from the west, and they won't blow over."

"Happy to," Laura says as she lays them center of the gravestone, covering the dates of Daddy's birth and death, *Harold Jasper Wells* clearly visible on the granite above them. The gravestone has not weathered.

"Don't think I've ever seen more perfect flowers, Laura," says Mom, her smile as radiant as the daffodils.

"Thank you."

I stare at the grass-covered ground to the front of the gravestone. Beneath that grass is where I took one last look at Daddy dressed in his gray pinstripe suit. In my mind I see him with creased skin, brown hair, a faint smile on his face. I promised myself I would never forget and I have not. At this moment it doesn't seem long ago. We are quiet. The wind is not; it's whistling and howling. A naked oak limb above creaks. The sky is gray. I shiver from the cold. I shiver inside. Someday I will have grass over me.

***

That hum of tires beneath is steady; just a barrump every so often made by a crack in the concrete. I'm glad the radio is off. I don't feel like music or yak right now. Whoa, that gust of wind! They come unexpectedly. There, I've aimed the Explorer straight ahead again. There is little traffic coming or going. I took this road for the quiet, even though it will take us ten minutes longer than the route we came up on. We are seven miles south of Leland on Highway 61. It's a two-lane that goes from New Orleans to Canada that's associated with the blues. I'm feeling a touch of those; I just want to stay quiet and listen to the hum of tires, but I feel like I need to say something to Laura.

"Thank you for staying in the background today," I say.

"The focus was you and Ida. Do you know how hard it was to stay quiet? I always want to be in the thick of the conversation. *Always.*"

"Yeah, I know," I say. I instantly smile. "I'm surprised you haven't been talking the whole way since we left."

"I've been thinking about your mom. I've been thinking about us. Ida's adult life was so different than ours; thirteen years of marriage and we've had almost thirty-five. I'm not sure I would have handled the widow-life with the commitment she did."

"What? You would have been dating the next week? You would have written a prospect list at the funeral home?"

"Walker, be serious. Sometimes your sense of humor is ill timed."

She's right.

"It's just that I would have been lonely; and incomplete."

I take my eyes off the road and look at Laura. Her green eyes are set within white skin, no hint of tan this time of year. Her skin is youthful for her age of fifty-nine; no fifty-eight. Her birthday's not for two months. Unlike me she could pass for a decade less than her real age. Her shoulder length blonde hair with a few strands of gray covers her ear.

"Keep your eyes on the road!"

"Can't resist looking at you," I say. I'm smiling again. It feels good.

"Usually you have sex on your mind when you say something like that."

Usually I do. This time I did not. I was just looking. However, she has planted a seed. Maybe I'll bring it up later. "I don't look at you often enough."

"That's because neither of us has slowed down this year. Even when I'm not working my mind is. This high school counseling is about to wear me thin. It's not just the kids who have changed; it's the parents. Half of them are stuck in adolescence. I don't know, maybe it's also my age. I'm not sure how much longer I can handle it."

Laura's brought this up before, more conversation than intention. But, again she has seemed worn down lately. Maybe I need to listen to what she's saying. And me? My entire adult life has been spent selling life insurance and investments, helping people plan their futures. It's been rewarding for the families I work with; and for me. I've been working with some families for over three and a half decades. These days I'm more a counselor than a salesman, people coming to me seeking advice for everything under the sun. I like what I do; *most* of the time. But, I haven't taken off a day since New Year's. Something's wrong with that picture. Natchez, Natchez, Natchez, I can't wait to get there Friday for my sixtieth. I want to be free as a bird that day. What I'm I doing? My mind is drifting. I've done that a lot lately. Laura needs a response.

"Let's see how this school year plays out. You don't have to sign a contract for another three months."

"Are you saying that to put me off?"

"In the past 'yes,' but not today."

"You really mean it?"

"I really mean it."

She smiled.

"Look what I brought," Laura says as she grabs her purse from the floorboard and pulls out the brochure for Monmouth Plantation in Natchez, a premiere bed and breakfast that people from all over the world come to. "Look at those azaleas!" Laura says as she opens the brochure. "They supposedly cover the grounds. I can't wait to get there."

She's beaming. I think she may be more excited about our excursion I am. No, that can't be. I've *got* to get away. My, those azaleas are something, purple on one page and pink on the next, the pink ones behind a concrete bench. I hope they are in full bloom. With the exception of the daffodils, everything is drab. But Natchez is a couple of hours to the south from our home, so maybe, just maybe.

"Walker, look at this."

Let's see if I can take another peek without running off the road. It's a photo of a massive dining room table; mahogany, dark-cherry? There are one, two, three…twelve chairs around it. What am I doing? Driving down a highway and counting the number of chairs in a photograph. Not real bright. "So that's the table we'll be dining at Friday night."

"It's perhaps the most elegant dining experience in the state. Somebody canceled so we got a slot. There will be five other couples."

"In other words we'll be seated with ten strangers. I don't…"

"Walker, don't try to weasel out of this one. It was your idea. You waited a bit late to make a reservation. Friday is the opening day of Spring Pilgrimage. Residents open up their homes in addition to the mansions that are open for tours year-round. That's why we only have one night. We couldn't even find a room for Saturday at a Motel 3. Next thing you'll want to do is wear blue jeans and jogging shoes to dinner."

I wear the suit-uniform five days a week. Laura's got me in a tux. I can't stand wearing those. And it's *my* sixtieth.

Culpepper Webb

"How about a blue blazer instead? I've got that Ralph Lauren…"

"Walker Wells, you're the one who picked this place. I bet you haven't even got your tux out from that upstairs closet. For all we know a family of moths is fat and happy from having dined on it. Besides, does it fit?"

"Of course it fits. I'll run over a thousand miles this year and…"

"Sweetheart, for a man of your age you're fit and trim; but you are not forty. I think that's when you bought it."

A man of my age?

"I'm picking up my little black cocktail dress at the cleaners tomorrow and I can drop the tux off, *if* it fits. Tonight you are trying on everything including the cufflinks. If it's not *just right*, it's time for a new one."

Settled.

"Maybe that's the room we are staying in."

Laura's flipped the page of the brochure and the conversation. That four-poster bed is huge. "Will you be sleeping in the same county as me?"

"What?"

"Look at the size of that bed. There's room enough to play hide and seek. Heh, listen…"

"I know that look of yours and I know where you are angling this conversation. This girl has already put forth today. Staying quiet this morning required more effort than any romp in bed we've ever had. If I'm in a good mood after you've tried on the tux, then tonight, *maybe*. Besides, in marriage there's always *tomorrow*."

Yeah, and *tomorrow* there's always *tomorrow*.

September 8, 1964

Leland, Mississippi

Ring…Ring…
"Take your seats. Take your seats. Take your…That's better," says Coach Petty.

I'm excited and nervous. This is my first day in the seventh grade, my first group of all males, just the guys, homeroom under Coach Petty. We're to meet briefly, then go to the next class where it will be guys and girls together. This is so different than my first six years of school where we had the same teacher for the full day. The teachers were *women*, every last one of them. I'll see Coach Petty three times today. I'm in homeroom now, and I'll have him again for science class this afternoon, followed by football after school. Since Daddy died it seems like I've been missing something. Although Coach Petty and my math teacher, Mr. Bowman, are no replacements for Daddy, I think I'm gonna like having some men teaching me. Coach Petty looks like he played football. He's muscular with his arms bulging from his short-sleeve white cotton shirt, his neck an inch too big for his button-down collar that has a one-inch wide black tie extending from it. He has dark-rim plastic glasses and a crew cut. I comb my hair to the side. Everybody's been doing that since the *Beatles* got to be big.

"As most of you know I'm Coach Petty. Welcome to junior high school. We will begin each day with the pledge of allegiance followed by roll call. Let's stand for the pledge," he says as he turns to the side to face the flag that extends from a spot next to the chalkboard. "I pledge allegiance to the flag…"

Bobby Fortenberry sways back and forth like a tree limb blowin' in the breeze. His tongue is sticking out. His thumbs are in his ears, with his fingers going back and forth. He's got it figured out where he's just out of Coach Petty's view; but I can see him out of the corner of my eye just like most of the class can. This is my first class with Bobby. He's moved up one grade in the past three years. At his rate he can join the Army before he reaches high school. He's never liked me since I shamed him in tetherball the day Daddy died. He scares me. The pledge is over. I take my seat like everybody else.

    Coach Petty has gone quiet, and he reached in his desk drawer and pulled out a paddle that looks like a board big enough to hold up a wall. He's not smiling. "Bobby, this year you didn't even make it to roll call."

    Coach Petty must have mirrors in his glasses. How else could he have spotted Bobby's acting up?

    "Let's step out into the hall so you can have a meeting with 'Ole Hickory'."

    Bobby's desk scrapes on the tile as he gets up and heads toward door. The smile on Bobby's face is like the one of that guy on the front of *Mad Magazine*. He has a little less swagger than during the pledge, but more than Coach Petty, who is following Bobby. The door closes.

    Whack. Whack. Whack!

    Ouch! I can feel those licks. I hear the paddle hitting Bobby's bottom right through the walls. Wonder if the doors to the other rooms on the hall are open? Bobby reenters the room, not an ounce of swagger in his body, no hint of a smile. Coach Petty follows, no smile on his face either, like this was not something he took pleasure in. Why in the world would Bobby have tried to pull a shenanigan like this on the first day of school; or for that point ever? It seems it was a regular event last year. From the sound of it, one of those licks would cure me for a lifetime.

    "Sorry for the interruption. We'll have to speed this up a bit to get it all done," Coach Petty says as he retrieves a spiral notebook from atop his desk, looking up for a moment and scanning the room through the dark-rim glasses. "Simply answer 'here,' nothing cute when I call your name. Abels, Benchley, Curtis…Wells."

"Here," I say, the last person to speak; as always. Usually I'm back of the class and last in line. *Wells*.

"You'll notice one of these pocket-sized student handbooks on each of your desks," Coach Petty says as he replaces the roll book with the handbook. He waits for us to grab our handbook. "Each of you gets a copy of the handbook to take home, read, and give to your parents. We adhere strictly to these rules, and you are to abide by them. Is that understood?" he asks, receiving only silence in return. "Is that understood?"

"Yes sir," I say in response, going along with the rest of the class.

"Open the handbook to page nine," Coach Petty says as he places his thumb in a spot in the handbook, and looks up peering through the dark-rims as he waits for us to reach page nine. "This book deals with just about every question that has ever been thought of regarding school policies. Page nine deals with the dress code."

"Why are we reading this? None of us wear dresses," says Henry David Nobles, his grin almost touching both ears, laughter coming from all directions, though not from me. Following on the heels of Bobby's experience, I'd do just about anything to stay away from Ole Hickory. Henry David's been blurting out like this since the first grade. He just comes out of nowhere with stuff, not a thought given to the end result. He must know how to laugh right, 'cause he seems to get away with it, always two inches away from the paddle.

"Class elections aren't until next week. Are you already running for class clown, Mr. Nobles?" says Coach Petty waiting for the laughter to die before going on. "As I mentioned, we're short on time. The handbook states that all males will wear long pants. The length of hair in the front must be at least one and a half inches above the eyebrows and on the side cover no parts of an ear. All females must wear dresses, the minimum length one inch below the knees. Oops, I read a bit too far. I must still be thinking of Mr. Nobles," says Coach Petty, cracking his first smile since we entered the room.

"Now, on to page ten. There will be no possession of alcoholic beverages on school property. Smoking or chewing of tobacco on school property is prohibited. Let me clarify," says Coach Petty. "Possession of tobacco is not a violation of school policy. If one decides to smoke before school or during lunch break there is a vacant lot across the street, although I recommend that you don't. Recent studies show that it causes cancer."

Seventh grade sure is different than elementary school. I feel more grown up just being here.

Ring...Ring...

***

I walk out to the hall. *First Period, Deborah Mabry, English, Room 106* says the slip of paper in my hand. It's different than last year, having to switch classrooms. I follow Henry David into the classroom and make my way to the back.

"Sit anywhere you wish," Mrs. Mabry says.

Wow! That must be Mrs. Mabry: pale white skin, dark black hair, red lips, and the straightest white teeth I've ever seen, pretty as they come; and young too.

"Sit anywhere you wish," she says again as I dart to a desk in the middle of the room, right next to Henry David.

Ring…Ring…

"Take your seats, class. Take your seats. May I have your attention. Class. Class," says Mrs. Mabry amidst the noise. The talk is finally dying, people are settling at their desks. "This is your first day in seventh-grade English, and my first official day to teach. I practice taught last spring, but that's different, isn't it?"

I see a few nods and bobs, but everybody's keeping quiet for the moment. She sure seems nervous and uncertain.

"I'd like each of you to tell me your name, and I'll check roll as we go," says Mrs. Mabry who is beaming, her bright-white teeth sparkling along with her face. "Well let's get started," Mrs. Mabry says, nodding at Camille in the front row, who immediately says, "How neat, I'm Camille Adams!" This followed by Susan, just to her left, "I'm Susan Baker."

Mrs. Mabry turns her beam up a notch, as though she's having the happiest moment of her life. And for the first time in their lives these two girls, both with off-pink pointed glasses, have the opportunity *not* to sit in the front of the class, but still choose to. The Bobsey Twins; perfect for an English class.

"Get me a pail, 'cause I think I'm gonna throw up," mumbles Henry David from just to my left.

"I think we need two pails," I come back as roll call continues.

"Henry David Nobles."

"Oooh, I just love your name!" says Mrs. Mabry, her joy going to a whole new level, as though she used to be cheerleader and wants to be again.

"I kinda like it too. I was named for my grandfather," says Henry David.

"What I mean is, one of America's best known writers is Henry David Thoreau," says Mrs. Mabry. "You'll read his works in high school."

"Never heard of him," says Henry David, shrugging both shoulders as Mrs. Mabry goes from bright to low beam.

"Walker Wells," I say, Mrs. Mabry offering no comment.

"Larry Edson, ma'am," says Larry from my right. I like Larry; and I admire him. He's not the smartest in the class. Matter of fact he repeated the second grade. But he's not like anybody else who's repeated a grade. He's courteous and kind. Larry's as big as any person in the class, and he's the best athlete. He's more a protector than a bully. And like me, he doesn't have a father; at least one that is around. I heard that his father ran off when he was little.

"We need to move on. When I call your name, please come forward and I will issue your textbook," says Mrs. Mabry. "Camille, you may come forward."

"Oh, neat!"

Bobby Fortenberry stands in front of Mrs. Mabry's desk, shifting from one foot to the other anxious as a horse before the race. "Bobby, this is the same book you had last year," says Mrs. Mabry as she stops writing and looks up at Bobby.

"Yessum," says Bobby.

"That's yes ma'am," responds Mrs. Mabry, her smile replaced with a frown. "This book appears unused," she says as she resumes writing his name in the book with Bobby offering no comment. Mrs. Mabry hands him the book as she attempts to smile and fails. Bobby walks to his seat, his pre-paddling swagger having returned.

"Walker Wells. Walker Wells. Walker!" says Mrs. Mabry, awakening me from my thoughts. "Come get your English book," she says, as I walk forward and stop in front of her desk. As I look down I notice the small gold band on her left hand as she writes with perfect scripted penmanship with her right, the letters forming beautifully as each letter hits the page, my name appearing in the book above Charlie Capicci's. Above Charlie Capicci's! So Charlie took this course last year and probably flunked it. I stare at Charlie who sits at the back of the room on the way back to my desk, as he glares back at me. Best not mess with him.

Mrs. Mabry begins to speak to all of us. "This year is going to be so much fun. We'll begin the year studying the basics, followed by the study of literature," she says, stopping midstream as Henry David's arm shoots up, his hand waving in the air. "Yes, Henry David."

"Why are we studying English?"

"What?" says Mrs. Mabry, in shock, before breathing deeply and calmly saying, "I meant to say is, what do you mean?"

"What I mean is, why are we studying English when we could be studying French or Spanish? I bet you that everybody in this room can speak English, and nobody, I repeat *nobody* can speak French or Spanish. Doesn't make sense to me, and I bet most will agree," Henry David says as heads, mine included, slowly begin to nod in agreement. "Aren't we old enough to learn something new?"

Mrs. Mabry's mouth is so wide open that I think I see her tonsils.

"Henry David, at this point the understanding of many of you for our majestic language is elementary."

Elementary is not a good word to use for seventh-graders.

"Many of you have only scratched the surface of your understanding and appreciation of our fine language," Mrs. Mabry continues. "There is such rich enjoyment ahead, and I think you will better understand the purpose of the class when we begin to study authors such as Charles Dickens."

"Charlie Dickings? Where's he from?" says Henry David.

I see Mrs. Mabry's tonsils again.

"He's from England," she says. "Please open your books to page one to begin reviewing parts of speech," she continues, pausing again to say, "Bobby and Charlie, if you have something to say, say it to the whole class. Do either of you have something to say?" her questions directed to Bobby Fortenberry and Charlie Capicci.

"No'm," says Bobby.

"That's 'no ma'am', young man," counters Mrs. Mabry immediately. "Do you understand me?"

"Yes ma'am," says Bobby following a long pause. Mrs. Mabry, whose face is now stern, stares at Bobby a good long time before going to the chalkboard to begin writing sentences.

I wonder which way Henry David's wheels are turning now, I think as I look at him. His focus appears to be some where in space. As for me I'm anticipating football practice after school, my first day of real football. Oh, I've played tons of football in the back yard and on the playground, but never with pads and a helmet. What will it be like to go up against Larry Edson, who sits next to me, or Charlie Capicci, in the back of the class, both of them older and bigger than me?

"Bobby Fortenberry, what do you have to say to the whole class?" says Mrs. Mabry, awakening me from my thoughts. My goodness, there are words all over the board. How long have I been daydreaming?

"It was just a few minutes ago that I told you that if you had something to say that you need to say it to the whole class. How good is your memory?"

"I was conceived in the living room," says Bobby, his smile again like that of the guy on the cover of *Mad Magazine*. Mrs. Mabry's face turned from pale-white to beet-red. A vein bulges from her neck. Boy is she steamed; and I don't have a clue what Bobby just said. I don't understand it, but evidently Mrs. Mabry does.

"Go straight to the principal's office," shouts Mrs. Mabry, her teapot releasing steam at full-force. "Tell him I will be there as soon as class is over."

Bobby slowly rises from his desk, the legs of the desk scraping on the tile floor and he ambles out the door, which thuds as it closes behind him.

Mrs. Mabry is breathing deeply, as though she has just run a sprint. She is quiet, searching for something to say. Her face holds a frown, wrinkles forming against her smooth skin. I feel sorry for her.

Culpepper Webb

***

Photosynthesis
Chlorophyll
Carbon Dioxide

 Boy, Coach Petty goes to work on that chalkboard, almost as fast as Mrs. Mabry, but nothing like Mr. Perkins, the math teacher. Male teachers are not all the same. Mr. Perkins is as thin as they come, and he wears the thickest glasses and a plaid shirt. He wrote his first and last name on the board at the same time, a piece of chalk in each hand. And when he added or multiplied he wrote on each side of the equal sign at the same time. Wow!

 Coach Petty draws a picture of the sun on the chalkboard, which he keeps calling the 'blackboard' even though it is green. Why? Anyway, his sun looks more like a glowing egg than the sun and its rays are aimed at a three-leaf plant he drew a moment ago.

 "Sunlight is essential for plant growth. It aids the plants with radiant energy, and without light photosynthesis could not take place; the plant would wither and die. The leaves contain chlorophyll, a green photosynthetic substance," Coach Petty says. These are the biggest words I've ever heard. Henry David talked about studying French or Spanish, and as far as I can tell the language Coach Petty is using is as foreign as either of these. This is so much harder than elementary school. He would have lost me completely if it was not for the fact that I'm so interested in the outside world. I can gaze up at the sky forever: clouds, stars, the moon, and the sun, constantly wondering how they were created and what keeps them going. No matter how much I study them, I'm not sure I'll ever fully understand everything. *Ever.* It's as if it is a mystery; at least to me. Every week at church Reverend Dixon preaches as though he has all the answers. I'm not convinced that he does.

 "You see, plants make sugar and starches by taking in carbon dioxide, combining it with water that they have obtained from their root system and leaves. During this process called photosynthesis, oxygen is emitted from the leaves. Class, what do we use oxygen for?"

Camille Adams' hand shoots into the air at the same time as Susan Baker's, both arms rising with the motion of a back stroke, each timed perfectly with the other. They remind me of members of a synchronized swimming team. I know the answer to that question. Henry David, Bobby, and Charlie probably know the answer to that one; haven't heard a peep out of any of them. Coach Petty has things under control.

"Breathing," they say in unison.

What the heck. I'll probably never be a scientist anyway; but I still want to make a good impression on Coach Petty. After all, he is my football coach. What's he drawing now, a worm? Yes, it's a worm, and that little critter is working its way between the roots of the plant loosening the soil, permitting water to reach the roots of the plant, as well as enriching the soil; or so Coach Petty says. Good thing we didn't cover this before I ate green beans for lunch today. Green beans and worms don't seem to go well together.

"Ooh, yuck gross. Ooh, yuck gross. It's a worm!" comes in unison from Camille and Susan on the front row.

Good grief, it's just the drawing of a worm on the chalkboard! Where does their thinking come from? The only thing I'm thinking at this moment is that it must be a hundred degrees in this room in the afternoon heat. Wonder what it's gonna be like with shoulder pads and a helmet on in a few minutes?

Ring…Ring…

Culpepper Webb

***

I sit on a bench surrounded by seventh and eighth graders in a football locker room, a place I've been waiting to enter for as long as I can remember. The school lumps seventh and eighth graders together, but keeps us separate from the ninth graders. I guess they want us to grow a little, afraid we might get injured by the bigger boys, although there are a couple in the room who are old enough to be in that grade.

The room is about as plain as it gets; concrete walls with a poster board on each worded *Team Pride,* a doorless group shower to my left just beyond the urinal, and a toilet with no privacy door. The smell is a strange combination of a bathroom, a hospital room, recently waxed floors in the school hallways, the school cafeteria, and the dirty-clothes basket at my house.

"Listen up," Coach Petty says, peering through his black-rim plastic glasses, his gaze fixing on each of us. He's wearing maroon shorts and a maroon cap, a white golf shirt, a whistle dangling form a leather strap around his neck, white socks that stretch to above his calves, with black leather shoes with rubber soles, his muscular arms, neck, and legs bulging. The entire outfit looks like it just came out of the package.

"Young men."

He called us gentlemen in class today. He's dropped the word *gentle.*

"We will play five games this season, and we will practice, practice, and practice to perform at the peak of our ability in those games," Coach Petty says, without offering a smile.

"Practice makes perfect, but since no one in this room is perfect, why practice?" Henry David whispers in my ear, causing me to think that those words may not be original, but Henry David is, truly one of a kind. He's got that deep-thinking look on his face again.

"Henry David, do you have any words of wisdom to share with the group?" Coach Petty asks.

"Oh, no sir; I've just got a habit of thinking out loud."

"That habit could get you some extra wind sprints. Does that sound like something you'd be interested in?"

"No sir."

"I'll expect y'all on the practice field promptly at 3:45, twenty minutes after school is over. That means you will have to hustle, and if there's any word you need to learn the meaning of it is hustle. If you don't learn the meaning of hustle, you'll learn the meaning of bench. You'll sit on it so long you'll have splinters in your butt. Also, if you're gonna be good in football, unlike the class room, on the field you'll have to go for *d's.* That's desire, discipline, and dedication. In this game, as in life, if you get the *d's* right, you've increased you odds for an *a.*"

Hmm?

"Horace will help you get your gear," Coach Petty says as he nods at Horace Thompson, a fellow seventh grader who stands in the doorway of the supply room, in the opposite direction from the showers. The dash is on, me in the middle of the pack, Horace, presently the one in charge, deciding who gets what. I wait my turn and finally come face to face with Horace, my noting that I am taller than someone in the room.

"We don't have much in your size, so these will have to do," Horace says to me as he bends over to retrieve a pair of pants. "And here's a jersey," he says, laying one filled with holes on top of the pants, just before placing a jock strap and a pair of socks that lost their elastic about the time I was in the third grade atop the pile. This is my first jock strap. I hope I can figure out how to put it on. He's laying the shoulder pads on, and a helmet that's so scarred I can hardly tell it's maroon. "What size shoes do you wear?" asks Horace.

"Eights."

"No way," says Horace before looking at my feet, his eyes lighting up. "Okay, Bozo, we've only got one pair of eights left," he says, laying a well-past-well-worn pair on top of the stack in my arms.

I make my way to the bench and begin to disrobe, starting with my shoes and socks, standing to remove my shirt and pants, then my underwear. I'm *naked!* What was the word Coach Petty used, *hustle?* I feel the need. Left leg, then right through the jock strap! I do this, then I put on the practice pants using the same method. These are shin pads, not knee pads, how am I gonna run without tripping? Now the T-shirt, shoulder pads, helmet, and finally my shoes. Wait, I can't bend over far enough with the helmet on; can't reach my shoes to tie them. There, that's better. Now, it's on to my feet. So, where's a mirror? What do I look like? All they've got is posters on the walls. Listen to the sound of cleats tapping on the concrete floor! I need to cover my ears, but I can't with the helmet on. I *hustle* out of here.

"Reach in there and grab a handful of those," Henry David says as I near the door.

"What are they?" I say.

"Salt tablets," Henry David says as he grabs a handful. "I hear they give you energy and keep you going when you sweat. I'm gonna take seven or eight; without water." Henry David tossed the whole handful in his mouth.

"Are you sure they work?"

"Ugh, ugh," Henry says, nodding. "You ever tasted sweat?"

"Yeah."

"Salty, wasn't it," Henry David says. He's grinning ear to ear.

I grab two, not a handful, and swallow as I head out the door, the clatter of cleats on concrete steady as my knee pads rub against my shins. I'm nervous.

***

"Hustle. Hustle. Hustle!" hollers Coach Petty as I step between a line of parallel-tread-less tires ten yards in length. I charge, lifting my knees high as my feet go in and out of the tires, kneepads flapping on my shins as I go. This is my fifth time, and this makes no sense at all. I'm breathless and wringing wet, the taste of salt in my mouth so strong I can hardly swallow.

"Ables, Benchley, Jones, Capicci, and Wells grab a tire and line 'em up here and here with enough space to run between," Coach Petty says, pointing to an area of half grass and half hard-as-a rock dirt.

Man this tire is heavy. I'd sure like to roll it, but that's not what the others are doing.

"Okay, listen up, listen up! Line up here and here," Coach Petty says. Half the team is staring at the other half, a narrow path lined with the well-worn tires between us.

What are we fixing to do?

"Those on my right are the runners and those on my left the tacklers," says Coach Petty, this time no holler in his voice as he tosses Henry David the ball. "When I blow the whistle, it's full speed at your opponent. Switch sides the next go around."

Tweeeet!

Oh no, Charlie Capicci is coming straight at Henry David with a full head of steam and Henry David is slowing down just before…before… Charlie's atop Henry David on the ground. I hope he's okay. I'm seeing movement on the part of Charlie. He's hopping on up; but Henry David…

"Hustle on up. Off the ground, this is not naptime!" says Coach Petty, no longer in soft-tone, as Henry David slowly rises, his helmet shaking left and right before jogging to the back of the opposite line, Charlie brushing his shoulder pad against mine as he passes.

Tweeeet!

Culpepper Webb

    This time it's Jimmy Gramatti, an eighth grader, tackling Aaron Jones who is not much bigger than me. Jimmy's quick to his feet, Aaron not so much so. "When you get knocked down, you gotta get up," says Coach Petty to Aaron not two feet from his face, just loud enough for all of us to hear. Aaron slowly rises and heads to the back of the line. His present fear of Coach Petty obviously greater than his pain.

    It's one, then another, and now it's me with the ball staring straight at Larry Edson, the biggest and best athlete in my grade, a one-time grade repeater who has a look of determination like I've never seen on him before, as though he's gonna show Coach Petty he's better than any eighth grader. My knee pads shake on my shins.

    Tweeeet!

    I tuck the ball hard in my hand and against my side and run forward. Larry comes straight at me with that look of determination.

    "Hit him in the numbers," hollers Coach Petty.

    Good, maybe that will throw Larry off. The numbers wore off this jersey years ago. I lower my head where I can't see him, and unlike Henry David I charge forward hard as I can, and… What's that ringing sound?

    "Sorry about that, Walker," Larry whispers above the ringing sound through the hollow circle in the helmet next to my ear, a dull ache within my head. "Didn't mean to hit you so hard, but I gotta do my best."

    "On your feet, both of you, we don't have all day," says Coach Petty as Larry rises from on top of me. I get to my feet and jog to the back of the line, the ringing sound still in my ears.

    Tweeeet!

    "Come this way," says Coach Petty, motioning with his arm for us to line up. "Because we were late getting to the field today, not all of you got the opportunity to run between the tires. So if I missed you today, I'll get to you tomorrow. For now we're lining up in a straight line in a three-point stance.

Jimmy Gramatti, take some eighth-grade leadership and show these seventh-graders what a three-point stance looks like.

"Yes sir," says Jimmy. He lowers his body, resting his weight on the extended fingers of his right hand, his fingertips planted on sun baked dirt. I take note.

"Everybody in a three-point lining up right here," says Coach Petty extending his arm to show an imaginary line, running backwards as soon as we have lined up. "Run to me when I blow the whistle. Run to me," he says as he keeps sprinting backwards.

Tweeet! Tweeeet!

"Sprint! Sprint to me!"

Man, he keeps running backwards. Not fair, the finish line keeps moving! I stop when the finish line stops, my lungs burning, my thighs aching, soaking wet head to toe, my mouth full of salty sweat. I feel awful.

"Okay, pause for a minute before we go the other way," Coach Petty says just after Tommy Wilson, the heaviest guy on the field, reaches the imaginary finish line.

Tweeeet! Tweeet!

Oh no, here we go again, and I think he's picked up speed. My thighs are getting tighter with each step, my lungs burning more. We're thirty yards to the goal post, twenty, ten…Surely we won't head back the other way. Surely not!

"As soon as you reach the goal post, that's it. That's it. Don't lie on the ground or your muscles will tighten and you'll cramp. Don't fall to the ground!"

Too late, half of the guys are either down on a knee or lying on their backs. And that big old eighth-grader, Tommy Wilson, just lost his lunch; all of it. I think I'll look the other way. Keep walking. Hey, the burning in my lungs is not quite as bad, the ache in my thighs not as deep; and I'm passing Coach Petty, looking straight at him, and he straight at me, right through those dark-rim plastic glasses that look half fogged up. He's poker-faced. I have no idea what he's thinking, but I do know this; I'm the first one heading to the locker room, and that's got to count for something. I'm feeling better with every step.

So here I am, the first to the locker room, the sound of my cleats on concrete and the roar of that big fan in the corner the only sounds in the room. The air from that fan feels so good. I'll take a seat on this bench in front of it and spend the rest of my life sitting here. I take off my helmet and then I pull the jersey over the shoulder pads. The soaking wet jersey gets stuck halfway. I'm about to suffocate.

"Can somebody help me?" I ask, somewhat in a panic as I hear sound of cleats on concrete and small talk, both muffled from beneath the wet jersey. "Can somebody help me!"

"Here you go, Walker," says Larry Edson as he yanks on the jersey. I feel immediate relief.

"Thanks Larry." Of all the people in the room it's no surprise that it was Larry who helped me. He's different in a good way, always kind to people. I bet he's the strongest guy in my grade and I've never seen him pick on anybody, not once.

"Will you help me with mine?" he asks and I oblige, although it takes three tugs.

A moment later, I've placed my helmet, shoulder pads, and shoes in a locker, and with the exception of the towel wrapped around my waist, I'm naked. What's next? How long will I be without clothes? I drop the towel on the bench and dash for a corner spot in the showers, turning the water on quickly, facing the spray so I'll be seen by as few as possible. My first day in seventh grade has been different than I expected. I'm beginning to learn that's the way life is. So much has happened today. The steady stream of water feels so good.

"Hurry up in there, I need a shower too!" hollers Tommy Wilson.

I bet he does. He threw up on the field. He's also the biggest guy in the room, so who am I to stand in his way. I head for my towel, leaving the water running.

A few minutes later I head out the door, books in hand. I stare at the huge pile of socks, jocks, and T-shirts, the smell unimaginable, all before Horace Thompson, the manager. I think I'd rather run head-on at Larry Edson again than have to deal with that pile. "Good luck," I say to Horace as I pass.

Coach Petty stands alone on the sidewalk just outside the locker room, his hands crossed, as I prepare to pass. "Let me have a moment," he says catching me off guard.

Have I done something wrong?

"Today has been an adjustment for all of you seventh-graders, a big difference from elementary school," Coach Petty says before pausing. "For you and Larry Edson, both of you without fathers present in your lives, life can be an even greater challenge. While I'm not about to cut either one of you any slack, I'm here if you ever need to talk to someone," he says, his look quite serious.

Coach Petty just showed a soft side. Didn't see that on the field, did I? I can't quite put him together in one piece: a law-and-order guy in homeroom, a genius from another planet in science class, a crack-the-whip man on the field, then a man who offers to be a counselor. This man is complicated. "Yes sir," I say, then, "I'd best be going."

Coach Petty nods and I head to my bike wondering how I'm going to balance my books on my handle-bars. I didn't have this many books last year. I better get a basket for the handle-bars. I start to pedal, almost spilling the books in the process. When I reach the street, the breeze begins to cool my face. I ponder what Coach Petty meant. In some ways he reminds me of Mr. Sandiford, tough and all, but he cares about me. I can just tell.

I can't believe it; just up ahead in that vacant lot across from the school, Charlie Capicci, who was just at practice, has met up with Bobby Fortenberry, and they're both smoking a cigarette. Bobby I can understand, but Charlie?

Culpepper Webb

My, that breeze feels good. Oops, better slow down, the stoplight is red. It's tough balancing the books and coming to a halt. There.

Two Negro kids, about my age, books in hand, are crossing the street not two feet in front of me, their eyes on mine. It's uncomfortable and strange. Wonder what it was like today at *their* school.

Monday, March 5, 2012

A Trip from Madison, Mississippi to the Mississippi Delta

I'm wide awake. What time is it? *4:01* according to the clock on the nightstand. Might as well go for my run. I edge out from under the covers without awakening Laura.

Ouch! The weight of my body on my right arch hurts. I tiptoe across the carpet, grab my jogging gear, and head to the den to dress and stretch. I close the bedroom door without hearing a peep from Laura. I lie on the rug and stretch my back and legs. There's that old joke about guy who goes to the doctor and says, "Hey Doc, I touch the arch on my foot and it hurts. Then I touch my elbow and my shoulder and it hurts again, both times. It even hurts when I touch my knee. What's the problem?"

Doctor says, "You've got a broken finger."

Yeah, but this time that's not the punch line, my finger is fine. I do some sit ups too. I feel better already. I disrobe and dress.

With me going out and running at this hour, most would say they are in better shape than I am above their shoulders; but they don't know that I decided years ago I was going to run twenty-five thousand miles, the equivalent of once around the planet; and I was going to do it before I reached sixty. I only have eight-hundred miles left to go by Friday. The other day I was thinking of football practice with Coach Petty, running wind springs. He'd run backwards and move the finish line. I'll move the finish line, maybe to say, age sixty-one? I've learned in life, it's good to leave yourself a backdoor to exit. In running, mine has been if I ever found an empty non-alcoholic beer bottle on the side of the road, I would have the option to quit running forever right on that spot. Imagine, I have run twenty-four-thousand-two-hundred miles and have yet to find one.

    I haven't run this far standing still. I hit the "on" button for the coffee pot and I'm out the door and down the steps, into the driveway, now out onto the street, a cold mist in my face, the fog from my breath and the pavement at my feet both visible from the light of the streetlight. It's up the hill, the greatest incline of my run, which in turn will be downhill on my return, followed by the pavement leveling as I head to exit our subdivision, on to a main road with no fear of a car. I can see headlights a half mile in advance. I now take a left on to the straight road, where if it were not for a rise in it, I could see headlights for a mile. That rise in the road is unnoticeable in a car. Not so when running. The pain shifts from my right arch and left knee to tightness in my thighs and a dull pain within my chest as the cold air flows in to my lungs and the warm air exits. I near the peak of the rise and keep gradually going downhill.

    Sometimes when running I am aware of dips and inclines in the road, the sight of my breath, the pain; other times not, my mind drifting to thoughts of all sorts of things, oblivious of the goings-on of the moment. It's a time I reflect. So many thoughts have gone through my head as I've taken these forty-million-plus steps, thoughts I would not have experienced in front of a TV, or in conversation. It's time alone, good in many ways. But of late I've felt *alone*, more so than any time in decades. I would have to go back to the wreck; and before that the death of Daddy, to have exceeded the aloneness I've felt of late. And, it's not that I'm that not surrounded by people, or a wife who cares about me, because Laura truly does. It goes deeper than my surroundings; it's me.

It's time to turn around and head home. Didn't realize I had come this far. I circle, because if I stop to turn, I might stop to walk, an unpardonable sin. Now it's up the incline, then down again, a right turn, then a left back in to the subdivision, now down the steep hill to the house, the best part of the trip!

I'm at my driveway breathing heavily, the inflow of cold air and outflow of warm frequent, I'm tempted to rest my hands and the weight of my body on my knees, but I know that it's best to stay up straight, so I keep walking. I learned that the first day of football practice in the seventh grade. I followed the advice of Coach Petty; and he was right. I read in the paper that he died, ten maybe fifteen years ago. I lose track of time. He moved on from my old school. And he moved up. He was quite a successful high school football coach. As I remember, he was not expressive in a touchy-feely way, but you could tell he cared. Men were like that then. The pain in my lungs continues to subside.

"Laura, I've got your coffee."

"Walker, why are you waking me up at such a dreadful hour?"

"Because it's Monday and work has your name written all over it."

"I told you yesterday I'm getting too old for this. I need to retire."

"And we'll spend the next couple of months deciding," I say as I walk toward Laura, about to touch her.

"Are you all sweaty? If you are, keep your distance."

"Sweat? Laura, I am completely covered with 'nectar from the sweetest fruit on the planet.' Any woman in her right mind should find me irresistible at this very moment, *as is*."

"Walker, go take a shower, preferably a cold one. I can't take this much enthusiasm on a Monday morning at five o'clock. Try me tonight."

"Tonight? Is that a promise?"

"In marriage, there's always tomorrow."

Laura's made it upright in the bed. I think I will hop in the shower. That 'nectar from the sweetest fruit on the planet' is causing me to chill, and it has my T-shirt stuck to my body. Man, the hot water does feel good.

"How is it?"

"Great," I say. "Want to join me?" All I hear now is running water. I've done enough joking for a Monday morning. I step out of the shower and grab the towel. Laura's gone to the kitchen. I dress.

"What's on the agenda for the day?" Laura says between bites of cereal.

"I'm driving to the Delta to see Randolph Hollings, at one time my biggest client. He called last week saying he needed to see me, not wanting to say exactly why. I didn't push. I just put his file in order so we can discuss whatever is on his mind. He lives 'out from out from' in a huge mansion atop an Indian mound with a view that goes forever."

"I remember him well," says Laura between bites of cereal. "Drive safely. Some of those Delta roads are narrow. At least they won't be driving the farm equipment on the roads this time of year. So, can I expect you home for supper at a reasonable hour?"

"Don't know. It's Monday, and of any day of the week, I *never* know what to expect on Monday."

In Search of Walker Wells

***

So here I am at the office all alone on Monday morning. There are no rings from the phone, no voices of conversations in the background, no interruptions to my concentration; the perfect environment for getting things done. I had to dig deep to get started. I always do on Monday; a lot of things change, but some don't. I've dictated task after task on a recorder for Kay, who should be here momentarily. Randolph Hollings' file is in my briefcase, next to the door. I'm prepared for the expected, and hope to be for the unexpected. I hear muffled conversation outside my door, a male voice and a female one. The office will soon be abuzz with multiple conversations, phones ringing, and printers printing, the conversations going from casual to business. I open my door to meet and greet.

"Kay, you're early," I say, just as I open the door.

"I thought you might be getting on the road early, so I'm here for instructions."

"Really?"

"Not really. The fact is I've been awake for hours, wired to the hilt. You're contagious, Walker."

"Perhaps," I say. "I've pretty much got things mapped out for you on the recorder."

"Walker, you have a guest," says a male voice in the background.

"Yes, Matt," I say, as I turn. "Who's here?"

"A Mr. Henry David Nobles. I asked if you were expecting him, and he just shook his head and grinned real big."

I had thoughts the other day of Henry David downing a handful of salt tablets without water. My blood pressure is rising just thinking of that. Yep, on Mondays "prepare for the expected as well as the unexpected." I guess I should have put Henry David's dropping by unannounced on the last day of the grace period of his life insurance policy in the expected category because he's done it before more than once.

"Kay, would you please retrieve Henry David's file and try not to injure your back when lifting it. Hey, you're not smiling anymore."

"That's because he could be my fulltime job. While he's here ask him if he has had an address change, switched banks *again,* taken on a new wife, or had any other minor changes. I'll put his file on your desk."

"See if anyone has made coffee so you can bring him a cup. And Kay," I say, pausing for emphasis, "I just know that pretty smile of yours will return when you do."

I know why she's not smiling; three letters and four phone calls over the past month, and Henry David just blows in with the wind on the last day of the grace period; an ongoing repeat performance.

"Hope you don't mind me coming by early," says Henry David, as he seats himself in a chair across from my desk.

"Since when does one define the last day of a grace period as early?" I say, as I seat myself across the desk.

"It's all a matter of perspective old buddy; all a matter of perspective," says Henry David as Kay enters the room, placing a cup of coffee in front of both of us, Henry David's cup loaded with sugar. Kay knows the routine. "Aren't we on the ball this morning," Henry David says to Kay, smiling that big grin of his. Kay closes the door behind her.

Here we are alone, Henry David and me; known each other all the way back to grade school. Oh my, I misspoke when I asked Kay to get his file. There are two of them, each five inches thick. I scoot both files to the side of my desk to where I see nothing but wood, the coffee cups, and Henry David. Look at him, the strands of hair on his head so few I could count them in less than a minute, his skin weathered as much by cigarette smoke as the elements, wrinkles in abundance on his face, but most pronounced around his eyes. He's wearing a partially unbuttoned shirt wrinkled enough to match his face, it covered by a light-brown leather jacket.

"Tell me the truth, Walker. When I took this life insurance policy out, did you honestly think I'd live this long?"

No. That would be the honest answer, not the diplomatic one.

"Are you there, Walker? A simple yes or no would be in order," says Henry David.

"Aside from your constant smokestack impersonation and frequently being 'over served' in the adult beverage category, why would I say yes?"

"So, you won't commit either way, and you're the one big on commitments, not me. You know it's been almost forty years since our wreck. You know I still have aches and pains from that, as well as nightmares."

I used to have the nightmares too, as well as day-mares, times alone when I would stare into open air reliving that event. It stuck in my mind like a bad song.

"Truth is," Henry David continues, "I didn't think I'd make it this far, and here I am stuck paying a life insurance premium I never thought I'd have to pay. So it doesn't have any more cash value in it to pay the premium?"

"Henry David, this is term policy. All the policies with cash value have long since been surrendered or lapsed, and the same thing is going to happen to this one at midnight if you don't make a premium payment." Henry David has that inquisitive look on his face, the one he gets when his wheels are really turning, after which he oftentimes comes out with a bizarre statement.

"Sudz, my car washes located beyond the burbs, haven't been the cash cows that I thought they would be. It seems that clean cars aren't a 'livin' necessity' in a down economy. Well, it's possible that success is just a couple of steps away since I opened Sudz'n Such next door to my best two. I told you about those little stores where I sell beer and cigarettes. Folks seem to be a whole lot more interested in those helpful goods than a clean ride. I have a little startup cost in the last one that should be resolved in a jiffy. And if not, I may go to Tierra del Fuego. Walker, what country is Tierra del Fuego in?"

Henry David never disappoints; Tierra del Fuego? I think it's in Argentina or Chile. His face displays earnestness within its wear and tear. "I'm not sure. So what makes you think that's where you might want to go?"

"My life-pressures seem to be growing, not shrinking, and that just doesn't seem right. I'm sixty years old. I figured things would have eased up a bit by now."

Hmm, one of life's great myths? Henry David has always shot before he aimed: three marriages, and now divorced, and he has a thirteen-year old daughter, that child the link with a true head-case, old what's her name? No, that was *young* what's her name. I have a hard time keeping them straight. Henry David's real-life issues have roots grounded in fertile soil that began to surface well before he walked down the aisle. A step in the wrong direction here, then there, then finally all over the place, footprints left in "don't walk on the grass" areas all over the place, eventually leaving him standing on ground that no human being should have stood on to begin with. Some outgrow their misguided youthful tendencies by their mid-twenties, a handful in their thirties, but if not by forty, unless they have an "on the road to Damascus experience," their die has been cast. Henry David's life's experiences have either taught him little; or he simply chooses to ignore those things that he knows to be true. Truth is, his present life circumstances are sort of like he struggled though a massive thicket of thorny briars only to wander into quicksand, an ultimate journey of self-infliction. I wish I could have helped him more. "So who's nipping at your heels?" I ask.

"Can't quite keep up with all of them, and I'm kind of scared to turn back and look. If I don't get straight with my banker, then the goose that lays the golden eggs flies or something dies. Walker, don't get that look of terror on your face. The flyin' part is about the goose and the dyin' part is about the eggs, not me. I need capital to keep layin' them."

"Your banker called last week about this policy that's assigned to them. If you decide to pay today, I'll have Kay contact him. So, is Tierra del Fuego symbolic for skipping the country?"

"Yeah, but I can't just go to Never Never Land. They don't have flights there anymore. I remember you took Latin in high school, while I was taking Spanish; a fat lot of good that's going to do for you in real life. They don't fly to 'ancient Rome' anymore, in case you haven't heard."

Henry David's making light of things, but his face says something different. This time I think he's serious. "So, if you get up to speed with your banker, do you think you'll stick around?"

"It depends; not all of life's burdens are financial. I went to buy Tori, wife number three, an entire witches' costume including the broom for Christmas, only to be informed that I was out of season and that they were out of costumes. Little did they know that Tori was in season and always will be."

I'm having an epiphany. As much as Henry David despised English, he married a girl name *Tori* and they named their daughter *Brittany.* He fired twice before aiming. At least he's consistent.

"Walker."

What's this, Henry David's about to tear up? There's moisture in his eyes and a tear rolling down his cheek.

"Everybody else I've known in life has given up on me: first my folks, later three wives, and now I'm afraid it's Brittany, the only child I have. That sounds strange doesn't it, three wives and one child? Walker, promise me you won't give up on me. Promise?"

Henry David, while I've never understood you, I've always cared for you. "I promise," I say. Now what is that, a genuine smile, not a façade, the veil lifted, a glimpse at the real Henry David?

"I'm not writing a check today for my banker. It's for Brittany, do you understand?"

"I do."

"The check is for two months, made out to the insurance company, right?"

"Yes."

"You got a bank draft authorization form that I can sign to put the policy back on automatic draft? That's the only possible way that it will ever get paid."

I slide the form that Kay has had prepared for two weeks across the desk for Henry David to sign. "Sign here."

"If the check doesn't go through, I'll give you another one with the next number on it, " Henry David says as he tears the check from the checkbook and slides it across the desk, my viewing the check to make sure he has signed it."

His veil is back on.

I'd best be going," Henry David says, rising. "You might even put in a word for me with the good Lord as I suppose I might be in need of it."

The veil came off again when he said that. At this moment he's as serious as I've ever seen him, no hint of humor to be found. This is not a casual passing of words. "Take care," I say as I rise and shake Henry David's hand, his grip firm, eye contact strong, both unusual for him, almost as if he has more to say but can't quite bring himself to do so. As he leaves, I fall back into the leather chair resting my arms on its arms as I place my hands under my chin and begin to analyze the happenings of the past few minutes. I've known Henry David since elementary school, and in some ways the only thing that has changed is his appearance. His trip here today was about far more than an insurance premium, so much more. I'll call him later in the week. I might be the only person on the planet to do so out of concern for his wellbeing. Now it's off to see Randolph Hollings. I grab my briefcase.

"Kay, I'm late. The check and bank draft form are on my desk with the files."

In Search of Walker Wells

***

It's forty minutes since I left my office and I'm approaching the town I refer to as kudzu city, a name I've given it in honor of the vines that cover the soft-silt of the hillsides on the bluffs that hover above the Delta. Kudzu, planted to combat erosion, has proved wildly successful, devouring all plants and trees in its growth-path. This time of year it's dormant, just scraggly-old- brown vines that define the word *ugly*. Give it a month or two and those vines will be showered with green leaves and they will be going after children in their back yards. Now I'm approaching the view I've been anticipating, just ahead.

Wow! Look at that full-view of the Mississippi Delta, land devoid of hills, save for the levee on the Yazoo River and a handful of Indian mounds, flat for fifty miles to the levee on the Mississippi. I go down the steep hill, houses on both sides of the street, the monotonous consistency of subdivisions lacking. I stop at the light at the bottom of the hill and look both ways at the downtown, much of it vacated, same story as across much of America. Now it's out of town and over the bridge high above the Yazoo River which grants me another view of the Delta, although not as grand as that from atop the hill. I'm now traveling across flat terrain, straight road ahead, open fields to my left and right, woods in the distance on beyond the fields.

What's that dangerously close to the road ahead on my right? It's a tractor, large, though not quite as massive as the heated and air conditioned models of late, a somewhat older Case. It must be broken down or maybe just out of gas.

Now, again it's the open fields with no houses. During my childhood those fields were dotted with shotgun houses, the homes of the tenants who worked the land. They were shaped like the barrel of a gun, so straight that if you opened the front and back doors you could shoot a shotgun through the front door and the pellets would come out the back. They were made of cypress wood that wouldn't rot.

Culpepper Webb

Just yesterday Mom mentioned a sermon about Noah. As I remember from childhood the ark was made of cypress.

I look at the woods in the distance, across a fallow field. Years ago woods covered all the land, cypress trees and hardwood forest growing in a land without peaks and valleys, the only variance in the terrain the sloughs, creeks, and rivers. The Yazoo and the Mississippi rivers on years of great rains and snow melts covered this entire surface with water, in some places deep, in others shallow, the shift in elevation oftentimes unapparent until the water rose. But rise it would. Still, the forest was all around, the water never covering the trees. In the story Noah saw nothing but water and a horizon for months on end. So much would a man long to see a single limb, much less a tree or an entire forest, his hope eventually restored by the physical evidence of a single branch delivered by a bird; or so the story goes. His hope was built on what he could not see or touch, so unlike me. If I can't see it, touch it, hear it, taste it, or smell it, as far as I'm concerned it doesn't exist.

What would a walk in those woods be like? I could trade these shoes for my rubber-sole leather boots, the ones where the rubber covers the tops of my feet. I'd need those because there's always water standing somewhere in those woods. With my boots it wouldn't matter. I could walk and it would be quiet, though not totally so, chirps of birds heard year-round in the woods, the sound of the patter of their feet on leaves ever so slight.

If I was quiet maybe I could hear a squirrel as it scurries up a tree knocking off hardwood bark; and perhaps a deer or a rabbit. How long has it been since I've been in the woods? I'm coming here soon, to that very patch of woods, and I won't tell a soul, not even Laura. She would ask "why" and I wouldn't be able to explain, even to myself, other than I feel led to them. I'll do it after it warms up a bit and the leaves start coming out. The ground will have dried, and there will be sunshine.

My, the time has flown. There's my turn up ahead with that convenience store that's been there for as long as I can remember. I'll stop in on my way back. Wonder if they still have that great fried chicken?

I'm not too far from Randolph Hollings' place, and it's so easy to see from a distance. One more turn and I'm heading toward it, a sight that looms as large as anything in these parts, a massive turn of the last century home that sits high atop an Indian mound. The hum of tires on asphalt turns to patter on the underside of the Explorer as I make the turn from the road onto the gravel drive of Hollings Row, the name of the home as well as the land it sits on. This view of the home on the Indian mound is, to me, the most majestic scene in the state. The enormity of the home grows as I near it. Man, this drive is lengthy, no trees on either side of it. Massive white columns arch at the top of the dark-brick of the home. It has always struck me as odd that in a land where woods are so abundant that brick was chosen.

I drive past the front of the house and enter the narrow drive at its back that curves as I ascend the mound. I park the Explorer and pause to collect my breath and thoughts, as well as my briefcase as I exit the car. The cold west-wind blows against my face and body, my suit coat and overcoat still on the front seat. The sky is gray, without a trace of blue. I move quickly up the steps to the back door, its height perhaps ten feet. The door opens before I knock.

"Hello, Walker," he says, almost before the door is fully open, followed by, "I have a pot of coffee ready," Randolph is now in full view. He's aged. Although I saw him last seven or eight years ago, my mental picture of him coming up the drive today was one of twenty-nine years ago when we first met and he was 55, tall and slender with a full mane of auburn hair with the most ice-blue eyes I had ever beheld. The ice-blue eyes remain; they are piercing, overwhelming his subdued smile. The mane is still full, but is as white as cotton, his body still lean, but his stature shrunken, his gait slowed, as he steps back for me to enter.

"Great to see you, Randolph," I say as I enter, the massive aged-cypress door causing a weighty thud as it closes behind me. He sizes me head to toe. "Been dying your hair?" he asks as his blue eyes settle on mine.

Is it that obvious? "Only the ones I have left," I say. "One bottle lasts me all year."

"And how old are you now, Walker?" he says, the ice-blue eyes squinting a bit this time.

"My late fifties." I ponder my reply for a moment then say, "Real-late fifties; I turn sixty this Friday," this time offering an abundant smile which Randolph returns prior to his heading for the coffee.

"Can you handle a cup and saucer with that briefcase?" he asks as he pours the coffee into each of the china cups next to the pot, his hand trembling a bit as he does so.

"I think so," I reply, as I begin the balancing act which is not as easy as I thought. I think I can make it to where he is leading me without spilling, a trip which is proceeding quite slowly toward the dining room to the front of the house. A solid-plank mahogany table runs the length of the room with the view of the land from the window at its far end seemingly endless.

"We'll sit here," he says, gesturing with one hand, the saucer laden cup of coffee in the other, seating himself at the head of the table, the massive window to his back, me to his left.

I carefully lay my briefcase on the floor, not on the mahogany, settle in and take a sip of coffee. Ouch, it's hot! I put the cup back on the saucer. I see a letter-size envelope to the front of him, *Walker Wells* on it. I look up and catch his ice-blue eyes now locked directly on mine. "One month, maybe two, the cancer is spreading fast through my lymph nodes." And just like that Randolph halts, so abrupt and to the point, allowing me to ponder the magnitude of his words.

And what do I now say or not say? I knew beforehand he had not summoned me all this way for a cup of coffee. I feel a sort of numbness, an inward lack of sensation. It's not that I don't care, for I do. Sometimes things don't immediately sink in with me. I have to let the fact of what he just said marinate before I can actually feel and taste the consequences.

"I'm sorry." Why did I blurt this out? My words sound so trite. I must say something. "Are you feeling much pain?"

"It's bizarre, but at this moment I feel none. The pain comes and goes as do the memories of my life. At times I wonder whether I'm asleep or awake, and also if this rapid-spreading cancer is real or make believe. The doctors have assured me it is quite real," Randolph says, pausing and looking away. Suddenly, he alertly turns back and says, "Is all in order with the life insurance policies?"

"Yes," I say, momentarily pausing before I speak. "All they will be need is your death certificate, the letters testamentary, and Alfred Robinson, your trustee's signature on the forms," I continue, thinking immediately of the oddity of saying "*your* death certificate," to a living man. "Have there been any changes?"

"No, all the addresses and phone numbers including my children's are in this envelope," Randolph says, handing the envelope to me. As you know my daughter, Amanda, and her husband, Richard, reside in Atlanta, while Randolph Junior and Sandra still live up the road in town. He and Sandra will be moving into this home soon, so this place won't become a museum. In some ways that's what I've felt like I've been living in since Agatha's death. I hope you can do some business with Randolph Junior to help him continue 'passing the baton,' although he quite frequently does his own thing; always has. Thanks to the life insurance, Amanda and her offspring will be well compensated. Neither she nor her spouse, Richard, care anything about this place, *place* meaning not only this home and land, but also this part of the world. It's a good thing we took out that additional policy back in the early nineties so that the she and Randolph Junior won't be squabbling over the crops on an annual basis. As you know he gets the home and land."

"I'll handle this with care," I say, the full gravity of this moment suddenly hitting me that this may be the last time I see this man alive. He seems so *human*. Now that's a strange thought, but it is so true. He's not an object, nor an animal. He's a human. Did Randolph simply want to see me face to face to make sure there are no hitches with the insurance? There must be more.

"Although you look different than the last time I saw you, in one way you haven't changed," he says, his face turning from dead serious to smile.

"How is that?" I say before taking a sip of coffee, no burn on the tongue this time.

"I can still trust you; always have," Randolph says, before going silent, the hook with the bait on it right before me, "the fish."

"I think you have more to say," I reply, realizing it might be after dark before Randolph gives in to completing what he has to say without some comment on my part. One doesn't run a place this size with just farming skills. He understands people.

"Although we are separated by a generation, I sized you up as someone I could trust when we first met. That's when I decided to do business with you, and I've never regretted that. I thought I might pass this along to you while I'm still above ground. There are many things I wished I had said to people over the course of my life, but did not. One can see this quite plainly at age eighty-four, especially when he knows that death is just around the corner. It would have much better if I had 'seen that light' at your age, or better yet much younger," Randolph says, coming to a complete halt, his smile dissipating, his look pensive. The gaze of his ice-blue eyes is distant.

I say nothing.

"Did I ever tell you that my burning desire growing up was to be an architect?" he says breaking the silence.

"No," I say, caught by surprise in Randolph's change of direction.

"I was born in 1928, and didn't turn eighteen until after the war ended. I was later overlooked for Korea. Anyway, my older brother, Oliver, was killed in Germany about a month before the end of the war, just after I had turned seventeen. I took it hard, but nothing like my parents. Following his death, Mother, during this bleak time of year, would have a despondent gaze. Father took to drinking. From December until well into March, there is only so much planning and paper work a farmer can do. In farming, the fallowness of time can be greater than that of the open-fields. And, look at that overcast sky. This time of year it's like that most days," Randolph says, nodding his head for me to look, which I do, immediately captivated by the gray sky against the empty field. If John Deere tractors define a color of green, then *Mississippi Delta Gray* is a color unto itself, so bleak and dismal against a cropless ground. No wonder this land is the "birthplace of the blues."

"I'm getting a bit off-track," Randolph says, "I majored in architecture and met Agatha in college. All through college father dropped hints. 'What will become of this place if you don't come back?' 'Running Hollings Row is not a job or a career, it's a way of life,' and so on and so forth on every trip I made home. In the end, my will to embark on my dream was not as powerful as my inability to stand up to Father. Within two months of graduation I married Agatha, and was reporting for duty on a daily basis. Am I boring you?"

"No." I say. "All along I've thought you were living your life's dream."

"For the longest time I hated this place: my work, the land, this home, my only consolation a small home I designed and built up the road in town where Agatha and I lived in until moving here. With a degree in architecture and dreams of building skyscrapers, that small home was the only structure I designed that became a reality. Moving on, Agatha and I had the two children, we were earning a healthy income, and I suppose you could say we were 'living comfortably,' until Mother died after a lengthy bout with cancer in the mid-fifties. That's when things began to deteriorate. Following her death, Father's penchant for bourbon became the controlling factor in his life. His judgment was clouded, his timing regarding planting and harvest out of sync, his management regarding the thirty-odd families that resided on and worked this place was at best negligent; and all the while he wouldn't allow me to assume at least some of the responsibilities. He wouldn't listen to me. I was as stressed and strained as one can imagine; or at least thought that I was. Father died in an automobile accident in 1962. It was alcohol related; right after we planted. I was thirty-four."

Randolph paused and I filter what he is saying, things that he's never shared with me, events I would have never guessed. He's the definition of serious, his gaze seemingly focused on some invisible object in the far distance. I wonder where he is going with this. Is he simply a lonely man wanting to share his life with someone and he thought that I, the man who helped insure his life, would be the person to listen; or is there more?

"Here I was, thirty-four years old with a wife and two children, two bad crops in a row, the crops for that year already planted, debt galore at the bank with the bankers looking over my shoulder at my every step, thirty families on this place with more marital, medical, and legal problems than I could count; and to top this all off, I didn't even want to be a farmer. Now, don't get me wrong; I had just inherited this home and nine thousand acres, a fortune by any standard. But I was in over my head; way over it."

He's gone quiet again. I wait a lengthy moment, then say, "Go on," followed by "something must have worked out," my offering a faint smile in the process.

"Do you know what this home sits atop?"

"An Indian mound."

"Yes. And thank God because of it, not one drop of flood-water has ever entered this home. But to the people native to this land it was more than a refuge from the high waters of the Mississippi. It was where they performed their religious ceremonies, an attempt to get closer to a creator. They sensed that there is more to life than what we see and touch. That's a basic human longing, and it always has been. We just come off the assembly line that way. During that year of 1962, I eventually 'came to the Indian mound,' so to speak."

He's gone quiet again. What now? I have an immense respect for this man. I've always valued what he has to say and I consider him a man of wisdom. He's quite alert, so these aren't simply unintelligible ramblings. Besides, I genuinely care for the man, and about what he's going through.

"I used the word *eventually*. I was not struck by a bolt of lightning that suddenly changed me. No, my transformation was gradual. In terms of struggles, that year was not day to day, but more hour to hour, each step I made and breath of air was an effort. Two o'clock in the morning was often my loneliest hour; not the best time of night for a man to confide with his wife. Until that year, my total spiritual experience amounted to no more than impatiently waiting for a sermon to end while staring at my watch, all the while wondering how long it would be until I could eat. I'm still not exactly sure why I was sitting in that pew to begin with. Habit? Social expectation? Agatha's expectations? Truth is, it was probably a little bit of each."

He has a kindly smile as he's gone quiet again, waiting for some response.

"So, what happened?"

"I came to realize several things, not the least of which was that I was at the end of my rope. I wasn't in a fox hole with shots coming at me; nor was I so desperate as to shoot myself. But I was in need; in need of strength and wisdom, and in need of something deeper, that to this very day I can't fully articulate. It was as if I had a bottomless hole within me that needed the cover removed and the hole filled. I gradually allowed the cover to be removed. Early that September, right before we picked the cotton, the cover came completely off. I was sitting in this chair. Out that window the sun was rising. There was no one in this room but me. At that moment I came to Christ. I surrendered myself. My hole became filled that day and it has never been empty since.

For the first time since sitting down with Randolph I'm discomforted. My life-experience has been just the opposite of his. I began to 'cover the hole' when Daddy died and completed the task following the wreck. We're all thrown together differently, aren't we? Yet, because this is a man I respect greatly, I continue to listen.

"My life didn't suddenly become a bed of roses. This place almost went under that year, and one of my tenants murdered another. You have no idea the degree of disharmony that created among the families. Somehow, I endured those challenges for another year of farming. Truthfully, I had to come back for another year, or I would have to have walked away from this place empty handed and dead broke. Life is not easy, but I had a peace within I'd never had.

"Life is not easy," I say.

"I began to find contentment in life, even in farming. I acquired a taste for it," Randolph says, smiling. "I finally got the fact of never designing a skyscraper out of my craw, and I gradually grew to love this place as well as farming; a good thing for Randolph Junior. All he's ever wanted to do is farm. I've found great joy in watching him work this place. He's so much better at this game than I ever was. Things worked out. Please note that I did not say that *I* worked things out."

It's interesting that Randolph said that. He said it genuinely. For a man of his looks, wealth, and intelligence I've never seen an ounce of pride or self-centeredness in him.

"I began to view people differently, although not overnight. It's amazing what happens when one seeks guidance beyond the top of his scalp. I'm ashamed to say that I once viewed the tenants as lesser-beings. Looking back I can't imagine that, but it's true. I viewed myself as more highly evolved than they, and with my higher level of wealth and intelligence, superior to most people I crossed paths with. I don't think I was very likeable."

He's offering a broad smile.

"Fact is, to my way of thinking, you and I are *people*, not just some other animal. We're the most precious cargo on this planet; each and every one of us. And each of us is planted here by God with a purpose. Walker, I believe that with all of my heart. And there's one more thing."

"What's that?" I say.

"In a matter of weeks someone will be shoveling some of this fine Mississippi Delta dirt in my face. If that's all there is, wouldn't that be sad?"

Randolph just took things from the vertical to the horizontal in a way I've never heard. I don't know how to respond. I simply nod.

"I look forward to seeing Agatha again, although according to Jesus we may be more brother and sister than husband and wife. But, that's all right. I look forward to seeing her under any circumstance," Randolph says, offering a deep smile that seems to go all the way to his heart. Now his ice-blue eyes are fixed on mine. "I have one great regret."

Randolph's gone quiet again, causing me to think. "What is your great regret?"

"I haven't told more people about my spiritual conversion. I hoarded the treasure, and I can see that now. Before I die I have a list of people that I feel compelled to share my story with. Walker, what do you believe?"

His ice-blue eyes are straight on mine. I glance out the window. I see gray sky and open field. I turn back to Randolph. "I believe in a god."

Culpepper Webb

According to the Bible, Satan believes in the existence of God. And Walker, do you know what else?"
"What?"
"It's always later than you think."

Monday, March 5, 2012

The Trip Home

  The constant patter of gravel on the underside of the Explorer gives way to the hum of tires on pavement as I turn from the drive that leads from Hollings Row, one final rock hitting metal as I head toward the tiny town up the road, fallow fields on each side of the road. My mind is flooded, more thrown at it than I can presently absorb, all of my thoughts concerning Randolph Hollings, both the man and what he said.

  The fact that I am soon to lose one of my biggest clients is of no present concern. Of all the people I work with, I can't think of anyone for whom I have more respect than Randolph, both his wisdom and his integrity. I told him this before I left. Soon he will be gone. Today this man who is standing at the door of death opened up to me in such a personal way. His conclusions about life are so different from mine. Oh, not in all ways. I truly believe in my integrity, doing what is right for others. I practice that or at least take a stab at it every day. Fact is, however, Randolph got to me, and I'm not easy to get to. His ice-blue eyes penetrated right to my core in a way I can't explain.

  What was that? I almost hit that old bomb of a car that I see through my rearview. Looks like an elderly silver-haired black woman sitting in the driver's seat all by her lonesome. Should I turn back? I mean, I've got an office to get back to. What am I thinking? That could be somebody like Mom out here with her car broken down in the middle of nowhere. I've got to turn around and head back.

  Oh, that wind coming out of the west is cold on the side of my face. Now it's biting at my body through my coat and shirt as I face the window gazing at a silver-haired woman, her perm-hair in a bun as if she just left the beauty parlor, glasses of medium thickness perched on her nose. Her skin is milk chocolate. She's dazed, disoriented. Is she suffering medically? She's staring at me as if I am a ghost. I open the door. "Ma'am, are you all right? Ma'am, are you all right?" I repeat.

"I don't want my daughter worrying. I'm supposed to be meeting her. She's taking me shopping this afternoon."

I love the way she talks. Her speech is deliberate.

"Name's Pearl," she says, with a huge look of relief on her face.

"My name's Walker. What do we have here?"

"The tire on that back passenger side is flat, and my cell phone doesn't get reception out here. I've been waiting for someone to come by; that is until the Lord sent you."

I'll not correct her, but if "the Lord" had sent someone it wouldn't have been me. "Why don't I get you over to my vehicle while I change your flat," I say. "Let me help you with your door."

"Yes, thank you," she says as she reaches to grab her purse and I assist her up, closing the door, accepting her right arm in my left as we move slowly toward the Explorer. I steady her step up to get in the seat, peering over her to see that there is no reception on my phone either. Now it's back to her car to retrieve the keys to open the trunk for the spare tire. This car's a Chrysler, an eighty-some-odd model in mint condition, the silver paint almost as fresh as my Explorer's. The rear tire is as flat as a pancake. I open the trunk.

  Wow, you could put a spare car in this trunk! Let's see, if I lift this cover there should be a spare tire under it. Good, a real tire, not a bicycle one like they put in most cars today; and it's full of air. There's the jack, but where's the lug wrench? Oh brother, it's missing. Wonder if the one in the Explorer will work? Oh, I'm cold; that wind is about to get the best of me. I'll grab my coat and my lug wrench. Look, she's peering in the mirror of her compact. She just put it down when she saw me coming. We smile at each other. "I need to grab my coat and also something from my trunk," I say.

She nods.

Excellent, the lug wrench fits. How fast can I get things done? I haven't had a flat in years. Watch me loosen the lug and jack this thing up. Ouch, my thumb! "Son of a …" Great, can't even finish what I was about to say. She's looking straight at me, smiling and nodding. I smile back. Okay, I've jacked this land yacht up. Now it's off with the old tire and on with the new, one lug at a time. tighten each one, *lay the lug wrench on the ground,* and plop the flat tire, hub cap, and jack in the trunk.

"You're ready to go," I say as I open her door to assist, her arm clasping mine, her purse in her other hand as we slowly trek to the Chrysler.

"Thank you," she says." The good Lord sent the right man."

There she goes again. My, look at her face; her smile seems to flow to her inner depths. It is as though I'm viewing a different person from the one of a few minutes ago. "You're welcome," I say. "Where does your daughter live?"

"Up the road, in town."

"That's the way I'm heading. I'll follow you," I say.

"For sure?"

"For sure," I say as I head back to the Explorer, the wind blowing at the side of my face. I open the door, start the ignition, and wait for Pearl to enter the road. She does. The good Lord didn't cause me to stop. The only reason I stopped was that there was no one else to do so. Back at home on the interstate when surrounded by people coming and going would I have stopped? The answer for certain is "no." Fact is, I wouldn't have stopped today if some one else already had. I'm a busy man, right?

I wonder if she ever goes over thirty-five. It will take at least ten minutes to go four or five miles.

Culpepper Webb

The silver Chrysler comes to a halt in front of a modest, well-painted, well-kept home. A lady perhaps my age comes out the front door immediately as though she had been waiting. I wave and head on.

In Search of Walker Wells

***

My bladder is full, my stomach and gas tank both almost empty, so it's fortunate that convenience store with the great fried chicken is right around the corner from where I just waved. I park to the side of the road and call Kay. Even though nature is calling me from two locations, there is no telling what has happened since I was out. It's a couple of minutes to one, so I might be able to catch her if she's back from lunch.

"Hello, Walker."

"What's going on?" I say.

"Nothing I can't handle. I'm working on the tape you left me. Nobody's called in."

"When was the last time that happened on a Monday?"

"Walker, I'm doing fine. Trust me; if Henry David Nobles had come back in I would have definitely called. That, or I would have left and you would never have heard from me again."

I smile. She's kidding, I think. "Well, I need to grab a quick bite to eat and gas up. I'll be back in about an hour and a half. Are you sure there's nothing I need to tend to?"

"Nothing that can't wait." Kay hangs up.

I ride around to the pump, hop out and open my wallet. What's this, no place for a credit card at the pump? You've got to be kidding. Whoa, that wind is cold. Glad I still have my coat on, and wish I was wearing the overcoat too. All right, nozzle in place and the gas is flowing. I think I can hold it til the tank is full. "I think I can. I think I can." How long is this gonna take? Good. Nozzle goes back in the pump and I dash for the door and through it. Great, the line is at the counter, not at the restroom.

I feel half-better now. Look at that mound of fried chicken in the glass container behind the counter. Problem is, there's still a line, and time is ticking. These people don't move fast enough. I've got an office to get back to, and regardless of what Kay said there's probably stuff stacked to the ceiling.

Culpepper Webb

These folks couldn't win a race against a turtle. They even talk slow.

"Freddie, what's it gonna be?"

"I'll have the box to go with this Coke, Tom."

What's this, a convenience store where people are on a first name basis, Freddie, the black guy in farm garb, and Tom, the white guy behind the counter?

"That'll be $4.79. What in the heck are you coming in here for so late today? You can't be plantin' anything yet," says Tom from behind the counter.

"Naw, but if I don't get that tractor fixed I won't be plantin' when I'm supposed to. I've got that tractor all tore down. Can't afford nobody to repair it, much less buy a new one. Tractors are about as bad as combines," says Freddie.

"How's that?" says Tom.

"Price of one of those big new ones is almost a half a million dollars," says Freddie.

"Imagine that," says Tom.

If these two carry on this conversation at this same speed, Freddie's gonna miss "the plantin'" anyway. Oh, I don't have anything to wash the chicken down with, and the container with the soft drinks is at the other side of the store. What to do? Behind me is a heavy-set white kid with *Chester* on his shirt who looks like he drives a route truck, and a young black kid in a blue shirt who looks like a mechanic. "Y'all mind if I grab a Coke?" I say.

"Go on ahead," says Chester with no hesitation, as the young black kid shyly nods and smiles.

I make it back while Tom is dispensing change to Freddie. "Thank you," I say. Chester nods and the black kid smiles. Hmm, there's no push, no shove, no facial expression of "hey buddy, why didn't you think of that ahead of time?" Back home I would have drawn a scowl from at least one of them.

"Whatilitbe?" Tom asks me as he nods to the two men walking in the door, white farmers dressed in khaki pants wearing windbreakers and caps with seed company emblems on the front. It's "Hey Carl and Carl Junior" before I can speak, followed by "hope you're not out of chicken, Tom," and Tom coming back with "not yet."

"We're still working on equipment," the older Carl says as Tom nods back.

"What can I get for you?" Tom says, turning back to me.

"I owe you for gas on the second pump and I need some chicken to go with this Coke. What's the best deal?"

"The box; it's a chicken breast and a drumstick with a potato log and roll. You goin' to a funeral or comin' from one?"

"Pardon?" I say.

"Nice suit."

Of course, fine as they come, suitable to walk into any law or accounting firm in the country. Problem is, this isn't a law or accounting firm. Until this very moment I didn't realize how conspicuous I was *and still am.* The only matching bit of wardrobe I have on is my shoes, totally caked in Mississippi-Delta mud, a reminder of my tire-changing. "No funeral. I had an important appointment."

His compliment was genuine. He wasn't making fun of me. He actually thought I was attending a funeral.

"Credit card?"

"Yes," I say as I hand it and he returns it with a smile.

"Drop back in on your next trip through."

I nod to Tom, then to Chester and the young black kid, to Carl and Carl Junior who are standing by the door. It's out the door, box of chicken and Coke in hand as I move fast to the Explorer because I'm in a hurry. Got to get to the office, work piled to the ceiling and all. I'll inhale this chicken on the road. I mean, folks back there have all the time in the world. A doctor would go to sleep checking their pulse, any one of them. Why, I bet they…What? Don't have anything to do, and they're grabbing a bite to eat at one o'clock? Probably got started this morning about the time I did. Maybe I'll pull around to the side of the store, park the vehicle, and eat the chicken instead of inhaling it.

    When was the last time I ate a meal in a vehicle when I wasn't driving? Is there a law against eating and driving? Maybe there ought to be. Oh, that chicken was good, but now I'm on the borderline of miserable, my stomach out of shape where I can't handle fried food. Growing up, if someone had offered me sushi, I would have demanded it be fried. I've changed. Well, I best get moving; back on the two-lane, and back to the office, maybe a little radio to keep me company. I cut the radio on.

    "Coke and Pepsi two dollars and ninety-nine cents a six pack. That's two dollars and ninety-nine cents a six pack. Plump and juicy whole chickens, and the finest pork to be found, along with potatoes, russet and sweet, along with turnip greens, fresh as they come. That's Red and Blue Supermarket on Old River Road, right across from Quality Auto."

    This station's half static. Now it's all static, a lull in the action between commercial and program. I'll switch stations.

    "Stop, don't touch that dial!"

    "What?"

    "Don't matter if you're big and fat like a refrigerator or long and skinny like an alligator, jumpin' over the hump or down in the dump, ready and rarin', or about to be child bearin', you need to be listening to Blues Man each and every afternoon, so listen up. This afternoon it's all about the late and great Yazoo Clay."

    Hey, I haven't heard a song of his in years. I like his music.

    "We got started at noon talking all about Yazoo, listening to his tunes and all. He began playing in the clubs all around the Delta in the late 1940s, movin' on up to Memphis in the early '50s playin' in the clubs all up and down Beale Street with an old Sears and Roebuck that wasn't even electric. Wasn't til the mid-fifties when he started playin' on an electric guitar and cuttin' 45s that he really took off. He got to playin' all over the place: Detroit, Chicago, all the way to Los Angeles, California. He was singin' up storms, in clubs and on the radio. Imagine, all the way from pickin' cotton in Mississippi to Chicago and Los Angeles!

"But life's got a way of turnin' on you; or you on life. After his wife Magnolia died of cancer his blues got bluer. Yazoo was bad to take to the bottle. Listen up to *Miss that Woman*.

Man that guitar is whining; sounds like it's crying real tears.

"Love that woman sho' enough
I was actin' mighty tough
Thought I's born to rule the world
And I sho' did love that girl
Sho' is lonely withya gone
Like a dog without a bone"
"Like a dog without a bone."

I like that. Yazoo sure had a way with words. I remember several songs by this guy. What were they? That's gonna bug me to no end until I remember.

"Miss that woman since she died
Many a night lay and cried
When I's young she caught my eye
Made my heart wanna fly
Didn't mean to up and marry
But my baby she start to carry
Sho' is lonely with you gone
Like a dog without a bone
Miss that woman since she died
Many a night lay and cried"

How long have Laura and I been married? Thirty-four years; no it's thirty-five, going on thirty-six. My, the years do pass. It was a bumpy the first few years. Before Rob arrived I had the roving eye. Just couldn't adjust to the thought of being tied to one person for my whole life. The thought of that robbed me of my sense of adventure. Wonder if Yazoo was that way? He had to be. Those blues guys all led a hard-living life. I would be devastated if Laura died. What do I mean *if?* I deal in life insurance. It's *when;* but it will probably be me first anyway.

>"Loved that woman day and night
>Always made me feel just right
>Til one day she took up ill
>And I tried to down that pill
>Was a pill I couldn't swalla
>Made me wanna cry and holla
>There lay my woman not too old
>Made me wanna bare my soul
>Sho' is lonely with you gone
>Like a dog without a bone
>Missed that woman since she died
>Came a time I no more tried
>Sho' is lonely with you gone
>Like a dog without a bone
>Miss that woman since she died
>Many a night lay and cried
>Many a night lay and cried."

"You're listenin' to Blues Man. Right when you think you're on top of the world, all successful and the like, somethin' sneaks up and knocks you down flatter than the Mississippi Delta. And there you are layin' on the ground lookin' up at a sky that one minute before didn't have a cloud in it, and the next minute it's full of gray. That's the time you gotta get up! Trouble is, Yazoo Clay never got up. From then on he just holed up in his room, and drank his life away. Never mind that his children weren't grown and he quit tendin' to 'em. No excuse for that at all. As was the case, relatives took up the slack. Seems like that's often the case, isn't it? Anyway, he did keep writin', and did a little recordin', though not much happened to it til he died. Ain't that the way it always is? They put you in the ground then 'fore you know it you're famous.

"Here's one of those songs that got to be real popular after Yazoo died."
Wow, he can make that guitar whine.
"Mogen David wine and the Schlitz Malt Liquor Bull
Sometimes I run half-empty, sometimes I'm runnin' full"
Oh, yeah! I remember this one.
'Cause since I took to drinkin', don't never seem to quit
'Cause since I took to drinkin', my life ain't worth cold spit
Don't never do no travelin', just stayin' in my room
I done got so lifeless, can't even lift a broom
'Cause since I took to drinkin', don't never seem to quit
'Cause since I took to drinkin', my life ain't worth cold spit
Don't never seem to get up, just layin' in the bed
Don't never seem to get up, got a pain in my head
Don't never play my guitar in front of folks no more
Don't never make no 45's, life be nothin' but a chore
I reckon my life be no count, ain't never really happy
I guess I'll up and die, just like my dear old Pappy
Mogen David wine and the Schlitz Malt Liquor bull
Sometime I run half-empty, sometimes I'm runnin' full
'Cause since I took to drinkin', don't never seem to quit
'Cause since I took to drinkin', my life ain't worth cold spit
My life ain't worth cold spit."

"Coke and Pepsi two dollars and ninety-nine cents a six pack. That's two dollars and ninety-nine cents a six pack. Plump and juicy chickens…"

I turn off the radio. I'm about to lose that station, almost nothing but static now. Old Yazoo Clay, what were some other songs he sang? They'll come back to me. Wonder when his life turned down the path of wrong- direction? Was it when his wife died, or was her death one large brick too many on life's wagon? Sort of like Henry David Nobles. A woman, or should I say women, didn't throw his life off-course. He was well along that path before a woman arrived, all the way back to grade school, a life full of tragedy. One wrong turn after another. And yet, I've always thought he would land on his feet. Today I came away with different vibes. Talk of going away to Tierra del Fuego. Where is that, Argentina or Chile?

So, when do the wrong turns start? Is it one big event in a person's life or a series of small ones? Take me for example. It's not like I've lived a life of perfection. More times than I can count I wished I'd done things differently. Unlike Henry David, I've kept some distance from the cliff of self-destruction, and in that respect I've been successful. In the end, will that be my epithet? "He never fell from the cliff of self-destruction; neither did he leap." Will that be all? Maybe. I've always been able to see the cliff before the edge, and I've always been strong enough to "will" myself the other way. *Always.* I'm a survivor, all on my lonesome. I overcome. I believe I always will; that is until I die.

What was it Randolph said? "In a matter of weeks someone will be shoveling some of this fine Mississippi Delta dirt in my face. If that's all there is, wouldn't that be sad?" And just a moment ago Blues Man talked about putting Yazoo Clay in the ground. One wouldn't think that Randolph Hollings and Yazoo Clay would have anything in common, but they do. We all die, don't we? Daddy's death, fifty years ago today made such a dramatic impact in my life. For some unexplainable reason, that's when I began to close the casket on the hereafter, on anything beyond the here and now. I shut it tight that December night my senior year in college. All there is is what I can touch and see. What do I believe in? *Myself.* I'm the only one that I can fully trust.

Hey, up ahead on the right is that patch of woods I passed this morning, the ones I'm going to visit as soon as the weather warms up. It will be special. It will be nice and peaceful just like this present moment. Up ahead, across the lane to the side of the road is that old Case tractor, same place as earlier; and there's a pickup, white, three-quarter-ton, approaching. Wait, that pickup is swerving toward my lane. Now it's swerving back to the other side of the road. It's going, it's going to hit that tractor! No! Turn; turn! It hit the tractor at full speed! Is what I'm seeing real?

    Settle down, Walker. Take a deep breath and collect your thoughts. Oh, that looks bad. The front of the truck driver's side looks like an accordion and there's a man slumped behind the wheel. The front glass is shattered. Looks like he tried to cut to the right before he hit the tractor, so I won't have to stand in the road. The door's part ways open, so I ought to be able to get in. There's blood all over the man's face. Nobody else is in the truck.

    "Ugh, Ugggh. Ugggh."

    Good, he's making noises. That's a relief. He's leaning away from the door. My, there's blood everywhere. I grab the door by the handle and tug. It won't open because the front end has pushed into the door. Yank harder; harder! It's opening more. I wedge between the cab and door and push it fully open.

    "Mister, are you okay?"

    "Ugggh. Ugggh."

    Blood is flowing out of that gash in his neck and his broken left femur juts out of his leg, That's awful!

    "Sir, can you hear me?"

    "Uh-uh," he nods. He's bleeding like crazy. I take off my coat and remove my tie. I wrap my coat around his leg and apply pressure above the break. I hold my tie hard against the gash on his neck. So far, so good. Man, he was losing blood, another minute and there would be no telling.

    He's somewhat alert now, not as stunned as a moment ago. He's about to speak. Appears to be about a decade and a half younger than me with a rounded-face, medium-length black hair, dark-rim plastic glasses leaning sideways atop his nose, a muscular build. This guy looks eerily familiar, as though I've seen him before. Where it would be, I have no clue.

"I was texting an appointment, and took my eye off the road, then saw a vehicle coming. I cut back the other way and I ran into the tractor," he says with great effort.

Gosh he looks familiar. I could say the same about his voice. I've got to call for help, but I'm afraid to release pressure. Oh no, in my haste I left my phone in the Explorer. I left my phone in the Explorer! Walker, you idiot, Why didn't you grab it?

"How bad off am I?"

He knows he's in rough shape. What are the right words? The worst thing I can do is remain silent. "Well you've lost some blood, but if I keep applying pressure on your neck and leg I think we have slowed the flow down. You don't need to move much, but can you move your arms and right leg?"

"I think so."

His right leg moves, and he raises his right arm as if asking to speak. He's not paralyzed. He needs to quit moving. "That's enough. Don't want to get too active, but you're not paralyzed." Why did I leave that cell phone in my vehicle? Why! I wasn't totally in control. His is on the floorboard smashed to bits.

"Texting and driving; it's always seventeen-year olds they show in the television ads. No one would pay attention to a forty-five year old; it wouldn't be believable. I'll have a hard time explaining this to my wife and two kids. My son, Mike Junior, drives. Now I'll be able to tell him 'see what happens when you text and drive.' I've got a daughter, Sarah, who just became a teenager, and my wife is Olivia. I'm Mike, but I guess you figured that out. What's your name?"

He's talking fast; didn't even stop to catch his breath. "Walker Wells."

"That's a unique name. Don't think I've ever heard it before," he says with great effort. "I'm losing blood and really hurting, mostly in my leg. Do you think I'm going to make it?"

His eyes filled with fear are locked on mine. It's uncomfortable. "Yes," I blurt without losing eye contact, yet truthfully within my heart I have no idea. If medical help doesn't arrive soon, "yes" could prove to be as hollow a word I have I have ever uttered. Yeah, at forty-five he should have known better than to text and drive, and at almost sixty I should have known better than to leave my cell phone on the front seat of my Explorer. I need to get my phone from my vehicle. Are you strong enough to hold the tie against your neck, the coat against your thigh?" I say, doubting his strength regardless of the reply.

"I think so," he says with total lack of confidence.

"Hey guys, what's going on?"

I flinch, startled. The voice from behind me is middle-age male, deep, calm, and deliberate. I turn my head to connect the voice with a face and see a fortyish medium-dark black man with neatly cropped hair. He's wearing a dark-blue dress shirt and khakis; and he's holding a cell phone, the sight of it giving me an immediate sense of relief. It's odd at this moment of crisis how I notice the details. Everything is so vivid, my senses so enhanced. So much is happening in such a short timeframe.

"He collided with the tractor," I say. "Call 911! Tell them we need an ambulance. He's not paralyzed, but he's got a broken leg and he's losing blood. And let them know the truck is not in the road."

From the corner of my eye I see him calmly touching the front of the phone and hear him relaying the information, adding the location of the wreck. He must have a GPS app on his phone. He doesn't live in the dark ages like me.

"A highway patrolman is within five miles, the ambulance is ten minutes away."

"I wish that were reversed," I say. "I don't think much time elapsed before you arrived, but we don't have time to spare. I'm Walker and this is Mike."

"I'm Hudson," he says. "What can I do?"

"Nothing," I say. "I'm afraid to let go of the pressure for even a second, and I'm almost certain that moving him would not be the right thing to do. Things are as under control as can be expected under the circumstances."

"Would one of you say a prayer for me?" Mike says, trying to sit up, as if to get our attention. His glasses fall onto the floorboard.

"Settle back down," I say, trying to calm Mike. He has a look of nervous fear on his face.

"I'll pray," Hudson says as he moves beside me and gently lays his hand on the top of Mike's head. Mike closes his eyes immediately. I pause momentarily then close mine also, out of respect I suppose; or so that if Mike opens his eyes he won't see me staring at him. Hudson is pausing, not jumping right into it.

"Lord, there is so much we don't understand, so many whys and wherefores in life. What I do understand is that You are present. You are real; and are seeing and listening. Mike is in physical danger. If You see fit within Your wisdom to heal him, please do so. You know what is within our hearts. Please touch Mike's heart; let him know Your presence. If Mike does not know You, grant him acceptance, if he is willing. I plead these requests in Jesus name."

My eyes remain gently closed. I'm not clinched in tenseness, my mind is floating, now coming back to the realness of the present, Mike's blood soaked through the cloth engulfing my fingers and palms, that sensation forcing me to open my eyes, to look at Mike, his eyes no longer partially obstructed by the glasses, but open and naked, fixed upon mine. His fear is gone. I can see that on his face and feel it in his body. This is all so vivid; so real. Mike's eyes cut from mine to Hudson's as he says calmly, "I've had God's acceptance since my youth."

I turn toward Hudson and ask, "Are you a preacher?"

"No, I'm the manager of a grocery store. I'm on my way to visit my mother."

"I'm glad you came by when you did," I say.

Hudson nods. He's looking at Mike.

I pretty much had to stop, didn't I? I mean, I witnessed the wreck. What kind of heartless person would have ridden on past in a situation like this. But Hudson, he was after the fact, how long I don't know, but after the fact nevertheless. He could have driven right on by. After all, he is going to see his mother.

Oh, here comes the blue circling light. The last time I was approached by one of those the patrolman gave me a ticket. Now, I'm anxious to see him. It's all about perspective, isn't it? He pulls up behind Hudson's Lexus and hops out quickly.

"Is that the ambulance?" asks Mike pleadingly.

"A highway patrolman," I say, noticing the change in Mike's expression. He's not looking forward to the upcoming conversation.

"Fill me in," says the patrolman.

"Mike needs medical attention. He has a gash in his neck and a horrible break in his leg," I say. "I'm applying pressure to both, and I shouldn't let go."

"How are you doing Mike?" the officer says, leaning over to take a view. "I'm Patrolman Watson."

"Everything hurts," Mike says. He clears his throat. "Is the ambulance far off?"

"It will be here any minute and it's a good crew. So what happened?" he asks Hudson and me.

"Might as well come clean; I was texting and swerved off the road," Mike says, his eyes on the patrolman as he confesses. His eyes are pleading for help.

"I'll take a peek at your driver's license when you're getting in the ambulance. For now, how do I get in touch with family? Who should I call?"

"My wife, Olivia."

Boy, Mike is struggling to get the words out. He's attempting to regain his strength before giving the phone mumber.

"662 555 1513, that's the cell. 662 555 4343, the landline at work."

His words have come to a halt. He's trying to catch his breath, literally, and he desperately desires to say more, much more. Man, my hands are drenched in blood.

"I'm forty-five. My two kids aren't grown."

I hear the sound of the ambulance, distant but rapidly approaching. From the corner of my eye I see Patrolman Watson.

"Walker?" Mike says, his words soft, his body weak.

"Yes."

"Olivia's cell number is north Mississippi area code, 555 1513. That's 555 1513. She works for Austin and Bailey, a law firm in town, just up the road. If the cell phone is dead, they can find her if you can't. You need to promise something. You hear me?" Mike says, grabbing my arm with every ounce of energy in his body.

"I hear you."

"I'm Mike Petty. It's strange, but at this moment I say that as much for me as for you. For forty-five years that's been my identity. It's what I'm known by, not what I'm known for. I've got a decent gift of gab, enough to be successful in chemical sales to farmers. I'm okay when it comes to selling. It's just…it's just, I can't express myself when it comes to the way I feel, the things that matter the most. It's not that I don't love Olivia or Mike Junior or Sarah. It's just, it's just..."

He's struggling. I want to tell him to quit talking, to save his strength, but I can't do that. He has something to say.

"I've never been able to tell them I loved them."

He's paused again, mustering his strength.

"If I don't make it, if I don't speak to them again, will you promise to tell them I loved them? Will you promise?"

I've never seen a more earnest plea in my life. "I promise," I say, looking him straight in the eyes, again struck with the thought that we have met. Wait! "Did you know a man named Robert Petty, used to be a teacher, and a football coach?"

"He was my father. He's been dead for some time. I still miss him. Why do you ask?"

Wow. It's like Mike got a sudden burst of energy. Look at him: rounded face, short dark hair, his nose rounded a bit, his neck muscular. It's as if I'm holding his father who taught and coached me, the man I thought of this morning as well as the other day. My hand against his neck is shaking, not wildly, but a tremor. I stare at my hand as if by doing so I can will it to stop shaking, but I can't. I can't! I can't!

"You knew my father?" Mike repeats himself, wanting to know more.

"He was my teacher, my football coach. He..."

"Out of the way, sir; out of the way. We'll take it from here."

I'm startled from in front and behind. I release from his pleading eyes and from his neck and thigh. My hands are cramped; the muscles in my lower arms ache. I continue to clasp the tie in my left hand. As I turn, a paramedic tosses my blood-soaked suit coat to the ground. I pause before picking it up to see Hudson who I had forgotten was standing behind me. He extends his hand to shake mine before retracting it upon seeing the blood that extends from my hands up both shirt sleeves to my elbows. Looking downward I see blood covering the front of my shirt. Until this moment I've lost track of the temperature. The whistling wind blows against chilled-blood. I shiver.

"Out of the way. Out of the way! We've got to get through!" Mike's body is strapped securely to the gurney. His eyes are closed, his chest moving up and down.

"We're taking this one to Jackson. He's trauma-patient all the way."

Culpepper Webb

They're by-passing the local hospital. What does this mean? I stare at the ground and in no time hear the siren of the ambulance, its sound rapidly becoming distant.

"I need to jot down some info," Patrolman Watson says, with me again startled by a voice.

So I give him my version of what happened, and Hudson his, phone numbers are exchanged. Patrolman Watson then turns his attention to the man in the wrecker who has come to get the truck, and I presume leave the tractor. Hudson and I talk for a moment, and although neither of us says, both of us of knows we will never forget this day and how we met. It's on to see his mother and far past time for me to be at my office, a place that doesn't seem as important as it did an hour ago.

A minute later I stand at the back of the Explorer with the hatch up and notice a knit shirt I had changed out of a couple of weeks ago on a day I thought no appointments were coming in. I start to place my coat and tie on the carpet before having the presence of mind to drop them to the ground so the blood won't stain my car.

As I strip off my blood-stained white shirt I realize I am again oblivious to the frigid wind, my mind so occupied by multiple thoughts that the cold is of no concern. What now? I can't litter, leave my clothing on the side of the road, something within tells me. But will this apparel ever grace my body my again? *Probably not.*

I place sheets from a legal pad on the carpet to shelter it from blood, laying the bloody clothes on top of them, then turn and gaze across empty fields against gray sky to the patch of woods in the distance, a spot I've committed to enter when the weather warms and the sky is sunny, at this moment realizing that I may not be able to wait that long. I have to go there and soon. I don't totally know why, only that I must.

My mind swims with thoughts; my body bursts with emotions, the most dominant at this moment the wellbeing of Mike Petty. Thinking back to high school, the football practice field, I remember Coach Petty's wife standing at a distance, time and again trying to constrain a toddler who wanted to charge on to the field, perhaps to participate; perhaps to be with his father. That toddler was Mike Petty.

    Until the past couple of weeks my life was on cruise control just like the Explorer was a quarter of a mile back. But recently there's been a storm brewing inside of me, sounds of thunder in the distance. Today, between my encounters with Henry David and Pearl, but mainly Randolph Hollings, the lightning strikes have been at close range. A few minutes ago the lightening struck me. The son of a man I thought of this very morning crashed before my eyes. I held his bleeding body. I stared at his pleading eyes. It's as if each of these people was placed in my life's path and I couldn't go around them.

    I slam the hatch of the Explorer.

***

It's a quarter of six. Best call Mom from here at the office. I might not have the energy to really talk if I wait til later. "Mom."

"How's it going?"

"I'm tired; the day was more than I bargained for. How about you?"

"Didn't go anywhere today; didn't cut the TV on…I tossed extra birdseed out the back door and watched the sparrows though the big window from my chair. They came in droves all day, as I sat here and relived my life all the way back to childhood, thoughts of Daddy, Mama, my brother, Anzel, and sister Mabel; all gone to the Lord. I was smiling one minute, wistful the next. I miss them, but nothing like your father, Harold. I got to that day when he died and I couldn't get off of it."

"Are you okay, Mom?"

"I'll be fine tomorrow. It's just that today is tough. You know what I am looking forward to?"

"What's that?"

"Seeing you and Laura again. It meant so much seeing y'all yesterday. I'll wake up tomorrow and each day until you come thinking about it. It's important to have something to look forward to. Are you looking forward to turning sixty Friday?"

I can see Mom smiling all the way across the phone line. "Not really; but I am looking forward to Natchez." I say that, but I haven't thought of it all day.

"You see, at my stage I'm probably more excited for you and Laura going there than you are. I'll be wondering all day Friday what you are doing. I'll want a full report."

In my mind I can see Mom's smile broadening. Rather than bring up anything about my day, especially Mike, Coach Petty's son, it is best to leave all of that alone. She needs to end the call on a smile. So do I.

"Love you, Mom."

In Search of Walker Wells

"Love you, son."

Culpepper Webb

***

  I lie in bed, my mind like a needle stuck on the same place on a record, the events of today replaying time and again. Henry David's visit was well beyond paying a life insurance premium. I'll invite him to lunch next week. That's what I'll do. Randolph didn't have me drive an hour and a half one way to cover his insurance policies. He wanted to tell me the *why* of his life. And today I changed a flat tire for an elderly lady, Pearl. I haven't changed a flat in over twenty years.

  You know, with all those things that happened today, I scarcely thought of anything tonight except the wreck. Can't even count the times I've thought about it. The facts of the wreck were different this time. I wasn't in the vehicle. How is Mike Petty? I called the trauma-hospital. "No Mike Petty." "Check the list again," I said. "Maybe you overlooked it." "No sir. I checked again. Not in ICU, not in an emergency room, not in any room." So I called the other hospitals and got the same answer. I tried Olivia Petty's cell about 7:00. "Voice mail has not been set up."

  I lie in bed. When I came home tonight, Laura looked as exhausted as I felt. I hadn't gone into detail earlier. We'll talk about it when I see you. I walked in the door wearing a knit shirt, mud-caked shoes, and a long face. Over the course of supper I talked more than I ate with Laura patiently listening. Along the way I told her Randolph Hollings had cancer and a short time to live. I didn't mention his testimony. She knows I hold back on some things. Laura places her arm across my chest and presses her body chose to me, breaking my thoughts. "Roll over, Walker."

  I hesitate then turn to face her, our faces a foot apart. Her eyes speak exhaustion. "I turned you down the last two nights. How about now?"

  "I'm depleted; physically, emotionally, totally. I'm as spent as I've ever been. Maybe tomorrow."

  "Sweetheart, that's my line."

"You've taught me well." I muster a smile. I cut off the light. Laura's body is again pressed against mine as I face the French door in darkness. As tired as she is I know she wants to say something, as she has all night. She wants to tell me that I have no one to talk to but her. She talks to God. It's been harder for Laura to refrain from that discussion tonight than it was to keep her mouth zipped yesterday with Mom. Right now I know she's tempted to speak, but she doesn't. She senses that it would only create friction, something neither of us needs at the moment.

It's strange. When we married, neither of us had a spiritual conviction. Hers came when Rob, our one and only, was a toddler. She drifted into church for his benefit and her life, unlike mine, changed. Rob. Rob. He's been on my mind lately; a lot. I've felt this compelling need to sit with him one on one. But he and Celia are three hours away in Memphis. He's an accountant and can't break loose this time of year; or doesn't want to.

Like those woods I saw today; the ones I've committed to go to. I need to see Rob soon, not in a few months.

So much on my mind. What were the words I said to Laura a moment ago? "Maybe tomorrow." Yes, maybe tomorrow will be easier than today.

Culpepper Webb

April 7, 1970

Leland, Mississippi

103 reads the number on the locker I just closed. I hold my notebook, English, and history books. For once I'm thinking ahead, the supplies for my final two periods in hand. I've had a hard time focusing recently with less than a month before graduation. Things have changed a lot in these twelve school years. When I entered school no man had ventured into space. When I entered school, the doctor's office had two waiting rooms, *Colored* and *White.* The town also had two schools, white and black. Later you could choose which school you wanted to attend. A few blacks chose to come to *our* school, and not one white chose to attend *theirs.* Last summer Neil Armstrong landed on the moon. Six months ago a federal court order landed on our town saying we would now have one school, not two. Over half the students in this hallway are black. I'm a minority.

"Move on to class. Keep it moving!" barks Deborah Mabry, my former junior high now senior high English teacher, the conversation of students uninterrupted. "Keep moving. Keep moving."

Oh great. I'm in her class this period, and she seems to be in a *more- lovely-than-usual* mood. I look at the scowl on her face, her wrinkles going all directions. She's in her late-twenties and before long that soft-skin beautiful face of hers will look like a road map of a mountainous state. So what contributed most to her demise? Was it having Henry David Nobles, Charlie Capicci, and Bobby Fortenberry, all in the same seventh grade class? Or was it her personal life, a divorce, she married to a two-timer who left her for that blonde with breasts larger than the pyramids; and with the responsibility a baby girl who is now three or four? Probably all of these.

"Keep it moving!"

I nod at Coach Petty in passing. Man, his role changed; seventh-grade coach when I enter junior high, and head high school football coach by the time I was a junior, our having gone undefeated year before last. We didn't fare quite so well this past fall, a team composed mostly of players like me. Larry Edson was the lone exception. The team was mostly white. The schools became one in January. Times change.

I edge into the classroom and mosey toward the back to sit with Horace Thompson, Larry Edson, and Henry David, guys I'm comfortable with, all white. It's not that I have anything against the black guys; it's just that these are the fellows I grew up with.

The door closes and Mrs. Mabry enters saying, "Be seated," followed by a slight delay on Henry David's and my parts, followed by, "sit down immediately."

Mrs. Mabry eyeballs the class, relying on memory for attendance, no roll call necessary, time to get down to business as usual. "Can anyone tell the class something of interest about William Faulkner?"

The hands of Camille Adams and Susan Baker on the front raise. These two future members of a synchronized swimming team with twelve years of practice now are nearing perfection.

"Susan, I'll let you go first today," says Mrs. Baker.

"He won the Nobel Prize for Literature. Although not required, I *did* read his biography."

"Susan, does the fact that he won the Nobel Prize make him a great writer?" Mrs. Mabry looks like she's a powder keg that's about to ignite. Hey, wasn't Nobel the guy who invented dynamite? I've got a feeling today we're gonna have an explosion.

"I suppose," says Susan, her answer tentative.

"'I suppose.' What does that mean?" says Mrs. Mabry abruptly.

"I guess he must be a great writer, or he wouldn't be in the textbook. I *did* read his biography. I can tell you all about him," Susan says, her eye contact moving from Mrs. Mabry to a tile on the floor.

What's this, nearing the end of twelve years in school and the first hint of non-affirmation from a teacher toward Susan? I think she's going to cry. And right next to her, Camille's face is covered in bewilderment. Although I'm in the back of the class, I'm sitting a bit to the side, just perfect for seeing all of this. Neither of them has *ever* failed to answer a question correctly and neither, to my knowledge, has ever been reprimanded. I'd buy a ticket for this. Hey, I'd like some popcorn.

"One's opinion of greatness regarding a writer is subjective. What is your opinion, Susan?"

"My opinion? Opinion? I don't know," says Susan, too flustered to think.

This is refreshing. All these years, guys like Henry David, and worse yet Larry Edson, as nice a guy as I know, have had to wear the dunce cap. It's nice to pass it around.

"William Faulkner is considered by many to be the greatest writer of this century," resumes Mrs. Mabry. "Personally, I consider him somewhat of a nut. However, I'll attempt to limit most of today's lesson to his work, not my personal opinion of the man. Most critics consider his work extraordinary. I have never heard his work described as mediocre. What does the word mediocre mean?"

The synchronized swimmers are taking a breather. What's this, Larry raising his hand in English class? He put a kind look on Mrs. Mabry's face when his hand went up. He has that effect on people.

"Yes, Larry."

"Coach Petty uses that word all the time. Most people would define it as not being very good. He defined it as not doing one's best. I like his definition better."

Larry may not have satisfied Noah Webster, but I like his and Coach Petty's definition. The textbooks have always come hard for Larry. Wonder how he'll do in the classroom as well as on the football field at Alabama. I can say this. He doesn't have an ounce of mediocrity in his body.

"That's excellent, Larry. You gave a dictionary and personal definition for the word. This shows you are thinking," says Mrs. Mabry, a smile on her face. I don't remember the last time I saw her smile. "Although, I said a moment ago that we would concentrate on one of Mr. Faulkner's works, I will acknowledge Susan's mention that he won the Nobel Prize for Literature, one of only six Americans to do so. He..."

What's coming now? Henry David raised his hand, perhaps emboldened by Mrs. Mabry's encouragement for Larry.

"Yes, Henry David?" says Mrs. Mabry, somewhat patiently.

"So where in America does this fella Faulkner live?"

"Henry David, Mr. Faulkner was a resident of our state of Mississippi."

"Was a resident? Where'd he move off to?"

"The cemetery, he is dead."

"So when did he up and die?"

"Henry David, one doesn't *up and die,* one simply dies. That event occurred eight years ago. I'm going to have you all read his biography prior to class tomorrow."

Mrs. Mabry is attempting to be patient. Henry David tuned out, and started doodling on his notebook the moment he found out Faulkner is dead. Perhaps he thought he could watch him on television one evening. Larry listens.

"Walker, tell us about today's lesson."

Oops. I read the first half of the story, but not the whole thing. I thought she would have us read through it in class today. This high school-senior-second-semester-bug has bitten me hard. "*Barn Burner* is the story of a man who goes around burning barns with his son."

"*Barn Burning*," she corrects. And?"

"That's about it," I say. Yep. That's about it, *it* meaning that's all I know about the story. Last night I got bored reading it and started watching television. Come to think of it, the TV was boring too. It's about time for me to move on in life. I've never before been so ready for school to be over, so I can go to college.

"Your explanation for the story is quite incomplete," Mrs. Mabry says, knowing full well that I didn't read the whole story.

"Tommy," Mrs. Mabry says to Tommy Wilkins, a black kid near the front of the class; a nice enough guy, pretty studious.

"It's about a man who goes around burning barns of people who rub him wrong. He has a son younger than me who gets fed up with it 'cause it's wrong. In the end the boy has to decide between family and what is right. He chooses to leave his family.

"Did you enjoy it?"

"Yes ma'am."

"What did you learn from the story?"

"Well, I already knew it was wrong to burn people's property. The young boy, Sarty, also knew it was wrong to burn people's barns. He was put in a tough spot. Was he gonna stick around while his papa kept on being destructive to other people's things? Was he gonna bury his head in the sand like an ostrich? Was he gonna turn his papa over to the law? His tough spot was not of his own doin'. Seems like you see more of that when you get older than you do when you're little. Your eyes open wider, and you begin to see what is right and wrong. When I was reading the story, I began to wonder if you ever get to where you can't see what's wrong, like your sight starts goin' bad on you. Some old folks can hardly see at all.

Although Sarty's papa wasn't real old, he couldn't seem to see that what he was doin' was wrong. Leastways he didn't let on to it. He just kept on destroying other people's stuff 'cause he was resentful. Mrs. Mabry, do you think Sarty's papa knew what he was doin' was wrong, or was he just blind, like his vision had given out on him?"

Everybody's silent. Tommy's words have me thinking, not so much about the story as his words. Maybe I would have been better off reading the lesson, rather than watching TV last night.

"God knows," says Mrs. Mabry.

What does that mean? Is she simply using an over-used expression, or is she speaking literally, which I'm not sure I buy? She's walking to what all the teachers refer to as the blackboard, although I can clearly see it's green, *Major de Spain, Mrs. Lula de Spain, Abner Snopes, Sarty Snopes* inscribed in yellow on the board. Henry David's hand is slowly rising. What now?

"Yes, Henry David, what do we have this time?" says Mrs. Mabry.

Those folks up yonder, are they from Spain?'

"Henry David, in response to your question, I will answer it by saying 'Faulkner knows,' or did know, as he is deceased. Wait, maybe he never did know," Mrs. Mabry continues with testiness in her voice. Also, your grammar is atrocious. Yes, atrocious! Why do you say, or should I say all of you put the word 'up' in front of everything? First, Mr. Faulkner 'up and dies.' Then you are pointing 'up yonder' at the blackboard."

The board is green! Why does she say black?

"The word 'yonder' is sufficient, nothing further needed," continues Mrs. Mabry, as Henry David chimes in with "where'd a word like 'yonder' come from? I use it all the time?"

"It's Elizabethan English; Shakespeare and the King James Version of the Bible! While in the Garden of

Culpepper Webb

Gethsemane Jesus instructs most of his disciples to stay behind while he selects three: Peter, James, and John to accompany him as he goes to pray 'yonder,'" Mrs. Mabry answers.

I've heard that story countless times, the last time at Easter. It's moving; but I've never been moved to buy into the rest of it, although at times I've tried. An internal conflict ebbs and flows, and this has troubled me greatly at times. I've never come to the point of God being so personal as to send a human to be sacrificed for others, and I've never falsely walked down a church aisle. This troubles Mom greatly. She's done her part, all but having taken those steps for me. But that's not the way it works, is it? Oh, I do believe in a creator of sorts. There *has* to be one. But, it's sort of like my taking a whack at that tetherball when I beat Bobby Fortenberry the day Daddy died. I remember so much from that day, not the least of things that I took one last whack at the ball, then stepped back and watched it go round and round the pole. I think that's the way it is with God and the earth as he watches it go around and around the sun; at least so far. But things can change, can't they? And maybe someday I will.

"Unfortunately, all those three do is sleep, as I'm afraid some of you do figuratively in this class on a daily basis," says Mrs. Mabry, hoping to now get back on track with the lesson, only to have Henry David's hand go 'up' again.

"Henry David?"

"Does that mean Jesus spoke English, since he knew not to put 'up' in front of yonder?"

"Aramaic, Henry David. The words were spoken in Aramaic!"

"Do you know what 'yonder' is in Aramaic?"

"No!'

"Do you know anybody who speaks Aramaic?"

"No, Henry David. I've never met anybody who does, and probably never will! No! No! No…no! No! No…no!"

And what else was Nobel known for other than giving away prizes? Dynamite; and Henry David just lit her fuse. In a way I feel sorry for her.

Culpepper Webb

***

My heart and mind are both racing. Henry David is as calm as can be. What about Mrs. Mabry? Should someone take her to the emergency room with chest pains from Henry David's antics? She's presently in front of a new class, final period, no Henry David around. I know for a fact he will pass senior English, and for that matter every course this year. What teacher with any sense of judgment would fail him, only to have him back as a student next year? He's home-safe.

Amending the Constitution, with *i* below it are on the board behind Albert Thomas, government teacher extraordinaire who is currently seated in his chair eyeing the class. He has that uncanny ability to make you think he's looking at you at all times; yes, each and every one of us, his eyes all-encompassing and penetrating at the same time, his voice deep baritone, his skin color light chocolate-brown, his hair full-crop with puffs of cotton-like hair within the black. This guy is as good a teacher as I've had; *ever.* He's made me use my noggin for something other than the interior of a football helmet.

The commotion settles, no need for Albert Thomas to raise his voice. Noise and movement stop naturally in his class.

"We continue our discussion of amending the constitution," Mr. Thomas says. Students are attentive. He has a way. "When I was your age my mother couldn't vote," he says.

There he goes, dropping his hook in the pool of students, patiently waiting for a nibble or bite, the kind of guy who could easily wait, if needed, until the bell rings. Wait, wait, wait. Look at those eyes; we're all under surveillance.

"She was black!" blurts Patricia, a somewhat oversized black girl, from whom Mr. Thomas steals her goat on a near-daily basis. I forgot to pop the popcorn for last period's viewing of Henry David and Mrs. Mabry, and now I wish I had it for this event, butter included. I look at the smile of Mr. Thomas, no teeth exposed, just ripples of dimples that let you know that he's smiling deep inside; Patricia, with no smile, is excited to no end. She already knows she's going to get shot down; brave girl.

"Yes Patricia, my mother was black, God rest her soul. She was one marvelous woman who has long since gone to be with the Lord; but that's not why she couldn't vote. Black folks, at least in theory, have been able to vote for over a hundred years, and although I'm advanced in years, I'm not that advanced.

He's paused again, all of us digesting and pondering, save Patricia who's having an exasperation attack.

"I say, 'in theory' because in our state it depended on which county you lived in. One was supposed to be 'literate.' In one county you simply had to be able to read, while in the next you had to be able to read in Chinese. Weren't too many black folks around these parts who had mastered Chinese, so it got 'em every time. It was an underhanded way of prohibiting people from voting. It wasn't so much the law as it was the way some folks manipulated it. So do any of you *girls* want to take a stab at what the nineteenth amendment is?"

Hey, he jumped ahead. Yesterday we were discussing the seventeenth. He's always keeping us off-balance, always a step ahead. He's walking to the board, writing *Women's Suffrage, Amendment 19/1920,* just below *i*. He never capitalizes *i*. "I was about you all's age when this amendment passed. With it, a woman could not be denied the right to vote due to her gender," says Mr. Thomas.

Patricia's hand shoots up quicker than the rocket that launched to the moon last summer, her voice in motion same as her hand. "Does that mean white women couldn't vote?"

Mr. Thomas' head goes north and south with a single bob, "whole-room surveillance" again in effect, no words flowing, none planned until… Henry David's hand goes up. Get me a fresh bucket of popcorn, extra salt this time.

"What do we have this time?" Mr. Thomas says, a hint of "what now?" inscribed on his face. Mr. Thomas handles Henry David better than all others, hands down.

"Last week we were talking about needing to be age twenty-one to vote. Do we have to know that for the final?"

"Is that all you are asking?" responds Mr. Thomas.

"No sir; but I usually like to take one step at a time. I can remember things better if I do it that way."

"This answer as always is 'maybe.' Now what else pray tell do you want to know?"

"Well everybody, you included, is so hung up on age twenty-one like it's magical. I think the big age is thirty. Maybe that's when you're too old to vote.

"Too old to vote! What's got into your head this time, son?"

Things are *always* getting into Henry David's head. The question is not so much "what," as from "where?" Obviously, it's from the far reaches of space, well beyond our galaxy.

"Well, some folks out in California say 'don't trust anybody over thirty.' So what do you think about that?" asks Henry David matter of fact.

Chatter abounds. Henry David, the master of chaos, has spoken. How will Mr. Thomas respond this time?

"Charles Evans," says Mr. Thomas.

Wow! That skinny black kid with the telephoto-glasses jumped.

"So Charles, now that I woke you from your afternoon nap, what do you have to say about not trusting anybody over thirty?"

Charles fidgets before speaking. "It seems to me that adults don't listen enough to what we have to say. It's like we don't know nothin' about nothin'." Mr. Thomas cringes over Charles' misuse of English; a true educator, a perfectionist. "So maybe the people out in California got it all figured out. If old folks, meaning people over thirty, don't listen to what we have to say, then why should we trust them?"

"Charles, I'm listening to you. A moment ago I listened to Henry David and to Patricia. Have I ever not listened to any of you?"

Come to think of it, he does listen to each of us, even Henry David's asking whether we "need to know to know this for the final," for the thirty-fifth time. I've learned a lot from this man. There are people to observe, to emulate. Mr. Thomas is one of these.

"I've passed the thirty-year mark twice with several years to spare," says Mr. Thomas, no pride in his demeanor. "Do you distrust me?"

Deliberate-Charles, just the opposite of Henry David, thinks before replying. "Maybe the people out in California should have said 'don't trust *almost* anybody over thirty.'"

Charles smiles, beaming the bright-beam. He has a future in politics.

"Yes Larry, would you like to say something?" asks Mr. Thomas in his soft baritone.

Larry Edson, shyest of shy, speaks in two classes in one day.

"I've had people over thirty be good to me. In your class I mostly listen, and I've picked up wisdom, things I can carry forward, same as with Coach Petty who's helped me a lot. He pointed me in the right direction when I was going the wrong way back in junior high. Fact is, I don't know if I would be a senior in high school if it weren't for him. Pardon my saying so, sir, being that he's a lot younger than you; but he is over thirty and a mighty good man, same as you."

"Listening to Larry's kind words about Coach Petty just helped me make a decision. You all have asked me since the first day of classes why I never capitalize the letter "i" except at the beginning of a sentence; and I told you someday I would tell you. I think today is that day. Years ago, while seeking spiritual direction, I was reading from the King James Version of the Bible when I stumbled upon something that seemed out of kilter, something quite peculiar; no, it was far more than that. Jesus is in the wilderness having an encounter with the devil. The devil takes Jesus to a high mountain to offer him the 'kingdoms of the world' in exchange for worshipping him. In the text, the word "I" is capitalized when the devil refers to himself, and 'thee' is not when referring to Jesus; same as in other translations, except it is 'you' instead of 'thee.' We are unquestioningly taught to write this way from the moment we pick up a pencil, all of us. Seeing those words written in that context seemed so incongruent to me, an elevation of one's self-importance above that of others, the ultimate source of self-pride countered against the most self-giving of all."

Mr. Thomas takes a long pause, looking pensive. The room goes quiet.

"Coach Petty is an excellent example of a man who doesn't think solely of himself. Self-centered people make for bad countries. They make for bad businesses. They make for bad families; always have and always will. When we have an overabundance of "I's" on a planet of four-billion, things don't run smoothly. I hope I've taught you, you can't be number one every time. It won't be too much longer and I'll be pushin' up daffodils, same as we all eventually do. It all passes fast, something I didn't see at your age. Won't be too much longer and those folks out in California will be saying 'don't trust anybody older than thirty-five.' Then it'll forty, then fifty, sixty-five; then finally *than* myself. Yeah, then they'll say, 'I don't trust anybody *but* myself.' Finally, some of them will come to realize that they don't even trust themselves. In life, one chooses where to place his trust. I hope that..."

"May I have a moment?"

Man, I just jumped a foot. All of us did. That's Mr. Sandiford, high school principal, booming loud and clear over the intercom. He's another one of those 'good men.'

"Earlier this afternoon I received sad news, quite sad. Bobby Fortenberry, who attended this school from the first grade until this past fall, was killed in Vietnam."

What? No way. Bobby Fortenberry?

"At this time I've been given no details in regard to arrangements. Needless to say, this came as a great shock to me, as I'm sure it does to you. Having served previously as the elementary school principal, I had known Bobby since his early years," Mr. Sandiford says with a break in his voice. "I ask that we all have a moment of silence for Bobby," Mr. Sandiford says followed by a hum from the speaker perched on the wall to the front of the room.

Mr. Thomas nods once without speaking, a sign to observe. I close my eyes and my mind floats. As with all tragic news, I don't have an immediate sense of grief, nor any other depth of emotion. I don't absorb quickly. So where do my thoughts start? It's the tetherball game the day Daddy died. I won the game. I beat Bobby who was older than me, although at the time I didn't know that he was so much older. I was somebody important. I was on top of the world, until I found out Daddy died. For the longest time I thought that because I, a younger kid, had beaten Bobby, that he had it in for me, that I was his rival. As time passed, I realized that he had either long since forgotten my achievement, or it didn't really amount to much in the scope of his life. Truth is, he probably never gave me much thought. Book-learning was difficult for him. After he was abruptly pulled from school last fall, I reflected on Bobby. His acts of disruption probably came more from frustration than defiance. He just couldn't measure up in the classroom; there was no way.

I remember well the day last September when Bobby was plucked from tenth-grade history. That's right, tenth grade. Bobby starts out a few years ahead, and last fall was a couple behind. He wasn't special education; he just didn't have the brainpower or the attention span to keep up. Word has it that Charlie Capicci, who had dropped out of school and was drafted, got word out before shipping overseas that Bobby had never registered for the draft. Charlie was envious that Bobby was still loafing around. So in September some army officers showed up and escorted Bobby out of fifth-period. Come to find out, Bobby was twenty-one and never should have still been in school. None of us knew Bobby was that much older. Mr. Sandiford was in shock. The school usually does a good job of keeping up with things like that. Bobby had slipped through the cracks.

"Amen," says Mr. Sandiford over the intercom, his voice not as big a surprise this time.

The room is quiet. The white kids all knew Bobby, and probably none of the black. He left before the schools became one.

Mr. Thomas looks at the class and says, "Bow your heads 'cause I'm fixin' to pray. God, there is so much to life that we don't understand. I see that more and more with the passage of time. There are those in this class who grew up with Bobby. They walked these halls with him. For those who knew him, it's going to take awhile for what's happened to sink in. There will be reflection. Within this time of reflection, may Your Spirit offer guidance to those students who seek it, a guidance and source of comfort that only You can give. If Bobby's parents are still on this earth, may You offer them comfort, for they most of all need it. In Jesus name. Amen."

Ring....Ring.

In Search of Walker Wells

***

The mood as I walk down the hall is mixed. A black guy in a different grade says, "Who was that guy?" as the other replies, "Man, I don't know." A group of black female students carry on a conversation, seemingly as usual. They didn't know Bobby. Had I not known him, I have no idea how I would act or feel. The white students for the most part are silent. I guess they, like me, have no idea what to say. I pause at my locker to make sure I get the right books to study tonight. I'll try not to be as unprepared in English class as I was today.

"If you want a ride to your house you'd better hustle 'cause my truck is about to pull out of the parking lot, with or without you," says Henry David as he flies past both me and his locker.

Man, Henry David is moving fast with Larry in tow just trying to keep up. I speed up to avoid the mile-and-a-half walk home. I follow Henry David out the door, into the parking lot, and to his pickup, a light blue Chevy that's fifteen years old, and runs; most of the time. He opens the door and puts the key in the ignition. I scoot next to Henry David as Larry piles in after me closing his door. Henry David peels out of the parking lot into a side street, then on to the main street, just catching the traffic light in that brief moment between orange and red as he moves the truck into second gear. The breeze from the rolled-down window circulates spring air as we pass houses on either side of the street for the two-block trek downtown. The truck needs a new muffler.

The cab is a tight fit, with muscular Larry taking up more than a third of the space and Henry David needing elbow room to drive. We make the jaunt downtown to the drugstore, a stop of necessity for Henry David. Nobody says a word. What are they thinking? Finally, Henry David speaks. "I need liquid worse than the Sahara Desert. Can't get there quick enough to get the biggest Coke they got."

Larry sits quietly, not all that different than he normally does, his mouth idle, not running. He speaks seldom in all settings, his comments in two classes today a true rarity. His words were not only public, but also personal. They were not so much about himself as they were of others. Usually when people speak personally, it's either to brag or complain. That's not Larry.

"That's got to be the slowest light in the whole state of Mississippi, and it gets slower every day. I need an extra-large Coke and quick," Henry David says, as he revs the engine.

This truck *definitely* needs a new muffler. Good, the light is turning green and it's off to the races, but there is no place for a pit stop, all the spaces in front of the drugstore taken. So we go seven or eight spaces beyond, right on the edge of the part of downtown where the shop owners turn from white to black.

Henry David is out the door within a blink of an eye with Larry's pace of exit deliberate, same as his speech, my gait similar to Larry's, as I smell the aroma of fried chicken flowing from the open door of the restaurant in front of the truck. Within, a rotund black man sits arms folded on a stool next to the counter. The man obviously enjoys his product. He nods and I nod back as I pass.

By the time Larry and I reach the drugstore, Henry David has a saucer-eyed stare on the largest drink I've ever seen, the man behind the counter asking for money, Henry David dispensing the exact change, then grabbing the drink with both hands and raising it to his mouth to begin to gulp. He momentarily removes the drink from his mouth to catch his breath and utters the words "I think I'm gonna live," then resumes his consumption, this time more vigorously than before. I watch in amazement as he downs the remainder of the Coke without taking a breath. "Dang, except for the ice, it's all gone. They ought to make these things bigger!"

Now he's munching on the ice. I should have looked at my watch and timed him. I think I'd like a Coke too, maybe the big one like Henry David's; that is if I can afford it. "How much are the Cokes?" I ask.

"We've got small, medium, and large; fifteen cents, twenty-five cents, and forty-five. What will it be?"

It depends. What do I have in my pocket? A quarter and two pennies. "I'll have a medium," I say, as he scoops ice into the cup, places it under the tap, foam rising to the top as he lets it settle before giving me one more shot from the tap.

"That will be twenty-six cents with tax," the man says. I hand him a quarter and a penny, leaving me one copper coin. I clasp the penny firmly in my palm before placing it in my pocket. For some unexplained reason it seems large and significant. I drink the Coke in non-Henry David fashion, the foamy delight sweet to my mouth, the acidic liquid exhilarating as it flows through my chest. Man this is good!

From the corner of my eye I spot Larry slowly turning a display carousel filled with post cards. He's not drinking anything. "What are you looking at?" I say as I edge toward him.

"Oh, just some post cards?" says Larry. "You wouldn't think folks in other parts of the world would want to receive a card showing a man in a mechanical cotton picker riding through a field, would you? Maybe it's just that people around here *think* that folks elsewhere would like to get a card like that. Do you know what looking at a cotton field on the post card makes me think about?"

"What's that?" I say.

"Bobby."

"Bobby?" I say, Larry's uttering of Bobby's name, the first mention of him since Mr. Thomas' prayer.

"Yeah, I bet he was lonely over there. If he got one of those post cards, it would have probably made him homesick enough to cry. Doesn't matter now, 'cause he's dead; died on the complete opposite side of the world. You know, he and I used to hang out together until junior high. We grew up just around the block from each other," Larry says, before pausing.

"Yeah," I say, feeling like I need to say something, although I don't know what.

"That's the time our lives started parting directions, Bobby drifting backwards and me moving forward. I'm not the smartest guy around, but in that regard I was always a step ahead of Bobby. You know what?" Larry says.

"What?"

"I truly think Bobby could have made it through school, although it would have been by the skin of his teeth. Me, I had athletics going for me. I've also had a mom and teachers who've cared. My dad left us when I was two and we haven't heard from or seen him since. Mom works two jobs just to make ends meet. On the other hand, Bobby's dad was a drunk who beat him every chance he could until he got too big to beat. I don't know which was worse, his situation or mine. All I know is, without some encouragement, I could have dropped out of school, and it could have been my name over the intercom today. So at this moment I've got mixed feelings. On the one hand I'm grieving over Bobby, and on the other I'm grateful to be where I am." Larry goes quiet.

"You're not gonna get a Coke?"

"Nope, it costs too much. Even with the scholarship, I'll need every penny for college this fall."

My foamy delight suddenly doesn't taste as delightful. I'd buy him a drink, but suddenly that penny in my pocket has shrunk to economic reality. I feel guilt. "Want some of mine?" I say, shaking the cup before Larry.

"Naw."

Hey, I guess Larry is glad to be where he is. He's heading to Alabama on a football scholarship. If he stays healthy, I know he will make it. Nobody will outwork Larry. "You sure?"

"I'm fine," Larry says, smiling that shy smile of his. "I'll catch up on Coca Colas at Alabama this fall."

"Y'all gonna spend all day lookin' at post cards of cotton pickers?" says Henry David, who walks up minus a cup. "If I'd had the money, I'd of drunk three of 'em."

"Three of those might not have been good for you," I say. Henry David is more hyped than usual, a feat I would not have thought possible. He's thinking about Bobby's death. People react in different ways.

"Good old Henry David could've drunk six of those and it wouldn't have hurt me. Y'all about ready to go," he says, not asking, as he waves the truck key and heads for the door, Larry and me in tow, lest each of us enjoy the walk home.

Back on the sidewalk, I hear music flowing from the restaurant as I head toward the pickup, the words becoming audible as I near its door. It's Yazoo Clay singing.

"Been runnin' round in circles since I don't know when,
Been runnin' round in circles, don't stop or begin.
I'm a rabbit on the run, aimed at with a gun.
Runnin' round in circles since I don't know when,
Runnin' round in circles, don't never stop or begin."

"Walker, you gonna stand there til midnight? All the good reruns are on TV in the afternoon, and you're about to cause me to miss 'em. Of course, this being a free country, you're welcome to walk home if you want."

"Been runnin' round in circles, since I don't know when."

"Henry David, do you know who that is on the jukebox?" I say, wanting to hear the rest of the song.

"Nope, and I don't care." Henry David revs the engine.

"That's Yazoo Clay."

"Yazoo who? Look, that's loony music, not even number one thousand on the charts. You wanna ride or walk?"

I want to ride. Larry's already moved to the middle, so I hop in and close the door, the truck moving in reverse by the time the door shuts. It's out into the street, Henry David shifting from reverse to first gear as we make a circle and head toward my house.

It is generous for Henry David to give me a lift. I live in a different neighborhood than he and Larry, a better one, my house a bit out of the way. I toss in for gas every once in awhile. I wish I could have heard the rest of Yazoo Clay's song. Is life just about "runnin' around in circles?" What is life about; the bottom line? I've thought of this, more so lately with high school graduation, a transition taking place, then off to college in the fall. On the one hand, I do want to think about my life, and on the other not, most of my days now spent wanting to be carefree. What I see, as I found out in English class today, is that life is not free of cares. A consequence rears its ugly head almost every time.

The breeze through the open window sure feels good, my hair flowing in the air, cars coming and going, scarcely a parking space available as we cruise down Main Street. Henry David stops, taking a brief look one way before turning at the red light. We cross the railroad tracks, Henry David looking neither left nor right. TV reruns are beckoning. To the left we pass oak-covered front yards, the leaves the tender-green of spring; to our right a creek, almost large enough to call a river, the oaks towering above the stream, a wooden footbridge crossing the creek just ahead. It is the whitest of white. This is the photo that should have adorned the post card. This is a moment worth remembering. It is a peaceful scene.

Henry David stops in my driveway, revving the engine. I open the door, hop out, and begin to close the door when Larry's eyes catch mine, his expression earnest, serious, sincere, if in fact a facial expression can be all of these. I can tell he's thinking about Bobby's death, same as me.

I watch as the truck heads up the street. Henry David takes a left turn with no turn signal, no arm extended from the open window.

Tuesday, March 6, 2012

Madison, Mississippi

It's twenty after eight. Kay and the rest of the crew will be here in no time, and I've accomplished more concentrated tasks in the past hour and a half than I probably will the rest of the day. My dictation is completed and I've looked over the files for my appointments, all here at the office at 11:00, 1:00, 2:00, and the last at 3:00, a wild assortment of planning financial needs, each family different. Might as well pause for a moment; quite likely I won't have that chance again until tonight. I'm running on nervous energy. Last night I slept hard and fast. This morning I ran five miles in the dark, not three. I drank coffee like it was water. My hug with Laura was quicker than an eye-blink. I dashed here. *Mike Petty.* He was on my mind with every step I ran.

It's odd that I spend so much time in this room and seldom if ever observe the details that surround me such as the rich grains of wood on my desk. It's usually covered with files. The chairs in front of my desk are upholstered in light blue leather. The only time I normally look that way, someone is sitting in one of them. The bookshelf to my left is filled with reference books that I, with the exception of the dictionary, haven't opened in years. These days I go online. There's a plant with large, smooth green leaves that sits in a brass pot to the right of my desk. Where did it come from? I know I didn't buy it. Who gave it to me? It was Kay, that's who, two or three years ago for my birthday; said my office needed "sprucing up." How ungrateful am I? I've never nurtured it, never one time given it an ounce of water. I walk down the hall to get some water in the coffee carafe, hoping to take care of this before Kay arrives. I find the carafe in the dishwasher. I run it under the tap and hustle down the hall. I pour a few ounces of water on the plant, hoping I haven't overwatered it.

"Walker, what are you doing?"

I jump. I didn't know Kay was behind me, and I spilled water on the carpet. "Gracious, Kay, you startled me."

"Why are you watering that plant?"

Why the look on Kay's face, her mouth wide open? "Truth is I don't think I contribute enough on some of the incidentals around the office."

"The plant is plastic."

At a moment such as this, what does one say? Nothing.

"I was going to get you a real plant for your birthday, but your office doesn't get sunlight, so I settled for a fake plant. Besides, Laura said you are the one person she knows who can't grow kudzu; that's what sealed the deal. Here, let me have that and I'll go and make some coffee. Would you like a cup?"

No, what I need is a dunce cap. "No thank you, but thanks for asking." I was only trying to be helpful. "I've set the files on your desk for dictation."

"How's the man who was in the wreck?"

"I don't know. I've tried everything but calling his wife's office. I'll do that right at 8:30."

Kay nods in concern, then walks away holding the carafe.

Olivia Petty is as bold as it can be on the first line of my legal pad, the phone number of her office beside it. It's 8:30. Over the years there's no telling how many times I've reached for the receiver and dialed the phone. Sometimes it's quite easy, other times the weight of it almost too heavy to lift, my reluctance to touch the numbers as pronounced as if each button was a searing-hot coal that would scorch the tip of my finger. Such is the present. My hand is on the receiver, but I have yet to lift it. I quickly lift the receiver and hit the buttons in rapid fashion. My heart pounds; my stomach churns.

"Austin and Watson, Chaz Austin."

One of the lawyers answered the phone. It's a small town, so I guess that's not too unusual. He doesn't sound too chipper. How should I approach this? "This is Walker Wells, the person who stopped to help Mike Petty at the wreck yesterday. He said his wife Olivia works with you. I've tried every resource I know to find out how he is doing. Would you mind giving me an update?"

Nothing but silence. Could it be I caught him off guard by calling?

"Your name again?"

"Walker Wells; I stopped to assist Mike Petty at his wreck, and I wanted to check his status. I believe his wife, Olivia..."

"Mike didn't make it. He died."

How can that be? I ran to assist him. The paramedics were taking him…

"He died on the way to the hospital."

What were Randolph Hollings' words? What were they! *It's always later than you think.*

"Mr. Wells?"

"Yes, I don't know what to say. Although in my mind I knew this was possible, it's not what I expected, not with the level of medical expertise that we have today. I have come to expect things to always work out. I…"

"She was contacted here yesterday afternoon by a highway patrolman. He was a real pro, so calm, deliberate, and comforting. He asked to be alone with her for a moment before he explained what happened, but she said it was all right for me to remain in the room. Look, I'm sorry but it would be inappropriate to go into more details. I really feel sorry for her and her two children."

Her two children? Yesterday it was *their* two children; how quickly one becomes past tense. What should I say or ask? I promised Mike that I would tell his family he loved them. I promised. "What are the arrangements?"

"As far as I know, none yet; Richmond Funeral Home here in town is in charge of those. For certain there will be nothing today. Maybe if you check back later they'll let you know. Look, I have to run. You can imagine things are in disarray around the office."

"Thank you for taking the time, Mr. Austin."

I've gone blank, nothing in my mind but thin air. My next thought is of Mike's face, mostly the look in his eyes, a vivid plea for help within them. Now I feel his pulse, the pumping of blood. Yes, his blood was everywhere. I pressed as tightly as I could. The whole process was like a reflex, one movement following another: stop the vehicle, run across the road, make sure I can open the truck door without getting struck by a passing vehicle, try to open the door, try harder, get it open, speak to Mike, see the flow of blood, stop the flow, all the while my cell phone lies on the front seat, across the road. What if? What if the ambulance had arrived three or four minutes earlier? Nothing I can do to fix things now. He is dead. My heart is pumping wildly. I breathe deeply, once twice, a third time. The pumping is subsiding. That's better.

Olivia. That's what it says on the legal pad. She's probably early to mid-forties, woke up yesterday, says bye to Mike and sends the kids off to school; just another day among many in a lifetime. Today she woke up in bed alone; that is if she ever went to sleep. Wonder what she did when the patrolman told her? Did she go blank, like I did a minute ago? Maybe she went berserk, screaming uncontrollably. I appreciate the attorney's discretion. And *her* two children, each old enough to comprehend death as much as anyone can fully comprehend the loss of human life. What did they do, how are they doing?

Back to Mike and the promise I made him. Right now, my thought of him is that of a toddler trying to run onto the football practice field, his mother constraining him. Yes, that thought, and that of his father, a man I've thought about recently several times. It's a small world. Coach Petty was one of those men, so common in past generations, whom you knew cared without his ever really saying so. Knowing that I had lost my father, he attempted to open the door by availing himself to me, offered to do so following the first day of football practice in the seventh grade. I never took him up on it. Larry Edson did. Yeah, Coach Petty was one of those tough guys who never went all mushy, but when it was all said and done you knew he cared. Maybe that's the way Mike was too. Only problem is, that doesn't work so well with family.

There's a knock on the door. "Come in," I say as Kay opens the door.

"Walker, you look pale."

***

It's been two hours since I called Laura and told her Mike died. I called right after school let out. "We'll talk about it more tonight," I said. I walk up the steps and open the back door. Laura stands behind the kitchen table. Shadows of flickering candles on the table dance on her face, a face that is both pensive and empathetic. I slide off my coat and undo my tie and lay them on the back of the chair. Laura rounds the table and places her arms around me, her breast against my chest. She looks me in the eyes, kisses me on the cheek.

"I'll serve tonight," she says, motioning me to sit, as I do. A moment later she places tea, a green salad, and meat loaf before me, and I reach out and grasp her hand ever so briefly before she seats herself. We eat in silence. There is no tenseness in the silence. She's trying in her own way to care for me, and to a degree it helps. Through the flickering of the light I pause, looking at Laura's face in detail, her rounded nose, ever-so-slight creases in skin, a sign of almost six decades of life, blonde hair mixed with streaks of gray covering her ears and touching her shoulders.

In a business sense the day was a success. I took a life insurance application, and helped two couples set aside monies for retirement. I stayed busy all day without a moment to spare, which was good because it helped keep my mind off Mike Petty and his family. Mike's visitation is tomorrow with the funeral Thursday at eleven. I'll show up for visitation to see the family well before the crowd starts to show at 5:00. They have no idea who I am. I know what I'm to say, but I don't know how to say it.

Normally, my mission of delivering a message to the Petty family would have been the first thing out of my mouth when I came in the door. But tonight is different with Laura "lighting the candles." I eat every morsel slowly. Neither of us is in a rush. "Go to the living room and make yourself comfortable on the couch. I'll get the dishes," Laura says.

I obey. I retrieve a novel, and Laura meets me on the couch. She leafs through a magazine.

"Walker, as tough as the past two days have been, we've got Natchez to look forward to," Laura says as she lays her magazine on the coffee table in front of the couch.

Laura's opening the door for conversation. The room is quiet; no TV tonight. The trip to Natchez? It was on my mind all last week, but it hasn't crossed it the past two days. I lay my book on the coffee table. "Yeah," I say, then, "the funeral visitation is from five to seven tomorrow."

"Although the family doesn't know you, it would be nice for you to go."

"I must go."

"Must go?"

"I'm going to tell his family that he loved them."

"That's nice for you to say, but how do you know?"

"Because he told me so. He had me promise if he died I would tell his wife and children. I said 'yes.'" I pause and look at the bookshelf across the room.

Laura tugs on my arm. She looks me straight in the eyes. "You didn't tell me this last night."

"I didn't know he was dead last night."

"It just seems you would have mentioned this minor detail," Laura says as she edges away from me. "Why didn't you tell me?"

Because there's a lot of things I don't tell you. That's the truth, but I can't say it; or won't. This time, why? Was it because I didn't want to believe he was dead? Was it because if I got into this, I might have talked on, telling about Randolph Hollings' testimony? That would have opened up a whole other discussion and Laura would have talked all night. Fact is, I'm not sure. There are times I like to keep my guard up. A lot. I don't get hurt that way. Hurry up, she's waiting. "I guess it's because I didn't want to believe he was going to die."

Laura's evaluating what I said. Usually I can tell when someone has bought, particularly Laura. Right now I don't know.

"So what are you going to do?" Laura keeps her distance.

"I'll get there before visitation. The words will come. They always do."

***

During our conversation about the Petty's, Laura's warmth cooled to well below room temperature. She wasn't angry; she was hurt that I had not told her the full story. We didn't talk much after that.

Later I called Mom. We talked longer than usual. Today she grocery shopped and played bridge. "Didn't have the best hands this time," she said. "But I got together with friends."

Rob, my one and only, has been on my mind of late. I've got to spend some time with him in person. It's not that we aren't on speaking terms. It's just there's friction. Normally, Laura makes the call. She's anxious for a grandchild; overly so. Rob and Celia don't seem to be in a hurry. Laura bites her lip; most of the time. I shocked Rob. I made the call, unplanned, spur of the moment, caught him off guard. After a while of this and that we actually talked. I'll make the call again, soon.

I lie in bed, my face turned towards Laura, my head atop two pillows. Wonder what she's dreaming? I raise myself and reach for her magazine, attempting to delicately slide it out from under her hands as not to awaken her. I slide it free as she mumbles something inaudible. Good, she's still asleep. And now, what am I holding in my hands? There's that actress, what's her name, on the front cover. She's what, twelve maybe fifteen years my junior; still looks pretty good. Hey, how much touch-up did they do for the photo? What does it say under the picture? *How I Finally Learned to Smile on the Inside/ Divorce Has Been Good for Me. Finding More Time to Do What You Want. Ten Ways to Help Balance Your Life. Healthy Eating/ Healthy Sex. Having Trouble Sleeping? We Have the Answer.* I bet that's the one Laura was reading. It worked well. I smile. I set the pamphlet of wisdom on the nightstand and cut out the light.

Culpepper Webb

Thursday, December 20, 1973

Leland, Mississippi

"I'll be watching every minute of it," I say to Larry, the well-worn windshield wipers work rhythmically against the glass in front of us. The rain is just beyond a mist. Henry David is having a rare moment of silence on the back seat with the radio off, permanently. I thought all football players drove big new cars, not clunkers, particularly at Alabama, a team poised to play Notre Dame in just over a week for the national championship in the Sugar Bowl.

This is mine and Larry's senior year in college. Unlike Henry David and me, Larry is the pride of the town, home for three days between exams and practice, a Christmas break this year without Christmas. For the first time in history the game is on New Year's Eve. Larry has to report back for practice prior to Christmas Day. Hey, but Christmas Day or not, this is the opportunity of a lifetime for Larry.

"Man, I'm exhausted," Larry says, "You wouldn't believe how hard I've had to study to make my grades."

Yes I would. School never came easy for Larry. If ever there has been an overachiever it's Larry, particularly in school. Academically, he had to fight to succeed in junior high and even more so in high school. I can only imagine how difficult college has been, and now here he is a senior, just like me. I don't have a clue what I'll do come spring; with a degree in marketing it will be something in the business world. The War in Vietnam is over, neither of us now required to pursue a career in the military. Henry David by-passed further academic advancement, the attainment of a high school sheepskin no small feat for him. His draft number was well into three-digits, so he was free to do whatever he wanted. He works for a large retail store that moved to the area about the time we graduated. The store is doing well; four downtown retail stores have closed since it opened. The world is changing.

"It's good to get the old gang together," I say, as Larry nods and Henry David remains silent. "There's no telling where we'll be in a year, much less twenty."

"I'll probably be teaching and coaching somewhere," Larry says. "I'm two inches too short and a step too slow to go pro. Heart and desire have served me well, but they've carried me as far as I'm going. The coaches and pro scouts say the same thing. 'Finish your education.' So, which light do I turn at, the one straight ahead or the following one?"

"The following one," I say. My mind has been drifting in thought. We entered Greenville, the county seat, three stoplights back. The rhythm of the well-worn wiper blades against the glass is hypnotic. I hadn't noticed we had entered town. We make the next light on green and come to a halt at the following one, then turn right. In no time we are downtown weaving around shrubs encased in curves that were placed in the broad street to "revitalize" it. It doesn't seem to be working. Look at all the shops that have closed.

"I don't recognize this place," Larry says from behind the wheel.

"Yeah, it took two years to redo the street. It makes you wonder whether it hurt the businesses more than it helped them," I say. We approach our destination, a bar filled with college students and young professionals, unlike the juke joints of our home town ten miles back; at least those were the inhabitants a year ago, the last time I came here. Larry spies a spot about a hundred feet before the bar and pulls in between two cars. The place must be crowded.

We hop out into the mist, the windy gust piercing through my sweater. By age twenty-one I should think I would have more sense than to simply wear a sweater in December. But hey, it's stylish, and that's what is important. I might meet a girl. The sound of muffled music and voices turns raucous as we enter the dimly-lit, smoke-filled, two-room establishment. The bar is in the room to the right. At the far end of the first room, a shoulder-length-haired male a few years my senior strums on his guitar as he sings into the microphone, the amplification of both the voice and instrument full-volume. Man, he's loud; this whole place is. Alas, where are the girls? They're outnumbered two to one, and all present appeared to be with a guy. This has been the story of my life so far.

"I'm heading to the bar for a beer," I say. Larry and Henry David tag silently behind as we enter the adjacent room, the bar concealed by bodies, all male. I raise my hand from behind the mass, waving in an attempt to catch the attention of the girl behind the bar, a perky blonde, a real looker. The guy who owns this place is no fool; a typical one of this bunch, myself included, would order a drink just to talk to her.

"How about a Schlitz," I holler, as she cups her hand to her ear, then shakes her head. "A Schlitz," I yell, and she nods. "What would you like, Larry, you paid for the gas, I'll get the drink?" I shout, although he stands next to me.

"A Coke," he replies, cupping his hands in the process.

I shout, "And a Coke," catching the perky blonde's attention.

She nods as Henry David screams, "And a Budweiser." The perky blonde picks up Henry David's message from amongst the noise. She's astute, and she's getting rich.

She returns momentarily, yelling, "Thatlbe two-ten." I reach in my wallet and retrieve a five dollar bill, the total amount I have on me, and almost the grand total of my money. I ran a bit over budget the previous semester. I pass the five over the shoulder of the guy in front of me, a Schlitz and a Coke coming the other way as I wait on the change wondering what to tip, somewhat bewildered as to why the Coke runs the same as the Schlitz; or at least it seems that way. If I give her all the coins back for a tip, I'll turn up ten cents short if we repeat this performance. I'll have to be a cheapskate and pass fifty cents back her way, which I do, carefully pocketing enough for a second round.

"Man I'm tired," Larry says as I hand him the Coke. I take a sip of my Schlitz and the liquid cools the inside of my chest on its descent.

"Sorry, but I can't say the same," I say. "I got home from school yesterday and slept til eleven. I better enjoy this routine while it lasts. I'll probably be living real life starting in the summer and eleven will be three hours into a work day."

Larry smiles a tired smile before changing his expression to pensive. "Man, I could use eight or ten of these," Henry David, who is always thirsty these days, shouts between gulps. Larry shakes his head in bewilderment, and I sip slowly on the Schlitz, hoping this beer and the next will last for the duration. Henry David grows animated for the first time this evening, all of this amidst the noise of the mostly males crowd.

I thought I would see some folks here I knew, home for the holidays. I recognized two somewhat familiar faces when I walked in, but aside from them this place is full of strangers. But hey, the main reason for coming here this evening was to get together with Larry and Henry David, to catch up with two guys that I once saw daily but haven't visited with except for a handful of times since high school graduation. I need to make the most of this evening.

"So, Larry, are you gonna make it out of college unhitched?" I ask.

"No question about it." Larry replies, smiling a broad smile, dimples forming around the corners of his mouth. "I thought for a while that Susan, the girl I was dating last year, and I might end up together. But you know what?"

"What?"

"As lonely as I've felt at times I knew it wasn't right. I don't know just what it was; maybe that she came from money, a pile of it; or that we would always end up arguing. And Walker, I don't argue, ever; except I did with her. That's not a good sign, is it?"

"I guess not," I reply. "I haven't dated any girl long enough to have an argument. That routine worked out pretty well until last semester when I ran out of prospects. My current definition of a date is a fruit they grow in the Middle East."

Larry's smile is brief before he turns pensive again and begins to speak. "I don't ever want a girl to go through what Mom did. I'm gonna treat the girl I marry like a queen. I'll do everything I can not to argue with her. I'll treat her special; and I'll treat the kids we have extra special, not like my dad treated me. I haven't laid eyes on him since age two. No memory of him whatsoever. For all I know he's dead."

This is a strange conversation, in the sense that I don't recall any conversation like this with another guy. Most of the guys I hang with can't think beyond daybreak about a girl. Larry is different in a refreshing way. He is so sincere. He's not the coolest guy on the world, but I respect him.

"Budweiser!" Henry David shouts catching the blonde's attention, no ear-cupping required.

My can of Schlitz still has weight in it. "You okay with that Coke?" I ask Larry.

"For now; I might need another in a while to perk me up."

"Just let me know," I reply as Larry nods back.

"Hey, are you that big tough football player who had his picture in the paper 'cause you're gonna play in some big, bad football game? Yeah you; look at me when I'm talking to you!"

I turn and see a big burly guy that I have to look up to; way up. I've never seen this guy before. No way to miss him. His unkempt hair and beard are fire-red, a perfect match for his current temperament. He's wearing jeans, a plaid shirt, and a scowl, and he's accompanied by two guys six inches shorter. He's drunk, plastered to the point of no return. And I thought this would be a nice evening with friends, a somewhat upscale establishment; and that I would meet a girl.

Larry remains stone-faced. The guy says, "What's your problem? You hard of hearin'?"

Larry shakes his head. "I guess my picture was in the paper this week. Mom showed it to me."

"Yore mama showed it to you! So the big hero is really a mama's boy. Ha, ha. You really aren't that tough are you? At least not without shoulder pads and a helmet."

Uh-oh, Big Burly just struck the wrong chord. Larry would go to the grave for his mother. I've never known a guy who cares more. His jaw is tense, a vein jutting from his neck, his fist clinched. Gosh Big Burly is big; maybe six-five or six-six, at least two-seventy-five, some of it gut, but plenty of it muscle, some of it between his ears. He's also bigger than Larry, and unlike Larry he has both fists clinched. He lunges at Larry and swings straight at his face.

Larry ducks and backs off. Man, he's quick as a cat, all reflex. He knows that the offensive lineman is coming to level him, and that the lineman will miss and end up on the turf, or in this case the floor, which is where Big Burly lands, face down.

Larry's fist is ready, just in case, his jaw tight as tight as it can get, the veins in his neck protruding to the point of bursting, until suddenly he takes a deep breath and unclenches his fist, his jaw loosening. The swelling in his neck returns to normal as he says, "Let's get out of here, Walker. Now."

I'm caught off guard, the rapidness of events almost more than I can absorb. I shake my head in a daze as Larry heads toward the door. Big Burly is now face-up shaking his head and shouting, "Yore nuthin' but a chicken."

Truth is, this guy looks like a fool.

"What about my Budweiser?" Henry David shouts, just before Larry reaches the door.

"Forget it unless you want to walk," Larry answers without looking back. I lay the unfinished Schlitz on the table of some unsuspecting onlookers as I walk toward Larry. Henry David follows as we walk out into the cold mist and toward Larry's car. The gusty breeze causes me to shiver. When we're all in the car, we sit in silence, the yet-to-be-turned key in the ignition, Larry's hands gripping the steering wheel. He is deep in thought, about what I'm not exactly sure, but it is an unmistakable fact. Even Henry David is, for the present, quiet.

"That kind of stuff happens more often than you think," Larry says, the only other noise now the patter of rain on the car. "It's such a temptation not to walk away, especially because I'm so competitive. But nothing good, other than feeding my ego, can ever come from taking the dare. I'd never forgive myself if I didn't get to play against Notre Dame because of something stupid I did. It's just that this time he brought my mother into the fray, and nobody does that. You don't know how hard it was to walk away from that guy tonight. I could have kicked him senseless when he hit the floor. But I chose not to."

With that, Larry turns the ignition and we back into the street. The rain begins to pelt the car, the well-worn wipers functioning minimally. Larry turns the car in the opposite direction as we head home weaving between the scrub-encased curbs, the wipers moving hypnotically, with no one saying a word. Halfway through the downtown section Larry again breaks the silence saying, "I was thinking about Bobby Fortenberry the other day. He just popped into my head."

"I haven't thought of him in a couple of years," I reply.

"He didn't make it eight months," Larry says, almost before I complete my comment.

No he didn't; dead over three years now, killed in Vietnam. It rattled me at the time; not that we were close, because we were not. But it was the fact that someone I had grown up with died; sort of a wakeup call. Anyway, it was on my mind greatly at the time, but after a few months thoughts of Bobby faded. After all, he was not family or a close friend. Until the day I learned of his death, I viewed him more as an enemy than as a competitor, thinking he held a grudge against me because I beat him at tetherball. How ridiculous could I have been? Had Daddy not died that day, I would have probably long since relegated that moment to the nearly-forgotten, as I'm sure he did. I find it strange that Bobby has been on Larry's mind. I wait to see what else Larry has to say. Thinking of someone not having much to say, this is the quietest I've ever seen Henry David.

Out of Greenville's downtown and back on the highway leaving town, Larry says, "I'm about as tired as I've ever been." We're stopped at traffic light, and Larry adjusts his neck. I can't tell if it's just to loosen it or if he is trying to stay awake.

"You okay?" I say.

"What time did you say you got up today?" Larry replies.

"Eleven."

"Tonight I'll break your record," Larry says, smiling a tired smile as he speaks. A couple of more stoplights and we're on open four-lane highway, no median, heading home to Leland. The cars and trucks coming and going are sparse. The rain falls gently as the windshield wipers go back and forth. The car begins to edge from the outside to the inside lane, then into the lanes of the oncoming direction.

The oncoming direction! Lights are coming at us! Now we're running off the road heading at some trees! "Larry!"

***

Where am I? I hear muffled voices from behind, I open my eyes. The light! The ceiling is plaster. I quickly close my eyes. I try to sit up to see what's going on. I can't, I'm strapped. I'm strapped! And oh, my head! And my chest too! It feels like it's been crushed. I'm so thirsty. My mouth feels like it's stuffed with cotton. Where am I?

"They think this one's gonna make it. Just waiting for him to come to; and one of the others hardly got a scratch; pretty amazing from what I've heard. It's a shame about the other one."

"Sure is."

"They say he was some kind of a football player, a college kid."

"Yeah, his mama went berserk when she found out he died. You just wouldn't believe. The woman was shrieking at the top of her lungs. Then she started pounding her head against the wall. The orderly finally grabbed her before she injured herself."

Football player? College kid? Dead. Mama shrieking and pounding her head on a wall. An orderly is restraining her. Yes, an orderly, I'm in a hospital.

The last thing I remember is the car running into the tree. We were going fast. It all happened so quickly. And now, I'm strapped in, but I can move because I could move upward against the strap. And I can feel the pain against my chest and in my head. I can see, although I don't want to open my eyes, the brightness of the light is almost more than I can bear. I can hear the nurses. My senses are in order. My consciousness is returning. Yes, my consciousness is returning. And what does all this mean? Larry is dead! I've got to take a moment and let that sink in. He'll never play another down of football, never have a career, never marry, and never grow old. His life is over, finished.

Life is not fair! And it makes no sense. I concluded both of those the day Daddy died. Tonight verifies that. No, this night puts an exclamation point on it. Of any person that I grew up with, Larry was the least deserving to die young. He overcame abandonment by his father. He was soon to graduate from college on time. I never heard him once speak unkindly of others. And strong as he was, I never saw him use that force to abuse others. Why tonight, if it had been my mom that guy was talking about, I'd have charged straight at him. But Larry didn't. And tonight he wasn't drinking. I guess the only thing you could have accused Larry of is studying too hard and coming home to see his mom.

So there you have it. A fine young man, as fine as I know, crashes into a tree; and dies. That's all there is to it, nothing more. Oh there is something more. Henry David, who single handily could keep Budweiser in business, hardly has a scratch. And me; I'm alive, and as far as I can tell, have all my senses intact, as well as my brain. I'm glad to be alive, I suppose. Right now I'm angry. I wasn't that way when Mr. Sandiford told me Daddy died; I didn't comprehend the *finality of that moment.* But I do now! I've got experience. Been there before, and I'll be there myself someday. Years ago I began closing the coffin on a personal god as they closed Daddy's coffin. Tonight I nailed it shut. You are nothing more than a spectator. "Damn You, God. Damn You!"

Wednesday, March 7, 2012

Madison, Mississippi

So, why am I running this morning, to get closer to that magic number of twenty-five thousand, a number I know is unattainable by my deadline? No, this morning I'm running because I need to. While the rest of the world sleeps I'm thinking, evaluating, questioning, and working up a sweat, my mind running faster than my tired body. Today I awoke with Larry's death on my mind. I could taste the Schlitz. I could feel the pain in my chest as I tried to raise myself against the strap. I could hear the nurses in the background and feel my heart pounding. And yes, most of all I remember cursing God.

I must redirect my thoughts. Today I plan to meet the Petty family and deal with the aftermath of a wreck two days, not nearly forty years, ago. I will show up at the funeral home, and hope that my years of people- experiences will serve to my advantage, and that I'll have the right words to say. I'll need to be at my best.

As I trek back to the house, streetlights shining on the early-morning street, I feel the ever-so-gradual incline in my thighs. The entrance to a school parking lot comes into view on my right. I always go straight, stick to my daily path, right on past that parking lot entrance to the school; *always*. But today I feel an urge, a calling to turn right, and I enter the parking lot, to run beside the school, to take the unlit service road behind it.

I'm a mile from home. So it's down the drive, and turn left, run through the lighted parking lot, and onto the service road with no streetlights. It is strange running without the aid of streetlights, a faint glow of the lights of a commercial district in the distance to my right the only sign of human-made light, stars illuminating the sky above. This morning there aren't any clouds, not a one. The sky is pure and stars are everywhere. Should I stop before the end of my run, something I never do? At this moment I feel compelled to stop and view stars. I come to a stop, place my hands on my hips, and look upward.

I watch the stars that cover the sky. I don't know the last time I saw a sight like this; stars, stars, and more stars, each a sun like our sun, some smaller, some significantly larger, and there are so many that exist that I could never count them all, so many that I can't see without the aid of a telescope, so many I could not see with aid of the world's most powerful telescope. These facts are more than I can comprehend. This planet I inhabit is so small, so insignificant when compared to the vastness I see above. And I am so small, a mere speck upon this planet, one of billions that currently inhabit it, one of more billions who have come before and died.

All of this is more than I can understand. I have never had the faith to believe that all of this vastness simply happened. *Never.* I do struggle with where I, as well as other humans, fit within this scheme. At this moment, I feel so insignificant compared to the immenseness surrounding me.

***

I pick up the phone receiver.

"Walker, this is Bob."

"Hey, Bob, what's going on?" I say, immediately thinking a negative thought regarding our appointment for tomorrow at 10:00. A call like this usually means there's a hitch. I've left the whole day free to complete the paperwork, which will be massive.

"We're still on board for the life insurance for the buy/sell agreement and we're ready to move ahead. Problem is, Fred has been called out of town for tomorrow, and I think you said all three of us will have to answer the questions and sign the papers, is that correct?"

Good, they're still ready to move ahead. "Yes. It would definitely be better to have all of you there at once. When can we reschedule?"

"What do you look like Monday at 2:00? We'll all be in for sure."

Where's my calendar? There it is the other side of those files. "That will be fine, Bob."

"Sorry for having to change the calendar, but Fred absolutely had to see this customer. If we don't make money, then we can't pay for the insurance, right?"

"That's right," I say. Bob's reply brings a smile to my face. He's repeating what I said to him last week. "See you Monday."

This is strange. If these policies go through, this will be the largest sale of my career. Any other time in my life the thoughts of this appointment would have occupied my entire being. I would have thought about it when I went to sleep, as well as when I awoke, and dreamt about it in between. And yet the events of this week and thoughts of my youth have consumed me. Something is happening inside of me, and I don't know where it's leading. A few hours ago I was pre-dawn star gazing with thoughts of my puniness compared to the vastness of the universe bouncing around in my mind. I was…

"Walker, your eleven o'clock, Marci Kern, is here. She's in the large conference room. It's the only one available."

"Thanks, Kay. I'll be along in a minute." I take a moment to collect my thoughts, to redirect them from stargazing. I reach for her folder. She was referred to me by a friend of a friend, same way I meet most people these days. She's in her late twenties, divorced with a young daughter, a school teacher who took the day off to "take care of things."

I open the door to the large conference room. Marci is wearing a pale blue dress and seated at the head of the far end of the long conference table, her hands crossed on the fine grains of mahogany. So strange, the conference table seems "cumbersome for the occasion," better suited for a dozen people rather than two, but my office is a mess, so here we meet. My, her features are strikingly familiar to Deborah Mabry, my junior high English teacher I thought of recently; dark-black hair with pale-white skin, youthful and, with the exception of a scowl, stunningly attractive. She also eerily reminds another woman of years ago. Don't need to go there; I really don't. Thoughts of her and of that time bring an ache to the pit of my stomach and a deep pain in my chest. Push her from my mind. I haven't thought of her in years. Push her out! There.

"Walker Wells," I say. Did Kay offer you coffee or water?"

"Yes," she says before shaking her head in rapid nervous fashion and saying, "but I didn't want anything."

I need to put her at ease, as best I can, so I nudge the chair to her left down a space before seating myself, leaving enough room to speak conversationally without being "too close." My, this room is overkill for a meeting of two. In addition to this massive table, the walls are dark-paneled with old-South paintings, a two-story antebellum home on the wall behind Marci, and a steamboat traveling the Mississippi across from me. "So you're a school teacher. What do you teach?"

"Third grade at the elementary school up the parkway; this is my seventh year," Marci says, offering little more than the answer to my question.

"Tell me about your daughter," I say.

"Alison is five." Her scowl dissipates and a smile replaces it. She reaches into her purse and pulls out her phone, showing me a picture of her daughter. Alison's smile is almost as large as her mother's, one tooth missing from the front. Unlike her dark-haired mother, the child is blonde.

"She's as cute as they come," I say, offering a smile, a real one not fake.

"I think so," says Marci as she takes one more look at the screen before placing the phone back in her purse.

Life would be so much better for Marci if she could freeze this moment, the mention of her daughter lighting up her being. But life doesn't work that way, does it? It is filled with heartache as well as joy, and I could tell from my first glance at Marci that the scales in her life tip more towards heartache. "Marci, how may I help you?" I ask.

"I'm struggling to make ends meet. I'm sure you know that teachers aren't overpaid. It's hard to provide for the two of us, at least to live in this area where the streets are safe and the schools good. It's month to month. I care for Alison more than you can imagine. I want to see that she is provided for if I die. Our mutual friend, Barbara, said you were the person to help me, someone I can trust."

Trust. That word keeps popping up. Mr. Thomas, my high school history teacher, whom I've recently thought about, harped on that subject. Who do we trust? And what do we trust? In the end, do we trust anything? For the moment, she trusts me. I know I can't take this lightly. There was that time years ago when I attempted to redefine that word for my own liking in my relationship with Laura, didn't I? "You can trust me," I say.

"Good," says Marci, her face displaying she is deep in thought.

"First, I need to jot down some basics such as each of your dates of birth, addresses, telephone numbers, income, assets, and liabilities," I say, proceeding with recording the information smoothly, seamlessly, until I get to Stuart. her ex. "What can you depend on Stuart for?"

"Mr. Wells, if Stuart jumped off the top of this building, I couldn't depend on him to hit the ground," she says, almost before I can finish asking the question. "All Stuart cares about is Stuart. He's been late on every support payment since the first. If it weren't for the legal expense, my lawyer and his lawyer would be visiting as we speak. Fact is, threatening him legally hasn't fazed him one iota. I can understand if he has resentment towards me, but his own flesh and blood, our daughter, Alison? Not caring for her? He was so fun loving when we were dating. But he was only in love with 'having fun.'"

Wow! Marci's natural beauty, which is immense, is again overshadowed by that scowl, her veins protruding on both sides of her neck. Too many of those scowls and her smooth white skin will age prematurely and look like that old proverbial "road map of a mountainous state," scraggy lines and crevices covering her face in abundance. This poor woman is at the present a "trampled-on woman."

"Does the definition of the word *two-timer* include a husband who had two affairs, that being the number I'm aware of? Is there such a word as *three-timer?*" Marci says, the veins in her neck easily visible from a distance. "No, I'm afraid I'm the only one Alison and I can depend on for income. If I'm dead, I want her provided for, and I don't want Stuart to touch a dime of it. If I can't trust him to provide for her while I'm alive, I sure can't trust him to do so if I'm dead and gone!"

Ouch! Her pain runs deep, and it seems there is justification. She's seeking guidance, so I give what I can. "I'm not an attorney, but I can tell you the courts weigh heavily towards flesh and blood when it comes to guardianship. Whether or not Stuart behaves like one, he is her father. The best thing to do is have life insurance proceeds payable to a trust. You could..."

"Mr. Wells, I don't have another dime to my name to spend on legal fees, and trusts aren't free!" Marci counters, stopping me mid-sentence.

I pause, take a deep breath, reach deep inside and force a smile from within, a calm one, "You could name a custodian as beneficiary for the benefit of Alison. Do you have someone you could trust with the money?"

"My sister, Sylvia," Marci says without hesitating.

"Is she married?" I ask.

"Yes, her husband is Al."

"How far ahead of the bill collectors are they?"

"What do you mean?"

"Perhaps you have no way of knowing, but are Sylvia and her husband in good financial shape?"

"Yes," Marci says. "Her husband, Al, is Mr. Discipline. He still has the first dollar he earned in the eighth grade. Used to be she complained that because of his discipline he was 'no fun.' Of recent, she's come to be just like him. Mr. Wells, it's *less fun* being broke."

"In the event you died, what would you want to provide for Alison?" I say, maintaining focus and trying to keep things on-track.

"The basics: food, clothing, medical expenses, and college," Marci says. "Right now fifty dollars a month is pushing it. Can you help me?"

"I think we can come up with something," I say. "I'll need a little time to work on it. Because of your schedule, I know you can't just come in anytime, so let's try it after school one day next week. How does Thursday sound?"

"But, Mr. Wells, I have to pick up Alison at 4:00, and..."

"Bring her with you. I have a son who was once five," I say, smiling. "Besides, I'd like to meet her."

"You would?" Marci says, flashing her biggest smile yet.

"Absolutely."

We stand up and I gather the file, assisting Marci out the front door, my view of her now from behind, doing so with no sexual allure, none whatsoever, my thoughts of her purely those of human concern. Prior to her marriage, how large were her doubts about Stuart? Surely there were some, but were they overwhelming? Did her misgivings go to the core of her being, or were they so slight that she overlooked them? Or did she simply ignore the obvious, and go against her better judgment, her desire "to be married" so forceful that she chose to suppress that better judgment? Clearly, she didn't envision her current life-difficulties.

Without Stuart, she would never have had Alison, a ray of joy in her life. I was my mom's. I hope that Marci can overcome Stuart. It would be a shame if she lets the actions of that man wreck her life. And now my thoughts shift from Stuart and Marci to me, events of long ago of my own making that created the ache in my stomach and pain within my chest a few minutes ago. I block these thoughts.

Culpepper Webb

***

I sit in a wing chair in the foyer of the funeral home. It's almost 6:30 and I got here well before 5:00. I've left the building twice and walked around the parking lot. I feel conspicuous being here among people I don't know. On the drive up I questioned whether showing up first in line as a total stranger to talk to Olivia and the two children was in their best interest. I decided it was not. The timing might have been ill advised. Fact is, there is no perfect time. So here I wait until the crowd dwindles so I can be last in line. I stand, then walk the short distance and peek into the side room. Olivia, a woman of medium height, medium age, with medium-length brown hair, wearing a navy dress, stands next to a six-foot-or-so boy with sandy hair and next to him, a dark-haired girl who is scarcely a teen. An elderly couple turns and walks by me, the man nodding as he passes. I stand before the Pettys.

"I'm Walker Wells."

"Yes," says Olivia.

She's exhausted. Her eyes show it. "I stopped to help Mike at the wreck Monday. I bet you all are tired of standing. Could we sit for a moment?" I say, as I manage a smile and nod toward a couch in the corner of the room with wing chairs to the side.

Olivia hesitates then says, "Yes." She walks to the couch and takes a seat, Mike Junior and Sarah to her side. I scoot a wing chair to the front of the couch.

Olivia's tired eyes are straight on mine. Sarah surveys the room. Mike Junior stares at the carpet. "I have no way of knowing what the past couple of days have been like for you."

Olivia offers no response, her eyes still locked on mine. What do I say? I usually come up with the right words, spur of the moment, but at the present I don't have them. I have no idea what is going through Olivia's mind or the children's. I...

"Thank you for trying to help Mike." Olivia's words are soft spoken. Her voice is southern, but not country. She offers a kind smile. "It's nice of you to come. I don't recall our having met. Are you local?"

"No, I'm from Madison. I was coming back from a business appointment when I saw the wreck."

"You drove that distance this evening to see us. That is quite thoughtful. You saw the wreck?"

One time in real life and a hundred in my mind. "Yes, I saw it happen. I ran to help and tried to do what I could. I'm sorry for your loss, I truly am."

"From what the report says, Mike made a mistake. Mistakes don't *usually* cost one their life."

I don't know whether I should reply. I don't.

"Anyway, it's been strange. Can you believe I've dialed his cell phone several times? I'm in a daze; I don't know up from down."

"I could say I understand, but I don't. I haven't lost my wife to death. My father died unexpectedly fifty years ago to the day of Mike's wreck. It's something one can't forget; ever. I can say that I *wish* you strength. I *hope* you will remember the good memories."

Olivia nods with no comment. I best say something else. "If Mike was anything like his father, he was a truly fine man."

Mike Junior looks up from the carpet for the first time. "You knew Pops?"

"You may have called him Pops, but I called him Coach Petty or Yes Sir," I say with a smile. "Growing up, he was one of the finest men I knew. He was my football coach; a tough man with a soft-side. Although he never said it, you knew he cared. I still think of things he taught me."

"I miss him," Mike Junior says.

You won't miss him like you'll miss your father, I think. But then again, I don't really know, do I? The teen years can be filled with friction, father to son and vice versa; same thing, wife to husband. The outside never really knows. I have a job to do. I clear my throat. "Mike wanted me to tell each of you something." All eyes are on me. "Right before he was carried to the ambulance he asked me to say something meant for all three of you. He…"

My voice cracked. I feel a tear on my left cheek. I don't cry; ever. They are staring at me. In my mind I am staring at Mike, his pleading eyes looking at mine. "He…" My voice cracks again. I clear my throat. "He said he loved you, each of you." I pause. "Looking back, I think he knew he was dying. If ever there is a time to say what really matters most, that is the time."

Olivia reaches in her purse for a tissue and wipes tears from both cheeks. "Mike could talk up a storm with men. He could talk football, hunting, fishing, and was a good as anybody when it came to selling chemicals to farmers. But when it came to sharing his cares and emotions he was mum. It's like he wanted to, but he couldn't. That's always been hard on me; and it's been hard on the kids."

"He sounds like most men, myself included," I say with a smile. "Mark my word, he meant what he said. If he had lived, he would have delivered those words himself. I have no question of that."

Olivia continues to wipe her cheeks. Sarah is again looking at the wall. Mike Junior's jaw juts. There's tension within him; there's more to his story.

"Mr. Wells, thank you." Olivia says.

"I've written my cell number on this piece of paper," I say, handing it to Olivia as I start to stand, but don't. Olivia wants to say more.

"Would you pray for us?"

I can't say, "No, I don't believe in that nonsense. I gave up on that after my own car wreck; maybe you will do the same."

"Yes," I say. I lie; it hurts.

We say pleasantries and I leave.

I sit in the Explorer and look at my cell phone. Laura has tried to reach me twice. I start to call her but hesitate. I need a moment to myself. How did I do? What are they thinking, each of them? Questions and more questions. You know what's strange? I just realized that Sarah did not say one word. She stared at me, but mostly at the wall. Did I ignore her? It wasn't intentional. I did talk with Mike Junior. Hey, he's male and he suddenly lost his father to death. Also, I had a son; no, *have* a son. Looking back as a father I wish I had said many things differently, but I can't go back. Finally, Olivia; her husband Mike is dead and tomorrow will be in the grave. No relationship is easy. Friction is part of the equation, and presently is she thinking more turmoil or peace? Over time what memories of Mike will dominate? For a while she may be as Mom was, reaching next to herself only to grab an empty pillow. Anyway, I did what I promised Mike. I'm a man who lives up to his word; most of the time. I probably won't for Olivia; and although she has no way of knowing, this bothers me. I hit autodial.

"Walker, are you all right? I was getting worried. I thought you would have pulled in the driveway thirty minutes ago. Where are you?"

"The funeral home parking lot."

"That's forty-five minutes to an hour away! What happened? I thought you were to show up before the crowd."

"I did. I thought my message might be a bit heavy beforehand. I didn't want it on their minds as they stood in line meeting folks."

"Tell me what happened with the family."

"I will, when I get home."

"But."

"I promise." Those words no more leave my mouth when I think back to me agreeing with Olivia to pray for their family. I picked my path of separation from a creator the night of the wreck years ago. Thus far, I haven't deviated from it, even to the point that I would go through a motion. It's just that at times such as when I ran pre-dawn today that I am lonely.

"Hurry home. I love you."

Culpepper Webb

"I love you."

***

"What's going on?" I ask after I enter through the back door.

Laura sits at the kitchen table staring at the burning candle. We hadn't had a candlelight dinner for six months, and now this is our second consecutive night. I lay my suit coat on the back of my chair and round the table to hug. Laura's return squeeze is halfhearted. She's obviously disappointed; it's going on eight o'clock and the ice in the tea in front of her has melted. She's prepared this for me, and the guest of honor is late. "I'll serve," I say, offering a smile as I look at Laura. A genuine smile goes a long way. Laura smiles back.

"Walker, I'm sorry. It's just that I envisioned this differently. I thought I would pamper you. I would serve you and listen to your every word. Right now I'm too tired to stand."

"Then don't," I say, as I grab both glasses of non-iced tea, and start them again fresh. I retrieve the stroganoff from the still-warm skillet on the stove and the salad from the refrigerator. We now sit eye to eye. Man, she looks tired.

"I started to buy wine for me and beer for you, but as hard as we've been going I thought it might have put us to sleep."

I could care less for wine, but I could have sipped a beer watching Laura. She gets looped sniffing the cork. It might have been entertaining. I start with the salad.

"So, start from the beginning."

"As I told you, I got there before visitation, but I decided it might be in the family's best interest to see them after the crowd left."

"Do you think that was the right decision?"

"That's the one thing I know I did right."

"Go on" Laura says before taking a bite of stroganoff.

"Well, I introduced myself and sat down with all three. I visited for a few minutes then delivered the message."

"Walker, you're not telling me a thing. Did his wife breakdown and cry, get angry, ask a hundred questions, nod in silence?"

Strange is it not that we look at things from our own perspective, Laura substituting herself for Olivia. "There was no downpour, but she did shed tears. I could tell there was pain in the fact that Mike didn't share his feelings verbally and that it bothered her greatly. It must have bothered him too or he wouldn't have asked me to do what I did. Beyond that I didn't have a read. Two days ago she was a wife, now she's a widow. I can't comprehend the array of thoughts and emotions she is experiencing. If I had to guess, his words may have as lasting an impression as any he ever spoke, their greatest impact coming at a time of reflection. And to think, they were delivered by a stranger."

"It had to be hard for you."

"It was. My voice cracked; my eyes moistened. All three were looking straight at me when I delivered the words."

"How did the kids take it? What are they like?"

"I guess Sarah's about thirteen. She didn't say a word."

"I presume you are speaking figuratively. She had to have said something, what was it?"

"She said nothing. I didn't realize this until I had left. I guess I messed up. Or maybe I didn't. In life you never know. Rob joined in the conversation when I mentioned his grandfather was my football coach."

"I thought you said his name was Mike, same as his father."

"Oh yeah; Mike Junior."

"Sweetheart, you just said more than you thought," Laura says, her fork poised mid-air, her look direct.

I guess I did. It's my perspective this time. Yes, when I saw him I thought of Rob at that age. Unlike Mike I'm still above ground. If I have something to say, I don't have to send a messenger.

"Walker, you're staring into space. I know exactly where your mind is. It was nice that you called Rob last night. We need to get him and Celia down here when he finishes tax season. The two of you need to go fishing or something."

Laura's right.

"Was there anything else? Did she ask for your help with anything?"

"No, that was about it." I lie. It hurts again. This is so uncustomary for me.

"Walker, you're holding back. I can tell. I *always* can. You've done so since the wreck; no, even before that. Fifty years ago Monday your father died. Anniversaries stir emotions as well as memories. That day you witnessed a wreck. Just the mention of the word wreck sends you into a tizzy. On top of this you're turning sixty, and like it or not, to most people younger than you that sounds old; *me* included. Is there anything you want to talk about?"

Want to, no. Need to, maybe. My gaze into the predawn-sky this morning the vastness of it all, the puniness I felt, brought forth within me a loneliness I can't describe. My life is unfolding and as much as I might think I need to talk with Laura, I'm not ready. "Not now; maybe sometime."

Laura's eyes hint she wants *now* not *sometime.* We eat in silence occasionally looking at each other, the candlelight flickering before us. Laura smiles at me.

Laura breaks the silence. "There's one big positive about you turning sixty in two days. We are going to Natchez, and I am leaving these crazy kids and parents for a day! Remember we talked Sunday about me retiring the end of this year."

"Yes."

"It got so bad this morning, I thought about taking early retirement today."

She quit smiling. Hmm? Natchez does sound good. Until this week, our going there was on my mind constantly.

"It's going to be great," Laura says, her smile returning.

Culpepper Webb

"Yes."

***

Laura and I sit on the couch. After cleaning the kitchen we collapsed here together. For the second night in a row the television is off and we are reading. Well, Laura is. I'm on the same page as thirty minutes ago. Of all the things that could be on my mind I've thought of nothing but Rob: his birth, birthday parties, taking him fishing when he was younger. We were close then. That changed during his teen years. The innocent relationship has yet to return. I'm stuck on thoughts of a night that changed things. I'm reliving it in my mind.

"It's after midnight, and unless you're married and in bed with your spouse, nothing good happens after midnight."

"Calm down, Walker."

"Calm down! My blood pressure is at stroke-level. This is the third time in the past month that it's past midnight and Rob is not here."

"Sweetheart, take a deep breath, it's only three after. Be a little more flexible. I hear the back door."

I toss the book to the floor, hop from the bed, and head from the bedroom. Rob stands in the den. He's smiling. He's smiling! I'm not.

"Hey, Dad."

"I told you to be home by midnight, no exceptions!"

"Dad, it's right at midnight, just a couple of minutes off."

"Have you been drinking again? Come here; let me smell your breath. Come here!"

"No, I haven't."

"Come here!"

Rob crosses the room and stops before me. As best I can tell, his breath is clear.

"I told you I haven't been drinking, not a drop since I came in late three weeks ago. You don't trust me."

"You're right, lately I haven't. You were late four weeks ago, three weeks ago, and again tonight. I'm grounding you for the next two weekends. Plus, I want you in by dark during the week. That's all there is to it."

"But Walker," Laura says.

"Laura, stay out of this. Coming in on time is between Rob and me."

"But…"

"Go to your room. Rob, go to your room now!"

"I can't believe this; coming in late by a couple of measly minutes."

"It was three minutes. Go to your room!"

"I'm never gonna forget this; never."

That's the way it happened. Rob was sixteen. I grounded him over *three minutes.* I acted in anger and I stood my ground. I'm a man of my word. I've never brought it up again; neither has Rob. It was such a little thing, that wasn't little. I should have gone back to him, loosened the curfew, perhaps have been more reasonable, apologized for my anger. I should have done something, even if it were a year later or five. I did not. I was the adult and he the teenager. Events at that stage are so magnified. I went by the book and stuck to it. What book, the one I dreamed up? We get together, talk football and politics; but that's as deep as it gets. I created a crevice that widened over his high school and college years; and although it has narrowed since, it is still there. I must sit down with Rob in person and make amends. It was my fault.

Three minutes.

Thursday, March 6, 2012

Another Trip to the Mississippi Delta

"Can you get the blood out of this suit?" I *never* take my clothes to the cleaners, just as Laura *never* carries out the trash. To this lady I am a stranger, for that matter perhaps a wanted criminal. Today I'm in hunting boots, rubber to ankles and leather above. I haven't worn them or hunted in years. The boots are a perfect match for my jeans, plaid shirt, and fully-lined windbreaker, not my typical apparel for a Thursday.

"It depends on how long the stain has been there," the lady behind the counter says.

I know she wants me to explain what happened. "Monday."

"Monday of this week?" she asks.

Heck no! I'm tempted to say. It was a Monday back in 1973. I resist. "Yes. Can you get it out?"

"Maybe, but it will take a bit of work. I'll need to get your name, address, and phone number," she says, with pen poised.

Do you want a photo ID? I'm tempted to ask. "Walker Wells." I hand her my business card.

"It'll be ready Monday," she says, giving me one more head to toe.

In no time I'm heading north. This morning I didn't run and I drank coffee with Laura. It was nice. I put on my suit and tie, as I do every day. I did, however, sneak this outfit I'm wearing in the Explorer. I feel a tinge of guilt for not telling Laura about my trip to the woods near where I witnessed

Culpepper Webb

Mike's wreck. This is the patch of forest I envisioned escaping into on my trip to see Randolph Hollings.

This morning I was to have presented my largest case ever, fully expecting to make the sale. Ordinarily I would be frustrated about the postponement of this appointment, but today I am not. I went to the office and left Kay enough projects to keep her occupied for the rest of the week as well as her paycheck. I then changed into my present outfit, hitting the road right after I turned off my cell phone. There's no telling what that lady back at the cleaners is thinking. Where was I? Oh yeah, this morning right before I placed my canvas chair in the back of the Explorer, I tossed the bloody shirt and tie in the outdoor trash can. But I couldn't do that with the suit; nor could I wear it again, not with Mike's blood soaked into it; not with the memories it would trigger. I'm giving it to charity. In a couple of weeks a homeless man will be walking around in style.

Yesterday was sunny and bright. Today there is mist. At least it's not overly cool. With this lined-windbreaker I'll mange fine. I'm crossing the tall bridge with full-view of the Delta ahead. For an unexplained reason, I hit the "on" button of the radio. I have not had the radio on since a moment before Mike's wreck. It's half-static; and it's Yazoo Clay.

"Nobody made me do it, I decided on my own
Could'a stayed in these parts and made myself a home
I took that bus to Memphis, a ridin' in the back
I took that bus to Memphis, with guitar and croker sack
Sometimes you make decisions that make a bunch of fuss
If you didn't want to go to Memphis, then why'd you get on the bus?
First it took a left turn, then it took a right
That bus took so many turns, I almost lost my sight
The bus it kept on goin' a ridin' up the road
I'm a sittin' on the backseat, thought I'd left my load
Only to of found out there's trouble up the road

> Nobody made me do it, I decided on my own
> Could'a stayed in these parts and made myself a home
> I took that bus to Memphis a ridin' in the back
> I took that bus to Memphis with guitar and croker sack
> Sometimes you make decisions that made a bunch of fuss
> If you didn't want to go to Memphis, then why'd you get on the bus?
> If you didn't want to go to Memphis, then why'd you get on the bus?"

Life is full of choices; and consequences. I turn the radio off.

It had to be here, although I see no old Case tractor, simply vacant fields on both sides of the road with woods up ahead on the left side, well beyond a fallow field. I slow the Explorer and come to a halt on the side of the road. Although there is no trace, I know that this is the spot. I open the door, check traffic, and hop out. The air is still, and it's not biting cold as it was on Monday. I see deep tire tracks in mud, both from the tractor and the truck, these between the patches of johnsongrass, the groundcover which lines every road in this part of the world. Is there any other sign of what happened? The cleanup crew did their job. No, wait; there's a piece of broken glass, almost too small to notice. To the rest of the world this place may go unnoticed, but not to me. I will never pass this spot without recalling the event of the day Mike died. It's time to go. I drive towards the patch of woods a ways up on the left, across an open field.

The road leading to the woods is gravel. I make the turn. The patter of gravel crunches against the underside of the Explorer. The field is much larger than it looked from the highway. This stretch of woods looks much larger as I approach.

I park the Explorer at the edge of the woods and cut the engine. I take a deep breath.

Culpepper Webb

***

  The canvas chair sinks into the soggy ground from my weight. This is the driest spot I could find; water stands everywhere. That must be why those trees have never been cut, this land never cultivated. This is so different from what I envisioned Monday when these woods beckoned me. In my mind I saw sunshine and dry ground. It was to have been a couple of months from now.
  So where do I begin? I turn sixty tomorrow; actually about one in the morning, although I would choose not to be awake then. I'm a planner and a plotter, although life has *never* turned out just as I thought it would. So why am I here? Truth be known, I don't really know for sure, only that I was called here, as if for an appointment to replace the one I was to have had today. My sitting here in mist in a sinking chair staring at a leafless tree makes no sense other than I feel compelled that this is where I am supposed to be. What's that? Oh, it's an eighteen-wheeler on the highway, a loud one. Where was I?
  My mind drifted because of the distraction of the truck. My mind…my mind; it's been filled this week as never before, so many events and thoughts. It started when I awoke Sunday morning with thoughts of Daddy's death and funeral. This unsettled me. Strangely enough, Daddy's funeral was the beginning of my disbelief in a personal god. The pain I felt when I learned of Daddy's death was far greater than any physical pain I've ever experienced, a pain to the core of my being that did not abate in the days following. Oh, it dulled over time to numbness, much as a pain killer gives relief to wounded flesh but does not heal the wound. His death has always lived within a far corner of my mind, much as a person who has experienced life-threatening cancer that "was cured." Cured or not, the memory of cancer returns, as does the thought that cancer will come calling again. No, the pain that I experienced, although distant, has been there, and its effect on my outlook of life immense. Sunday morning when I awoke

the wound was reopened by the sharpest of knives, the pain returning, it no less acute than the actual happening itself. Since that time I've had a concentration of life-experiences, and thoughts, one after another, that I've never had before. I've tried to "run them off" and that hasn't worked. I've tried to push them from my mind. I'm mentally tough. I can block thoughts out; but not the past few days. This week my inward goings-on are not just within my mind, but are all inside of me, head to toe.

So who am I? I'm a soon-to-be sixty-year-old man who is supposedly in great health, and who has more money and physical possessions than ninety-nine percent of the inhabitants of this planet. My wife is at my side. I'm well respected at what I do, one of the most successful in the state. "All is good" is what they say.

So what's bugging you, Walker? What's all the fuss? Can't handle life's pressures? Letting daily events and thoughts get to you? Can't handle turning sixty? No, while each of these may to a degree be true, they are not at the heart of what's eating at me. I feel a void, an empty pit. I'm lonely within, the pain of loneliness a rival to the pain of my father's passing. It is a storm that I've seen approaching from the distant horizon that has now come to engulf me, the events and thoughts of this week having brought it to a head.

Head? That's one of those words with multiple meanings. So right now, use my head. Think. That's something you're good at. Okay. It's crazy, I could never be an atheist. No way. There is a creator; has to be. Here I am sitting in a man-made contraption breathing air, staring at a tree, knowing that there are birds and animals within these woods, all the while listening occasionally to another human passing by in a different form of man-made contraption. Right, all this just happened out of nowhere. The universe is so vast, is it not, a fact that I was reminded of yesterday morning running in the pre-dawn when I stopped to gaze at the stars. My heart soared briefly before I was reminded of my puniness. The number of stars is countless, many unseen even with the aid of the most powerful of telescopes. They say that light travels fast enough to circle the earth six times in a second, and some of those stars are thousands of times the distance that light travels in a year. I can't comprehend that. And yet, I have always wanted exact answers, have I not? *Always.* I want validation, all answers neat and crisp: two plus two equals four, twelve inches in a foot, 39.37 inches in a meter, all scientifically verifiable. I want to know the exact number of stars in the universe.

I've been conflicted since early on, never doubting there is a creator, but doubting his involvement in the universe, much less man's affairs. The other day, in my thought of the day Daddy died, I took a hard whack at the tetherball and watched it go round and round the pole. Is that what You did? One big whack to set it all in motion, then walked away, perhaps looking back to watch the universe, the planets going round and round suns such as ours, a sport of sorts with You as the ultimate spectator. If that's the case, it's quite a game to watch, is it not? Countless stars, our sun just one of many, planets out there that I don't know about, plants growing, animals, birds, insects being born and dying, and humans *thinking* they are communicating with You. And how many humans are there, six billion going on seven, an ever expanding number, figures that don't include those who have come before.

Tell you what I think. You are beyond my reach, this universe so massive, and me so small. Fact is, You don't care. I began to lose trust in You when Daddy died; couldn't absorb what was happening, and couldn't understand what that preacher was saying. Why did Daddy die? To this day my answer has been "'because he had a faulty heart and all people die; *all* people. It just happened, and that's the way it is. Move on and keep going." Not even ten years old, and I began to close the chambers of my heart, that event the beginning of my journey. Larry Edson's death in the car wreck brought me to a conclusion of the journey, he no more deserving of death than my father; actually less so, Larry, a person who had lived his life as genuinely as anyone I knew my age. So he dies. Why? Driving while too tired. Mike Petty? Texting and driving. So there you have it, all people die and that's that: two plus two equals four, twelve inches in a foot, 39.37 inches in a meter, just the way I like things, all scientifically verifiable. Why can't I just accept this? Why? Why!

Settle down. Settle down. It was only Monday of this week when I was visiting with Randolph Hollings, a man I respect as much as any other, his death not only certain, but soon, his saying, "In a matter of weeks someone will be shoveling some of this fine Mississippi Delta dirt in my face. If that's all there is, wouldn't that be sad?" Yes, it is sad.

And yet, while my mind tells me to trust only what I can see, touch, or hear, I sense this inner void that defies my reason, a hollowness that neither sight nor touch can fulfill, a longing from within for more, much more, an emptiness of soul. What's a soul? What's a soul! No doctor has ever found one within a human body. It doesn't exist, right? And yet this inner feeling is as real as anything I've touched or felt. This defies me.

Trust, there's another word with multiple meanings. I mentioned to Marci yesterday that she might want to set up a trust. No, that's not the trust I'm thinking about that's so important in life is it? People don't buy from me if they don't trust me. Husbands trust wives, and wives trust husbands; to a degree. Can't trust another a hundred per cent, can you? Marci, who came into my office for advice yesterday, has no trust in her ex. It doesn't usually get quite that bad, but you can always gauge trust in another human as at less than a hundred per cent. Some say that the only one you can trust at all times is You.

Well that's a trust I've not had since the day Daddy died. There I was sitting in Mr. Sandiford's office with my legs not long enough for my feet to touch the floor. My world disrupted. Maybe if someone had sat down with me and explained things at my level, the preacher showering the air with platitudes beyond my understanding, and Mom too overwrought with her own pain to put things where I could grasp them, then the outcome may have been different.

Hey, get over it Walker, you're only a few hours away from sixty. Don't lay your lack of belief at the feet of others and their actions of five decades ago. You're in the here and now, and you're the one who needs to deal with who you are.

Well, others put their trust in You, and I don't. At least that's the way it's been for the past fifty years. My trust has been in me, the only one I can always count on. So, I place all my trust in a person who doesn't have the wherewithal to remember to carry his cell phone across the road when he sees a wreck, a man so brilliant that he doesn't remember to bring a bottle of water on his excursion on this very day, a man who is now thirsty, a man whom no one else trusts a hundred per cent.

At this moment my inner thirst is greater than my thirst for water, far greater. And yet, I'm not sure which way to turn, or to even turn at all. The most polar opposite of my view of life is Christianity, the religion that has surrounded me my whole life. Laura, my confidant of three and a half decades, is a Christian, as is Mom, and neither in a casual way. It is who they are. It's not the "do good" part that I'm at odds with. It's the rest of it, the divine in human form coming to this speck of dust in the universe. Why? Yeah, why? This planet is so puny, and I am so small. Yes, it is the most personal of all religions, for no other religion of today lays claim to the creator of the universe sending his son in human form. This story is so foreign from a distant creator, as far away from my beliefs as the most distant star from where I now sit. And yet I thirst.

If heaven is a mansion with many rooms, I want to open the door and know where the furniture is, right down to where the lamp is located and where the pillows are. I want to know what books are on the shelves.

What am I doing? I'm speaking from within to someone or something other than myself. No one can hear me.

In Search of Walker Wells

I'm not saying a word aloud. I've been carrying on a conversation with You, as if You are listening. I don't do that.

No, I like everything verifiable, just the opposite of faith. And yet, is it possible there are things that cannot be answered in full, no matter how hard one tries? Things that must be accepted sight unseen, and yet they are as real as that tree before me. And even if I could accept such a belief, would I then have an explanation as to why all things happen? I would not, for neither Laura nor Mom lays claim to that. Much of life would remain a mystery that I would not solve. That is so unlike science where there is a belief that *all* things can be explained, that this universe is just one big laboratory.

So, it is Laura's belief, as is Mom's, that your son, Jesus, accepted human form and was sacrificially slaughtered. It was the stone in front of the cave back then, not "fine Mississippi Delta dirt." Then he arose from the dead and later ascended, vanishing from human sight. In the interim a guy named Thomas asked for proof. He wanted to see and touch. I am Thomas, straight to the core. Again, if it is true, why did You do what You did? What is so special about a human, one of many animals on this speck of dirt called Earth? Just one of many animals, nothing more and nothing less, only that we are the ruling hierarchy on this planet.

In a museum I once viewed some skeletal remains that looked like a deceased duck-billed platypus and was informed that this creature was one of my ancient ancestors. For some unexplained reason I considered this an affront. At that moment I considered myself human, not in a prideful or gloating way, only that I was and am different from that pile of bones that lay on the museum floor; quite so. Yes, I am a *human*. And at this moment I sense something special about that fact, my insignificance not so great, a sense of importance gushing in my chest like a spewing geyser.

What's that? What's that sound! Oh, it's a squirrel scurrying up that tree before me knocking off a piece of bark, scampering out a limb, now soaring to the next tree. He startled me.

Where was I? I'm a see-it-to-believe-it-guy who completely severed my trust in You when I was twenty-one. I shut You out; I cursed You. Do You hold a permanent grudge? If I came to You, would You invite me in?

So where does all this lead me? I'm not sure. I am, after all, the ultimate see-it to believe-it guy. At this moment I am having a thought from my trip this direction on Monday. When I came down the hill to view this flatland called the Delta, I thought of the story of Noah, a man who built a ship on faith alone, although he had never seen rain, had never touched a Bible, and didn't know what a cross was. Yet he had faith in the unseen. At this point I'm not a ship builder building a boat in the middle of dry land. I am a person who is seeking more, a man who might possibly open the door to my heart's chamber; if You would accept a person who cursed You. Noah got a rainbow, but it came years after he began building a ship. For a see-it to believe-it guy could You send me a sign beforehand? Could it work that way? At this moment I'm feeling that pain within, same as when Daddy died. Right now I'm a conflicted man torn between what is ingrained and what might be.

Thursday, March 8, 2012

Madison, Mississippi

Sweet Dreams; I'm Turning Sixty

  I turn my head atop the pillow to view Laura, her breathing rhythmic and slight. She has a soft smile on her face, a look of contentment. I've lain here for thirty minutes alternating my stares between the ceiling, drapes on the French door, and Laura, my thoughts bouncing between my day in the woods, the fact I'll be sixty in a few hours, and Laura's and my trip to Natchez tomorrow.

  What was that, a snort from Laura? No way. Never heard one of those before. Will there be more to follow? I turn off the lamp, return my head to the pillow, roll onto my side, facing the French door in darkness.

  Before I returned home this afternoon I switched clothing, returning to my coat and tie, feeling guilty for having done so. I didn't want to open a discussion with Laura about my day. I didn't want to reveal, and that's truly strange for I have revealed so much through the years, my life's-book open much of the time, but not always. This is one of those times. I must work this out between the Creator and me with no middle-person involvement.

  I close my eyes. My mind drifts. It drifts...

The intensity of Laura's gaze is more than I can allow, her green eyes piercing mine. A steady stream of pressure flows from them through my mind and into my chest, all the way to the core of my being. I tilt my head downward, and gaze now upon the grains of oak wood of our kitchen table. I can no longer handle the intensity of her look. We sit across from each other at the round kitchen table in our apartment, the table's diameter too large for us to touch each other. We've done this for over an hour, most of it in silence, the muteness and stillness of the room in some unexplained way deafening as I yell at myself within.

"How could you?" Laura says, as I glance at the green eyes that at this moment I cannot read. No tears flow from them. Do they display anger, hurt, distrust, or all of these and then some?

My thoughts flow in all directions, mostly memories of the two of us, the shared experiences of life, as the thought of our first meeting suddenly comes to the forefront, me standing in a department store on a Saturday in the kitchen section looking for a set of drinking glasses. Of all things, a man shopping for drinking glasses on a Saturday; get a life, Walker. Yeah, I think I was down to two beer mugs and three glasses, none of which matched. She was buying a wedding gift for a girlfriend. From the corner of my eye, she caught my attention; her blonde hair, the green eyes, the shapely body, although strangely enough, I didn't look at her sexually. My attraction for her went deeper than that, and it was immediate. So I took a second look and a third, as I eyed her head to toe, noticing no jewelry on her left hand. "Which glasses would you buy?" I asked, holding two styles before her. She didn't respond immediately. Did I catch her off guard, she preoccupied with shopping? Did she find me less than appealing? I persisted. Two years in sales have at least taught me that persistence pays. "Do you like this one better, or that one?" I said, holding each glass out one at a time. "That one," she said pointing to the taller of the two. "That one," were the first words Laura said to me. In life, it's strange the things you remember. We still have those glasses. One of them is on the table before me at this moment. We talked for five minutes, maybe ten. My attraction for her grew rather than diminished as we talked. She gave me her number, although at first she was reluctant. So, two days later I called her, and we went to lunch the following Saturday, a "day date." It was then that Laura warmed up to me as I had already done with her. Truth is, I was lonely; quite so. She was too. We needed each other.

Laura's eyes are upon mine. They are so green. She does not blink.

At this time we are coming up on our second anniversary of marriage. I wonder if it will occur. I want it to, but that decision is not mine. I am the one who placed the event in jeopardy through my infidelity. Oh yes, Laura has been less than perfect. I think she is selfish at times, but so am I. I want my way, and she hers. She wants a child and I say "what's the hurry," a statement not a question. If that decision is left to me, a child may never occur. *Never*; at least that's what I thought until recently. You see, a child would be an additional infringement on my freedom, and a month ago I thought that more freedom was what I wanted; no *needed*. I needed to be free from the dual yolks of responsibility and commitment. Forget about loneliness; set me free, at least partially so. Have my cake and eat it too, to the nth degree; just so long as it goes undiscovered. But it didn't.

Summer, even her name is "seasonal." Her season didn't last three months; only one. Regardless of my outcome with Laura, my relationship with Summer is over and done with. She called on me to sell a typewriter, the fancy type that could do it all, just the type I needed for my growing business. She's quite attractive, not in the same way I am attracted to Laura, my allure for Summer ninety-nine per cent sexual, if not more. She's just the opposite of Laura, even in her looks; dark-black hair with pale-white skin to go with dark brown eyes that flow with sensuality. If one is tempted, why not go for just the opposite of what you have. I did. What's the old adage? "Don't take a second look?" Maybe it should be "don't take a second listen." She went beyond the call of service after the typewriter was delivered, checking back over the phone twice before dropping by one day to make sure the typewriter was working properly. It was that day, following an argument with Laura that morning that I took another look *and* listen, allowing my guard down. I never would have called Summer to instigate a relationship. She called on me, and my sales resistance was low. Is relationship the right word for an encounter that is ninety-nine percent sexual; at least from my perspective? I wasn't seeking binding kinship, and neither was Summer; or so she said. But humans don't work that way, do we? That is, if there is a repeat performance. Either one, or both, eventually long for something beyond the immediate. "No responsibility and no commitment." On the surface that seems so perfect. At this moment it actually hurts me to think of that. My regret is overwhelming, and I'm not sure whether this is due to remorse for my actions or of the thought of losing my life with Laura.

Laura isn't saying a word. She stares at me. I can't withstand her gaze.

So, they say that all good things come to an end. What about bad things? Is bad a never ending condition? At the moment it seems so; I'm about to burst. What I did, I thought at the time, was trivial. But it was not. Not for Laura. Not for Summer. Not for me. I was a fool. And Summer, how did I describe her, a fearless salesperson? It should have been *psycho*; she called the apartment tonight and spoke to Laura. She wanted to introduce herself, so she did. Laura had no idea. Now she does. That was over an hour ago. Laura is in shock; so am I. Where this will lead I have no idea. What's this? Laura is rising to her feet, the sound of the oak chair scraping on the floor breaking the silence. She rounds the circular table, tightens her fists and begins to pound on my shoulders, then on my chest. "How could you! How could you!"

I'm awake. What time is it, my pulse is racing? 2:49 on my clock. I turned sixty almost two hours ago. I haven't thought about that night in years. In real life, that night was just like I dreamed it. What a way to celebrate my sixtieth.

Culpepper Webb

Friday, March 9, 2012

Natchez, Mississippi

Honk! Honk! Honnk
What's gotten into Laura? She's been a terror in motion ever since she awoke.
"Got to get to Natchez!"
Honk! Honnnk!
Honestly, I wasn't willfully leaving behind the tux I hold in my hands, although that would have been convenient. I don't want to wear it. All I want is a day of escape. Just one day. I want to leave all my cares behind, all of my struggles, internal and external, emotional, physical, and spiritual; all of it. I didn't run this morning, I fell 800 miles short of my goal. I'm almost tempted to ask Laura if I can get out and run so I can look for an empty nonalcoholic beer bottle on the side of the road, therefore exempting me from ever having to run again. I best not push my luck.

Mom called me, and we had a "nice long visit." I think she had been awake for quite some time. I am, after all, her one and only. I think that today is as big a moment for her as it is for me. She carried me internally for nine months and nursed me after I was born. We men don't really have a sense of such things, do we? She was quite emotional.

I place the tux on top of Laura's "little black cocktail dress," close the hatch, scoot around and sit next to Laura who's in the driver's seat. Laura driving is a perk of my birthday, or so I think. We are in reverse before I close the door, speeding down the driveway with Laura slamming the brakes just before we reach the street. For the moment, I think I'll simply observe. The radio is loud!

"Sweetheart, there's mud on the floorboard," Laura says, cutting down the volume on the radio as she speaks, waiting for my response.

"Huh, sure is," I say. "Yeah, I stepped in mud; meant to clean it up before we left. Why don't I take care of that when we stop for gas. It's not getting on your shoes is it?"

"No."

I didn't lie did I? Perhaps I will tell her of yesterday's trip someday when things within me are more settled, if in fact that ever occurs; but not *today*. Today I wish to be totally free. Laura's reaches for the volume dial on the radio; wonder what she's listening to?

"Well Jack, we've had some great calls on 'Free-for-all Friday' where we let our listening audience pick the topics and we run with them."

Oh no, that's *Bob and Jack*, the loud talk show where everybody yaks about the…trivial. I gave up on them two weeks ago. All they do is rile me up. Absolutely nothing constructive has ever come from listening to those guys. Laura is listening to them? I thought that reality TV would more than satisfy her fixation for the ridiculous. Last night it was the two-hour kickoff for *Children, Pick Your Parents*. The only time she looked my way was during the commercials. And this morning she's listening to *Bob and Jack*.

"Do you listen to this show often?"

"Oh no. The radio was set on this station."

No it wasn't. The only time the radio has been on this week I was listening to that AM blues station in the Delta. So much for telling Laura about the mud on the floor board.

"Bob, we've got a caller on line one. Anna."

"I want to talk about the blackbird cannons."

"Oh yes, the devices that are designed to drive off flocks of birds that migrate in large numbers this time of year, settling in people's trees. They are a total nuisance, noisy beyond belief, leaving countless droppings on the ground, perhaps a health hazard."

"What about the bird's ears?"

Bird's ears? I've never seen a bird's ears.

"Sweetheart, are you more concerned about a bird's peace and rest or a human's?" asks Bob.

"Why of course I'm concerned about both. But the bird's ears are such tiny little things nestled under their feathers. I bet their ears are very sensitive, as tiny things oftentimes are."

What are we listening to; and Laura so intently? She's not even cracking a smile. Wouldn't some classic rock, blues, country, or even *rap* be better than this?

"Anna, thanks for your input. Next caller."

"Yeah, about those cannons."

That lady seems about my age, voice kind of raspy. She's been a smoker for years. I can tell.

Honk! Honnnk!

"Get a move on!" Laura says to the driver in front of us. "The light turned green over ten seconds ago."

Listen to Laura. What's gotten into her today? She's not usually this tightly wound. Must be she's had her fill of parents and students this week. "Laura, honey, can we cut that down for a minute?"

"But they're right in the thick of it. Can't we wait until the commercial?"

"Please."

"So, what were you going to say?" Laura says, as she cuts down the volume.

"We didn't discuss which route we are taking, the interstate or the Natchez Trace," I say. The route could set the tone for the rest of the morning, the interstate four-lane and 70 miles per hour, the Natchez Trace with a maximum speed of 50. Ah, the Natchez Trace, part of the National Park Service, the speed limit a part of the ambiance, the only signs on the road the speed limit and exit signs. It's two-lane, so peaceful…

"We're taking the interstate. That Trace is too slow for me. I'm ready to get to Natchez and kick up my heels!"

I guess that settles it; she's got the steering wheel. Hey, there's Henry David Nobles surrounded in a cloud of smoke in that old Escalade we're passing. I intended to call him, but I've had so much going on. "Laura, there's Henry David. Honk so he'll see us."

"Walker, I don't see why you keep up with that loser."

"He's not a loser. He's just suffered quite a few defeats."

"What's that old expression that the college football announcer used to say when a player tripped on a blade of grass? 'He's a victim of self-tackleization.' If that word's in the dictionary, it has his picture beside it."

"Perhaps, but we have a certain kinship of life-long shared experiences, one in particular quite dramatic. Honk," I say, as Laura responds reflexively.

I wave at Henry David, and he waves back. His smile is barely discernable through the smoke inside of the Escalade. I should have called him. I am truly concerned about his wellbeing, but I've been too wrapped up in my own life. At least he hasn't headed to Tierra del Fuego; *yet*. Oh, well. It's a good thing Laura that hasn't turned the radio back on. Maybe I'll be able to kick back and simply enjoy the ride, a nice component of my day of total freedom.

The traffic thins as we make our way down the interstate. The last remnants of city are now in the rearview, and the landscape shows a peaceful quality, mostly pine trees with an occasional dogwood in full-white blossom shining through the green of the pines.

"Walker, what's been going on?" Laura says, breaking the sound of the hum of tires on pavement.

I look to the side to see that her eyes are fixed on the road ahead, not on me; so she's not in full-attack mode, but she's probing nonetheless.

"So, what's going on?" Laura says, this time turning her eyes toward mine.

"Well, for one thing, this is the week I've turned sixty, so far beyond the midpoint of my life that I can no longer see middle age on the radar. It's a year and a few months off for you. You'll understand what I'm saying when you get there."

"That's not what I meant," Laura says, again taking her eyes off the road and aiming them at me. At this moment I look to the open highway ahead. Her eyes are still upon me. I can tell. Hope we don't run off the road. What a way to celebrate my sixtieth. So, what is she really asking, and how do I respond?

"It's been a dramatic week," I say. "I was in a car accident in college in which a friend died. I was fortunate to live through it. This week I witnessed a car accident, and tried to save a man's life. I did not, and I suppose I will second guess myself for the rest of my life as to whether I could have done more to prevent his death. I hope I don't see another car accident for the rest of my life. So is that what you're asking about?"

"It seems like there is more, something more than you turning sixty, and the trauma of experiencing another car wreck where someone died. I know that it might seem strange for me to say this, particularly with the car wrecks, but I feel like there's something you're not telling me."

What is it, three and half decades of waking up next to me or what? Maybe it's simply innate, a woman's intuition, that a fact, not merely a wife's tale. She's picked up that I have something brewing within me beyond the things I mentioned. So what more do I reveal? "I've had thoughts."

"Like what?"

"Oh, lots of things. Last night I dreamed we were playing dress poker at a nudist colony and I kept winning."

"Did you really dream that?" Laura says, again momentarily taking her eyes off the road.

"Of course not," I say. "You know how opposed I am to gambling. I wouldn't even dream about it." Deflect; that's what I do. Maybe she'll get the point that for now I've said all I want to say; at least I hope so. Truth is, in last's night's dream, the last thing I can remember was Laura pounding on my chest; pounding, pounding, and more pounding. The dream was real. So real. It was just the way it happened. I've tried so hard to block Summer from my mind, to completely blot out the night at the kitchen table, to forget the months there following; and I've done well until last night. Right now I feel a chill within, and at its root is guilt. Laura forgave me years ago. She's never really thrown it in my face. How she's done that I don't know. She forgave me, yet I don't feel forgiven. Why?

    All I want today is to be as free as a bird, free from the weight of the world. Right now I don't feel so. I turn to view Laura, her eyes on the interstate ahead. The hum of the Explorer's tires against the pavement is the only sound.

Culpepper Webb

***

Across the mighty Mississippi I see the flatlands of Louisiana from high atop the bluff of Natchez. A church steeple towers through trees beyond the levee across this massive body of flowing water, this view from one of the highest spots on the river until it reaches Missouri. The temperature is already in the sixties and rising, and there is not a cloud to be seen, the clearness of the blue sky rivaling that of the star-clustered sky of my predawn run a few days ago. Natchez is the oldest permanent settlement on the Mississippi, and I can see why. Why would anyone want to leave this spot? This is bliss.

"Walker, here's the brochure for the carriage ride," Laura says.

Carriage ride? I saved my well-worn feet for the walking tour of downtown. That's why I'm wearing my running shoes. "But I thought that the first thing we would do is take the walking tour," I plead.

"Whatever are you thinking? The first thing we'll do is ride in style. We'll walk later; to the antique shops. It's only two blocks from here to the carriage station, so let's get a move on."

The clop of horse's hooves on pavement is unmistakable. The sound of advancing horse and carriage can be heard from a block and a half away. *Clop—clop, clop—clop, clop—clop* come the horse and carriage until they halt next to the sidewalk just beyond Laura and me. Six people disembark along with the carriage driver who assists a lady several years my senior, steadily holding her arm as she descends from the carriage. All exchange pleasantries with the driver. Three open their wallets.

Laura and I walk to the carriage with our tickets in hand. There are three people in front of us and several behind. With Pilgrimage, the annual several-week event featuring the opening of private as well as public homes for tours beginning this day, the crowds flock. I take special note of the driver as he accepts our tickets. If I had to guess I would say he is about my age, gray hair flowing from his cap, with a full gray beard. He's wearing sunglasses, the silver-lens reflecting my image. We nod, and I follow Laura onto the carriage. As soon as we take our seats Laura grabs my hand and kisses me on the cheek, then smiles a broad smile, her green eyes focused on mine. "I've been waiting on this ride for weeks," she says.

 I didn't realize this ride was such an event for her. Now I understand why she didn't simply give in to walking the streets. We all play things out in our minds in advance, anticipating one scenario and then another as the excitement builds. Maybe this will be one she remembers for years to come. I grab her hand a little tighter and she kisses my cheek again, her smile after the kiss broader than the last.

 "My name is Fred," says the driver with the shiny glasses, his face turned toward the five passengers. "My horse's name is Brownie, and we've been together for quite some time. I'd like to start this downtown tour of the oldest permanent settlement on the Mississippi River by finding out where y'all are from. Could we start with you, young lady," he says to the woman with the brown hair who appears to be in her mid-thirties seated alone in the first seat.

 "Montreal," she says, her accent French. She's been taking notes on a pad. Wonder if she's writing a travel article?

 "Ve are from Germany," says the male member of the couple in front of us. They are at least a decade younger than Laura and me. They are a handsome couple.

 "Uh-uh," says Fred. "And what about y'all?

 "We're from here in Mississippi," I say. "We live in Madison outside of Jackson and drove down this morning."

 "We get folks from all over," says Fred. "Glad you all could make it. We'll mostly be touring the downtown area, buts there's more to Natchez than downtown. This little town of twenty thousand has around six hundred antebellum homes. Any of y'all know what antebellum means?"

I know the answer, but I don't feel like being the star student right now. Most folks think it means a big old southern home with columns on the front. In fact is means "before the war," and down in these parts it means "before the Civil War," a war that some folks were still fighting when I was born. Today, that is pretty much a thing of the past.

"It means before the Civil War. Folks around here think our buildings are old, although you all from over in Europe might think different. Come on, Brownie," Fred says, jostling the reins.

Clop—clop, clop—clop, clop.

Laura has tightened her clasp, and she's rubbing my calf with her foot, her sandal now on the floorboard. This is my kind of carriage ride!

"Here is the home of William Johnson, a black freedman and barber who amassed quite a fortune prior to the Civil War. If you go beyond the history books, you'll find that real life produces unique bedfellows. *Real history* is interesting. Over a hundred years after he died, thousands of pages of his diary were found in the attic of his home. He was a man of quite some influence around this town. His home is owned by the National Park Service."

Fred's a real pro. He's talking, steering a horse, and watching for moving vehicles all at once. A few blocks down we round a corner and come to a halt at a church, a real church, not a museum, the schedule of services posted tastefully and encased within a glass beside the sidewalk. "This little town has almost a hundred active churches. The church to our right is one, but it also holds an extensive museum of photos of the people of Natchez taken during the eighteen hundreds. Now across the street to our left is…"

"What's that?" I say.

"What's what?" says Fred.

"That," I say, pointing across the street.

"City hall."

"No, that," I say, hopping out of my seat, hitting the pavement, running across the street, then the lawn, and stopping in front of a grave marker, a tiny one.

"Walker Wells, what are you doing?" I hear Laura holler from the carriage. "Have you lost your mind?"

Tripod October 9, 1983 "The Citys Kitty"

Yep, that's what it says. And what am I doing? I just fled a carriage and am standing before a tiny grave marker in front of the Natchez city hall. This moment is so incongruent, so unlike me, *Mr. Always Wear a Funeral Suit to Work,* having done something spontaneous, no prior thought to my action. What the heck, I only turn sixty once. I think I'll stand here another moment and stare at the marker.

"Walker! Walker Wells! You're embarrassing me!"

Oh well, I guess I'll walk back to the carriage and not hold things up any longer. There's a "carriage traffic jam" forming behind our carriage. These drivers have to earn a living and Pilgrimage is their time of year to harvest this crop. Nevertheless I was drawn to that tiny grave marker, and I had to take a look. And now as I approach the carriage I am overwhelmed by my conspicuousness. Who knows what thoughts lurk behind Fred's shiny sunglasses? He's probably thinking about the plentiful nuts he has dealt with through the years on this job. He can now add Walker Wells, home grown native species to the list. The young woman from Montreal writes furiously. She'll probably want my picture for the travel magazine. The Germans nod, he whispering something to her in German like "if most people around here are like him, we'll be full of stories to tell our friends when we get home." Laura's mouth is wide open. I can't tell if she's startled or upset; probably both.

"Ve do not understand," says the man from Germany. "In Germany ve do not bury the dead in front of public buildings unless they are very important. Who is this one of great importance?"

Culpepper Webb

Fred turns to face us. "Well, thirty-something years back a little cat with three legs wandered into city hall. The little kitty didn't have a home, so the folks around city hall adopted it. This little feline-phenom was the toast of the town! Hung around city hall for years. Well anyway, when it up and died, the people of Natchez decided they ought to do something special. A local funeral home donated a gravestone. There lies Tripod, 'the city's kitty.' Y'all about ready to move on?" says Fred, as looks over his shoulder at the "carriage traffic jam" behind us, at the same time lifting the reins, signaling Brownie to move forward. The young woman from Montreal continues to write, as the couple in front of me nods and bobs in unison, conversing in German as they nod. Laura continues to stare at me. She's gone temporarily silent. I extend my hand as hers remains closed. *She'll come back around.*

We continue our ride through downtown, Fred talking the whole way, sometimes stopping, other times not, as he describes the buildings and the stories behind them. Past the downtown area the streets begin to narrow as we enter a residential area canopied in ancient live oaks.

"Whoa, Brownie," says Fred as we come to a halt in front of a massive home.

Laura extends her hand to mine and I reciprocate. "Walker, wouldn't it be neat to live here," she says eyeing the home. I glance at the home and back at Laura. She is viewing the roof, her eyes moving downward to the pink azaleas surrounding the home. I've been so involved in looking at buildings, I failed to look at her. Sometimes I can tell exactly what she is thinking, but this time I cannot. Is she wondering about the family who lives in the home, or is she projecting the thought of us living there? Either way, she is smiling, her hand in mine, her sandal again on the floorboard, her foot rubbing my calf.

"This was the home of Captain Thomas Paul Leathers. He was the captain of the steamboat Natchez during the most famous steamboat race in history, the 1870 race from New

Orleans to St. Louis between the Natchez and the Robert E. Lee, a race that took less than four days. Unfortunately for Captain Leathers his boat finished second. Rumor has it he bet twenty thousand on the race, a pile of money at that time. He died years later in New Orleans when his head hit on the pavement after he was struck by a bicycle. Only man I've heard of to go that way. Let's turn on up this street," Fred says, veering Brownie to the right.

Our next stop is at a home more massive than the previous, the grounds surrounded by towering live oaks. Fred turns our way and begins his spiel. "This home was built by Frederick Stanton in the 1850s. The roof is solid copper and the doorknobs on the cypress doors are sterling silver. Take a look at the sixteen live oaks that have survived from the original nineteen planted. As far as the home itself, you might recognize it from either postcards or movies, several of which have been filmed here. Any questions?" Fred asks.

I alternate between looking at the trees, the home, and Laura, her gaze fixed upon the home. In her wildest dreams she couldn't picture us living here. Her hand is still tightly within mine, her foot no longer rubbing my calf.

"The home took five years to build and Mr. Stanton died of yellow fever within nine months of moving in. If there are no questions, then let's head on up the street."

As we halt at the next intersection, I notice a live oak larger than those surrounding Stanton Hall. Fred's been inviting questions, so why not? "Hey Fred, any idea how old that oak tree is?"

"Two hundred and eighteen years."

Now how in the world did he know the exact age? Who planted it, Johnny Acorn? "How do you know the exact age?"

"'Cause when I started doing this job eighteen years ago they told me it was two hundred years old." He's staring stone-face at me. If I were three feet closer to him I could comb my hair in his mirrors. The German couple converses as they say two hundred and eighteen. The lady from Montreal writes.

Laura releases her clasp and views me from the side. This guy has reeled me in, sent me to the taxidermist, and mounted me on the wall. From behind the sunglasses he continues to stare me down. I think he's gonna wait through the green light to savor this moment.

One more nudge in my ribcage and one of them is gonna crack. I've opened my wallet and am pulling out a ten. Ouch! I think she's finally broken one. I replace the ten with a twenty, four times what I had in mind, and Laura nods. Somehow she got the notion I've been a nuisance and Fred needs some payback for his misery for enduring me. His simple nod is ever so slight. I think it's time to move on.

A moment later, Laura and I hop in the Explorer to get closer to the antique shops and restaurants that caught her attention during the tour. With the influx of visitors, the traffic has picked up and parking spaces are at a premium. Two doors down from one of the antique shops Laura had in mind, I wheel into a parking spot. A minute later we are inside looking at four-poster beds, tables, and armoires, all of either mahogany or cherry, each magnificent, yet far too large to be functional in our home. I must admit it is fun to look.

Laura finally zeroes in on a pair of lamps she thinks might go on the end tables on either side of the couch in our den. She's been onto me for years to replace the ones we have and the price the store is asking for these is less than I would have thought. But Laura isn't sure these are the ones; and if I might recall that's the reason she's been onto *me* for years for not having bought new lamps.

We amble down the street to the next antique shop, then a jewelry store, Laura almost purchases a wedding gift, but decides she doesn't want to lug it around. I feel certain we'll be back to buy it tomorrow. For the moment, she's having fun looking, and I must admit I am too. I've been going hard lately, as has she. Today, it's nice not to have a schedule. Hand in hand we walk, blue sky overhead. I can't remember the last time I moved at this pace. Down Main Street, a couple of doors past a hotel, I note the scent of food. It's time to eat. "Let's take a peek," I say, as we stop before a large glass window to view the interior of the restaurant.

"It looks fine to me," says Laura.

I struggle to open the solid-wood eight-foot-high entrance door. Inside there's a twenty foot-long mahogany bar to our left and tables to our right. The ceiling is at least two feet higher than those of today, and there's a spiral staircase leading to the next floor. This place we stumbled into has *character*. As a matter of fact, the same could be said of each place we've entered today.

"We've got two seats at the bar, or the table over in the corner," says a young man.

"We'll take the one in the corner," I say as he leads us that way.

"Someone will be back to help you in a minute. It's good you showed up now 'cause this is the last table in the house. Enjoy yourselves," he says, his voice trailing amidst the noise of others. There is a true assortment on hand. Those guys with ties look like lawyers and bankers. And there's a table of little old ladies dressed to a T, all drinking glasses of wine, and each appears to be having the time of her life. A few more glasses of wine and from a spectator's stand point this could prove to be an entertaining lunch.

"Hope you enjoy these," says a young girl, mid-twenties who plops a plate of biscuits on our table.

"What are these?" I ask.

"What, you've never seen a biscuit before?" she answers.

"No, what I meant to say is, do you serve these to everyone?"

"It's what we're famous for," she says, setting two menus on the table in the process.

"What do you suggest we order?" I ask.

"Anything that has catfish, oysters, shrimp, or crawfish in it. What would you like to drink?"

"Sweet tea," I say, as Laura says, "teemumble" with half a biscuit in her mouth. "Unsweetened for her," I say, serving as an interpreter. Laura nods and I say, "Give us a few minutes to order."

"Walker, these are marvelous. We'll need to order some more," Laura says, as she reaches for a second biscuit. I grab one too; while I still can. Hey, it is good. A moment later our tea is delivered and I beg for a little longer to look over the menu. Laura's hand is no longer securing a biscuit, but is again holding mine, her foot movement against my calf more aggressive than earlier in the day, this time purposeful and arousing.

"I've never been this close to a sixty year old," she says, as she moves closer, her hand removed from mine now upon my thigh, her foot against my calf still moving. "This is a wonderful day, and it's going to be a *wonderful night*."

Laura's eyebrow is arched, her face displaying a suggestive look.

Ouch! I flinched, a pain like a dagger in my chest. Laura's eyes are straight at me. It isn't the angry stare like that across the kitchen table within last night's dream. There's no hurt in Laura's eyes, only love. But she's looking into me, same as the dream, same as real life years ago. And at this moment I feel guilt within.

"Walker, what's wrong? Your face," Laura says with alarm, removing her hand from my thigh, her foot from my calf.

My face? Yeah, my face. I sidetracked Laura this morning when I quipped about playing dress poker at a nudist colony. I could never be a poker player. I'm too transparent, particularly with Laura. I certainly can't tell Laura why I flinched. "Summer;" I don't even directly refer to that season of the year. "Nothing, Sweetheart." This is to be a day of freedom, right? At this moment I feel like a prisoner.

"Walker whenever you call me 'Sweetheart' something…"

"So what have you decided?" says the young server.

Laura hesitates, takes a glance at the menu and says, "I'll have the shrimp po'boy with fries," before cutting me a look that could slice leather.

"I'll have the oyster," I say. The young girl retrieves the menus.

We sit in silence as two of the elderly ladies order another glass of wine. The bankers and lawyers stand and continue to carry on a conversation as they head to the door. Finally, before the girl delivers the po'boys, I begin to engage in small talk about the evening ahead, casual conversation finally coming from Laura's side of the table. She has chosen not to delve any deeper for the time being.

"What in the world caused you to jump out of the carriage?" Laura asks, in her own way informing me she's allowed the mood of a moment ago to pass. "Now that you're sixty, have you turned *squirrelly?*"

Squirrelly? Next thing she'll be asking me is if I'm wearing little boy underwear. *Do you have football players or spaceships on them? In your regressive state, I was just wondering.* No, today I desire to be as free as a bird. I want to escape, like that guy Jonah who headed in the opposite direction from the city he was directed to go. He took a boat, while I prefer to go by land. Today I desire to push yesterday, my trip to the woods, as well as other events of the week, completely from my mind. Until now I have. So block out the thoughts of yesterday. Block them out. I'll return to being "Mr. Responsible" tomorrow.

"Would you like for me to be squirrelly?"

"No!"

"Then I'll strive not to go that direction."

"Walker, I've been so looking forward to today. I don't want it to end."

***

Ring...Ring
901 area code; It's Rob.
"Dad, happy birthday. How does it feel to be sixty?"
"So far, so good. Your mom and I are having a blast in Natchez. We took a carriage ride and just polished off po'boys. Man we're full."
"You'll have to call and tell me all about it when you get back. I've never been to Natchez."
"You're kidding. We only live two hours away, and we never brought you here?"
"Not once."
"I recommend it; it's romantic," I say smiling at Laura. She smiles back.
"Tell him hi," says Laura.
"Mom says hi; she's smiling. I don't know whether it's because she's having a good time with me, or because you called."
"Well, I just wanted to wish you well," Rob says.
"Rob," I say, pausing. "I really want you and Celia to come see us as soon as tax season is over. I was thinking the other day that we could go fishing. I've got a client with a lake full of bass. He'd be happy for us to fish it."
"Sounds good. Well Dad, I've got to go. Tax season already has me hopping."
"So, we'll go fishing?"
"Yeah."
"Bye."
"Bye."

I don't remember the last time Rob called me. It's just like the other night when I called him. I need to make another call Sunday. I've got the opportunity of telling him about our trip. And when we go fishing...I've got to get beyond small talk. I need to go back to that night when he was in high school. I need to apologize. That would be a start.

I start the Explorer and we head to Monmouth.

Friday Night, March 9, 2012

Natchez, Mississippi

    We stand before a full-length mirror, Laura to my side finagling my bowtie for the third time. It seems that my neck has expanded since I wore it last. I tried one last time to convince her that going tieless with a sport coat would be fine, but she would have no part of it. This would *not* be a good night to alienate her affection. All in all it's been a fine day, about as fine as they come. We went to one more antique shop and toured two more antebellum homes. I've never held a hand so much in one day in my whole life.

    "That ought to do it," Laura says, backing away, tilting her head to make sure the tie is balanced, then turning to look in the mirror, she in her "little black cocktail dress," her hair up for the evening, her uncovered ears weighted with chandelier earrings.

    "Hey, we're a pretty good looking couple," she says, after turning her eyes to the antique mirror.

    "Not bad for a couple whose combined age is almost a hundred and twenty," I reply.

    "Walker, why'd you have to spoil my moment? I still think we're a good looking couple, *especially* if our combined age is almost a hundred and twenty."

    "I think we would look better without these outfits on."

    "Don't start into arguing for your sports coat again!" Laura counters quickly.

    "I'm not. I said 'I think we would look better without these outfits on.' How long til we're supposed to be downstairs? Maybe…"

"Three minutes, so don't even think about it. Besides, I don't want to deny you the pleasure of anticipation. Oh, and I've got one more thing to say since you've turned sixty."

"What's that?"

"Act your age. Let's head downstairs." She drapes her burgundy wrap around her shoulders and I slide on my standard black tux coat, the fit snugger than I recall. "Oh, but before we go, take a look at this room, the tall ceilings, the four-poster bed, the mahogany chest of drawers, and this antique mirror."

She's right. This room is really something else. A moment later I open the massive door for Laura and we walk onto the balcony that overlooks the courtyard below. A huge canopy covers the courtyard and it is abuzz with people hurriedly setting up tables and chairs. A gray-haired black man unloads champagne bottles near the bar at the far end of the canopy. He wears the trimmings of a tux, all but the coat itself, so maybe they do expect folks to dress up around this place. He smiles and nods at me and I nod back as we reach the bottom of the staircase.

From the courtyard I open another massive door, this one to the hallway that leads to the dining room. The broad hallway is lit by a massive chandelier and lined with wallpaper by Zuber similar to that found in the White House. The floor is aged heart-pine.

Before entering the dining room Laura stops before the antique mirror, causing me to do likewise. It is a moment of further inspection, this time in full uniform. I can't remember the last time Laura wore her hair up, and her chandelier earrings are a perfect match for the setting. There are chandeliers everywhere. My, she does look good. I stand next to her in my standard black tux, the creases of my facial skin far more evident than hers. My gray and brown hair covers half of what it used to. Did the creases become deeper; did more hair fall out today?

"Let's head to the dining room, honey," Laura says as she passes me an infectious smile, clasps my hand, and guides me into the dining room abuzz with whispers. Is whispering a requirement for this room? The people appear comfortable with the one they are standing with, but not with the group as a whole. This is a true assemblage of strangers, couples who have come here for a unique dining experience. Wait, there's the German couple from the carriage ride earlier today, so I do know them. No, I don't even know their names. Let's see, there are one, two, three, four, ten of us including Laura and me. No wait, one more just entered the room, the maitre d, a distinguished looking black man; his skin tone light, his grey hair thinned a tad. He's the man who nodded at me a moment ago when he was setting up the champagne bottles, and he's nodding at me again. And he's wearing a tux, unlike the three guys in sports coats, and those two funky-clad chaps standing together. With him, I don't feel so all alone, although I do feel "starched."

"May I have your attention," the maitre d says in a soft-baritone, before repeating himself, this time turning the volume up a bit, silencing the whispers. "We have made special seating arrangements for the evening that we hope you all will find enjoyable. We have set place cards on the table for each of you, so make your way to your seat, please."

Near the end of the table appear the words *Laura Wells* neatly inscribed on a place card, meaning that I will have the pleasure of sitting at the head of the table. And why not? I'm wearing a tux, the obvious "guest of honor." Yep, there it is. *Walker Wells*. I turn back to assist Laura with her chair that is so heavy it requires both hands to move. I take my seat, carefully lifting the chair as I scoot forward as to not scratch the heart-pine floor. The intensity of conversation has elevated to well beyond the whisper of a minute earlier, the group livelier, sounds abounding, conversation now enlarged to include a neighbor or two now that all are seated.

I survey the room beginning with Laura to my right, followed by a couple that appears to be in their late seventies. They have a sweet look, a grandfatherly and grandmotherly one that life has mellowed them to a point where nothing could upset their temperaments. *Right*, they're probably un-ignited powder kegs. You never know. Next are the funky-clad guys, definitely from "out of town." No, they're from "way out of town."

To the far end of the table sits a vacant chair, its wood so rich and warm, yet cold, lacking human warmth. I stare at the chair as it seems to reciprocate and I look away. I continue to circle the table visually as my mental impression of the chair lingers.

Next is a trim, handsome man with a thick-gray mane, his elegant companion of dark complexion with hair to match, a lucid "Rock of Gibraltar" atop her hand. The scent of high-wealth or extreme debt flows from their side of the table, as they continue to whisper in what appears to be a conversation reserved for a group more elite than the present. "No need to converse with the masses" is surely their motto. And next to me, the German couple is speaking at a decibel level that is nearly perfect for normal conversation, the clarity of words absolute, the language German, and I don't have a clue what they are saying. He and she are both serious, neither jovial, but in their own way friendly nevertheless. And they are both handsome, attractive in a practical way. And yes, they are younger than me by a decade or two. So if I counted correctly, there are only eleven chairs and ten people around the table. Someone removed a chair from earlier today.

"May I have your attention?" the maitre d says in his soft baritone voice, immediately silencing conversation around the table. "We're going to start you off on your five-course meal with lightly seasoned crawfish in a special wine sauce."

Back home we spell it crawfish, here probably *crayfish*. In this setting it would seem uncouth otherwise. Gosh, those windows are taller than the ceilings in our home.

"The green salad contains walnuts, grapes, mandarin oranges, with a light vinaigrette dressing. We'll serve a sorbet following the salad, followed by your choice of redfish, broiled and topped with lump crab and a wine sauce, or the twelve ounce filet mignon, which if you like, can also be topped with lump crab and a wine sauce. Be thinking about which of those you want," he says before leaving the room. Two female servers remain behind to pour our water and to further describe the meal.

Laura and I make small talk with the German couple who introduce themselves as Hans and Elsa, as we also do with the couple adjacent to her who happen to be from Midland, Texas. He has a booming Texas voice and her pronunciation of ice is "iiice."

"What would you like to drink?" the young female server says to me.

"I ordered pinot grigio," Laura interjects before I can respond. "She says it's the best wine to go with the redfish I ordered. It sounded so good I thought I'd go ahead and get started."

I hope Laura paces herself. "I'm going to order the steak with lump crab. What do you suggest?" I say.

"I recommend our pinot noir," she says.

I don't really care for wine of any type. I'd like a beer, but in this setting that would seem boorish. The couple down the table to the left would probably whisper "I suppose he wants it served in a can." Hey, sitting at the head of the table and wearing a tux, it's almost like I'm trading places with James Bond. I look her straight in the eye and give her my best impression. "I'll have a vodka martini; shaken, not stirred. Your house vodka will be fine."

"Yes," she says, moving on immediately to the German couple.

She looks like she can't wait to leave the room to talk about the "old idiot" at the head of the table who thinks he's so cute.

"Honey, maybe I ought to try one of those, a nonalcoholic one," Laura says. "What would that be like?"
"An empty glass with two olives."
"Oh."
"I'm only planning to have one."

***

"I'll have another one of these!" Laura says, holding the empty wine glass high in the air, moving it in a swirling motion. "Those high school kids were horrible all week. Perfectly horrible!"

"Sweetheart, if there's anyone in the parking lot, they just heard you," I whisper.

"Good! Maybe it's one of their parents. Hey, they are just as bad as the kids."

"Pinot grigio?" says the server politely.

"Yes!"

Wow, this is her third glass, more than I've ever seen Laura consume. "Sweetheart, don't you think you should slow down?"

She's leaning over, whispering in my ear. "Zoom, zoom, zoom."

I think that was her impression of a racecar. Now she's giggling in my ear. It tickles. The movement of her left foot against my calf is about to rub the hair off my leg. What the heck. I'm probably never going to Germany or Midland, Texas. These folks will never lay eyes upon us again.

"Your filet topped with lump crab and wine sauce. Watch out it's quite hot," says my server as she lays the plate before me. "Would you like another martini?"

"No thank you, just some more water," I say, waiting a bit to let the steak cool before beginning to dissect it, the texture of the steak tender, the lump crab and wine sauce adding a near-perfect blend of flavors. "How's it going?" I ask Laura.

"The redfish is delicious," she says, casting me a smile. It's a loving smile, one I've seen countless times, and never tire of. I think the food has served as a sedative. She's settled back to near-normal, her consumption of food replacing that of wine, her third glass still half full. The steak doesn't take long to devour. I was hungrier than I thought. I now await my bread pudding, as the maitre d makes the rounds to make sure we are pleased with the experience. The empty chair at the end of the table regains my attention while eating my steak, as it did while eating my salad, the same as during the drinking of my martini. It is obviously on my mind. At this moment I am peering and wondering, almost to the point of obsession.

"You and the Mrs. enjoying yourselves?" the maitre d asks from behind Laura and me, and I turn my face to his.

"This is sooo much fun," Laura says.

I lean toward the maitre d and gesture him to come closer, so as not to be heard by the group as a whole. "The empty chair, who is it for?"

He's pausing, a sudden look of sadness on his face, now speaking in his soft-baritone he says, "It's for a gentleman from Iowa. He and his wife have been coming down here forever, same time every year. Anyway, she died a few months ago. He came down alone, I guess searching for memories. I saw him peeking in this room this afternoon. It's sad, real sad. So there is the *empty chair*."

"Oh, that is sad," says Laura who has overheard the conversation.

"Anything else, sir?" says the maitre d.

"No," I say, looking at the chair, the emptiness so stark amidst the chairs filled with people. I wonder what that man is doing at this very minute?

"I hope one of us doesn't have to deal with that for a long time," says Laura pensively, her mood change absolute from a moment ago.

"Your bread pudding sir," says the server, interrupting my gaze at the empty chair as she lays the dish before me.

"Thank you," I say, offering a smile.

Conversation around the table picks up again. Earlier Laura and I had conversed with Hans and Elsa. This was their second trip to the United States. Their first had been a combination of New York City and California, "a flyover America" trip, quite a contrast to this visit where they flew to Memphis and are driving to New Orleans, making stops along the way. They have enjoyed their stay in Natchez, and are heading to New Orleans tomorrow. It all went well until he bought up my dash to Tripod's grave. Laura spent five minutes trying unsuccessfully to explain my action. "I've never ever seen Walker do something like that; *never*. He's not like that at all," she said before going on and on explaining. Give up Laura, after that lady from Montreal finishes writing her article, I'll be famous in Canada.

"So what brings you two fellas all the way from Los Angeles to Natchez, Mississippi?" says the man from Midland with Texas-boldness loud enough to wake up anyone who might be sleeping upstairs. His question is directed to the two funky-clad guys to his right. And I thought this couple from Texas was "Mr. and Mrs. Meek and Mild." This man sounds like he's fully prepared to drill for oil in Antarctica, or for that matter on Mars, anyplace they say oil can't be found. Compared to his wife, he's the quiet one. The two guys are looking at each other, each dying to go first.

"Sidney and I are in the movie business," says the one on the left.

The man just grabbed the crowd's attention quicker that a cross-eyed javelin thrower at a track meet. Even the "whispering couple" is attentive.

"Sidney and I are exploring the possibilities for a full-feature film; nothing small, mind you, something big, *really* big. We need an old-South look, and the prospects for this town are simply marvelous."

"What's this movie about?" asks the man from Midland.

"Oh, we can't give that away; not specifically at least. We keep the details of those types of things a bit of a secret," says Sidney, who this time verbally gets the jump on his companion.

"Oh, I guess we could tell them a little," says Sidney's cohort. "The story is set way back in the '80s."

"The seventeen or eighteen eighties?" I inquire reflexively, almost as spontaneously as my advance on Tripod's grave earlier in today.

"Oh, no, no, the nineteen eighties. It's about people turning up dead. They are being poisoned, and there is no particular pattern such as male, female, old, young, African American, white, Hispanic, Asian, Lapps, or whatever, all this adding to the mystery of the movie. They are *all* dying in this southern town. I think the uniqueness was what caught the eyes of our investors. They are looking for something other than helicopter crashes to send people to the hereafter. Back in the fifties and sixties it was six shooters. Then there were the car crashes of the seventies and eighties. It's mostly been helicopter crashes since, and I do think the routine is getting a little old, don't you, Marsh."

"Absolutely; no question about it," Marsh says, nodding.

"So, you probably ask, 'Why Natchez, Mississippi?' Think about it. You go around poisoning people in L.A. and they say, 'Oh, that's just L.A., no big deal. That kind of stuff could happen anytime.' Now, stop and think about it again. You set the story in a small-population town in the South, and you've got an instant winner! We *will* get some big-name actors," says Sydney before coming to a sudden halt.

"So what you gonna call this hoopla?" asks the man from Midland, almost loud enough to shatter the windows that survived the Civil War.

"The tentative title is *Dropping Dead in Dixie*."

"Huh," says the man from Midland.

The room goes momentarily quiet, followed by conversations, save Laura and me who remain quiet, these conversations again at whisper-level, each conversing with the person they came with, same as when we entered the room. The group has come full-circle. I scan the table again observing the people before I zero in on the *empty chair*. It draws me in, and as I stare at it, it seems to stare back. A chair staring at me?

In Search of Walker Wells

It's not possible, yet it seems that way. Oooh, an immediate chill is running down my spine, same as it did today at lunch when I had the flashback of last night's dream.

***

Laura and I stand at the head of the table, her hand in mine. With the exception of the servers who are clearing the plates, the rest of the group has vacated the room. Standing here reminds me of a football stadium thirty minutes after the game. I don't know why, other than this game is over too, and I'm standing here analyzing what has occurred. This room was and is remarkable, with or without people. The food was extraordinary. Laura had the time of her life, and I must admit that when I overcame my self-consciousness of wearing a tux at the head of the table, I enjoyed it too. The martini helped. Laura remains tipsy, the wine now more a sedative. Collectively, the group was strange, really strange, such an unusual assemblage. I wonder if the others thought likewise of me? A smile suddenly spreads across Laura's face, a happy one. She is having a pleasant thought. "To the room," I say.

"Sounds great to me," Laura says, her look direct, her radiant smile still present.

I can't wait!

As we head toward the door I'm compelled to veer left to *the chair*. All the chairs are empty now, but I am drawn to the one that has been vacant for the night, my hands now grasping the top of it, the wood now within my palm and fingers as I gaze at the grains. My hands feel no life. There is a certain deadness that I can't explain.

"Walker, I said 'to the room,'" Laura repeats, her look suggestive.

I release my grasp on the chair and I advance into the hallway with Laura before me where the collective group stands with Sidney and Marsh. Sidney continues to talk, mentioning the actress who adorns the magazine cover Laura has back in the room. He's speaking as though they dine together daily, and the group is buying every word of it. No one notices as Laura and I pass down the hallway going through the massive door out into the night, the temperature a bit cooler than earlier, a partying crowd before us with a three-piece band composed of an organist, guitarist, and drummer playing up-tempo music. People are dancing.

"Walker, when was the last time we danced?" Laura says with a burst of enthusiasm.

"I don't know, but we're not invited," I say.

"That doesn't matter to me," comes from a male voice behind me.

I turn to see who is speaking, a man about my age who is wearing a black tux. It's "instant kinship."

"Name's Sam Jones," he says, extending his hand and we shake. "Julie, my daughter, insisted the wedding be here, and that it had to be this week, the opening of Pilgrimage, the most expensive time to book this place. Her mama agreed, so I got outvoted. Go ahead, dance and drink up. One more couple's not gonna make a difference."

"Are you sure?" I say, hoping he will change his mind.

"Of course I am. Enjoy yourself."

"Thanks, Sam," I say.

Laura grabs my hand and leads me to the dance area. Wow, look at Laura! Is this a "mating dance?" It's certainly not the "high school-counselor waltz." She did finish off that last half-glass of wine, didn't she? Something has kicked back in. And me, I feel uncomfortable, and it's not just the starch in my tux shirt. Sam sounded like he's local. In this small state I could easily see him again someday. What the heck, I only turn sixty once.

"Let's get some Champagne!" Laura says as the song ends. She grabs my hand and leads me to the beverage table where she seizes a flute, downing her glass of the bubbly liquid as if she just finished running a marathon in July. "Yum, yum, that's good. How about a refill?" she asks the girl behind the table who obliges. I grab a bottle of beer; might as well. I approach my consumption at a much more leisurely pace. "Oh, isn't this fun? I don't want this evening to end!" says Laura before taking a gulp of champagne. We sit out a song or two,

Laura fortunately going from gulps to small doses as I continue to sip the beer.

"Oh, I like this song," Laura says, setting the empty flute on the table with me following suit with a half-full bottle, wishing I had a moment longer to down the balance. Laura's got even more jump in her step now. I didn't think that was possible. Hey, that might work to my advantage in a little while. I suddenly feel more pep in my step and glide in my stride!

Laura does all within her means to make the evening last, going all out on the band's last song. I feel an inner tug to send a substantial contribution to Sam Jones, father of the bride. *Poor Sam.* For obvious reasons I allow Laura to go first as we mount the staircase on the exterior of the home. I finagle for the room key as Laura leans on the wall, finally retrieving it and turning the key and doorknob simultaneously. Man these doors are heavy.

Laura flops backward onto the giant four-poster bed, her arms and legs outstretched. "I'm on a merry-go-round; haven't been on one of these since Rob was little. Wow! Roar, roooar, roooar! Are you ready 'Mr. Sixty Year Old?!" Laura says, signaling me with her forefinger, wiggling her hips in the process.

That's the most suggestive look I've seen from Laura since she was trying to get pregnant. "Yes," I say, removing my tux coat and slinging it to the floor as I advance toward her.

"You know what I'd like first?" says Laura.

"What's that?"

"Coffee."

"Coffee?"

"Tell you what. Go and get each of us a cup and I'll slip into a special outfit I bought this week. You're gonna love it. Roar, Roar!" says Laura, now on her knees wiggling her shoulders as well as her hips as she says, "roar" again.

What should I do? I actually backed up a foot on Laura's last roar. She half-way scared me. On the other hand is she singing the stanza "I don't want to deny you the pleasure of anticipation" one too many times? She did make the effort of buying a special outfit. Probably won't get one of those for my seventieth or eightieth, will I? She'll be singing the next stanza, "act your age" at that point.

"I'll get the coffee," I say.

"Rooar, I'll be ready!" Laura says, with one final wiggle.

I head down the staircase. The band is dismantling equipment and the servers are taking down tables. The guests of the reception now gone. Without my tux coat, I'm chilled.

Across the courtyard I enter a small brick building, separate but adjacent to the main home. It houses the service desk and the young man behind the check in desk is just about to shut things down. "Could I bother you for some coffee?" I ask.

That look he gave me is not "oh boy, I'm glad you showed up."

"I'll brew a pot," he says, quite professionally. He obligingly goes to a small room behind the counter, and within a minute the familiar sound of coffee brewing emanates from the background.

"Are you a college student?" I ask.

"Yes, I need the money."

"What are you studying?" I ask.

"Basic courses," he says. "It's my second year at Co-Lin. I plan to go to USM next year and major in business." The coffee continues to perk, its aroma sweet.

We wait a minute longer, this time without conversation. The young man is tired. He exits to the adjacent room and reemerges with fine china cups on a matching platter, creamer and sugar to boot, and starts to hand me the platter as I invite him to place it on the counter. I reach for my wallet and hand him a twenty. This is the first time I've ever tipped twenty dollars for coffee.

"Thank you," he says, a smile lighting his face, a burst of energy in his body as I lift the platter from the counter. He goes ahead to open the door as I embark into the cool air, crossing the now-empty courtyard, proceeding up the staircase, balancing the platter as best I can. Before entering our room, I lay the platter on the wicker table next to the door. Then I retrieve the key and open the massive door.

"Snunkkk, snunkkk….Snunkkk!"

Oh my goodness. Better grab that platter and place it on the table between those two chairs inside the room and close the door quickly before she wakes the whole place up. I do so, and now I stand before face-up-arms-and legs-spread-prostrate-Laura, still in her "little black cocktail dress" completely passed out.

"Snunkkk, snunkkk….Snunkkk!"

***

I don't look that bad, do I? I ask myself, turning sideways in the antique mirror, tightening my stomach muscles in the process, turning again with my face straight before the mirror. What to do with my time? There's no way I can go to sleep now; no way. I mosey to one of the chairs next to the table with the coffee cups on it and take a sip. Um, the coffee is rich tasting but cool. I think I'll drink both cups, as I have no one to share it with, so I do.

"Snunkkk, snunkkk….Snunkkk."

What is this on the table beyond the coffee platter, a Bible? For years I've had an aversion to reading from it, a personal prohibition as such, as though it would go against some personal code to read from it. With nothing else to do, I reach for the book and open it. There's a book marker three quarters of the way through it, but I choose not to pry where someone else last read. I read books from the start. Someone has written on the blank page at the front of the Bible: *If you have a drinking problem call the number below*.

"Snunkkk, snunkkk….Snunkkk.."

I'm bored. I dial the number.

"Thompson's."

"Pardon?"

"Thompson's Packaged Liquor."

I punch the "off" button.

What demented mind thought that up? That was bizarre; much of this evening has been. And all I wanted was to be *totally free* on this day and night.

What a way to turn sixty. Now what? I'm fully awake, no hope of sleep anytime soon. There's that magazine of Laura's on the table, the one that claims to solve all the world's problems, the one with what's her name on the cover that Sydney was singing the praises of on my trip through the hallway following tonight's meal. Yeah, there's that actress on the cover, probably ten or fifteen years younger than me. Hey, she does look pretty good. Wonder how much they touched her up? You never know. Let's see what words of wisdom she has to go with her good looks.

How I Learned to Smile on the Inside/ Why Divorce Has Been Good to Me "Oh, I'm really better off. No really. I've found marriage to be much too confining, too restrictive. I've come to an understanding of myself, my needs. I need my own space, and I really can't find that once I've made a major commitment. It's just not for me." Recently I had the rare opportunity for this interview. It's not often one gets to discuss topics intimately with a person of this magnitude. We were seated in an all-glass room in her Malibu home. We were not totally alone. Since Mallory's most recent divorce, Tofu, a Pomeranian, has taken up residency at the posh estate. "Personally, I think Tofu was an upgrade," she said, casting the Pomeranian a loving glance. Somehow I sensed she was not joking.

    I close the cover, placing the magazine on the table. I reach for a cup of now-cold coffee, and I take a swig. So she traded him for a dog, and called it an upgrade. Wonder if that poor fellow has read the article, or if he has simply left his ex's smiling face on the shelf at the grocery store as he placed a six-pack on the counter? Although I'm currently perturbed at Laura for spoiling the most anticipated event of my sixtieth, I don't think either of us would trade the other for a dog, not even at this moment. I do need relief from my current tenseness, and I think the best way to do that is to tour the grounds. The stars are out tonight, and I want to gaze at them. I rise to my feet, slip on my tux coat, open the massive door, and take a parting glance at Laura who is still sprawled upon the bed.

    "Snunkkk, snunkkk....Snunkkk."

    I close the door, letting it thud, unconcerned about awakening Laura. I head down the staircase, this time going in the direction of the gardens, stepping off the courtyard onto an antique brick path lined with full-blossom azalea bushes, their blooms all but glowing on the star-filled moonlit night. I look for the concrete bench Laura and I sat on this afternoon as we gazed at the azaleas and the blue sky. I find it and take a seat. It's chilly; I place my hands in the tux pockets to keep them warm. Wow! Look at the stars, not a cloud in the sky and all is quiet.

"So, what brings you out tonight?"

I almost jump; my heart races. The man is sitting on another concrete bench, down the path a ways. I wanted to take a stroll," I say. "I've had too much coffee and my wife has retired for the evening." *Retired for the evening*; I'm surprised the man can't hear her snoring all the way out here.

"I see."

"Yeah, just thought I'd take a stroll; the place looks different at night. Can't see the azaleas as well as in the daylight. The stars are really something tonight, aren't they?"

"Yes, they are."

The man goes silent. I'll do the same. A moment passes.

"My wife's dead. She died a few weeks ago."

It's the man from Iowa; the *empty chair*. The chair's in front of me in a flash, so vacant, so void of life, so real. My heart pounds again, same as a moment ago when I was startled by the man's voice. He's gone quiet again. Should I say something?

"Can't get out at home; it's cold, really cold," the man says, before taking another long pause. "We had been coming down here for years, same week every year. My wife enjoyed touring the mansions. I bet I've been through two dozen of them. I could have cared less about touring mansions, but she really liked it. You know, it's strange. As I sit here tonight I miss touring those homes. I used to get bored about her talking about this or that antique, or this or that lamp or rug. Tonight I miss that because I miss her so much."

He's gone quiet again. I feel for the man. "Why'd you come back?"

There is a moment of silence before he replies, "Already had the reservation; had it for a year. No, that's not it. I thought that for one last time I would walk down this path and sit on this bench. We sat on this bench more times than I can count. We'd come out here and view the azaleas. We even came out here a few times at night."

I remain quiet for a moment then say, "Your seat was open at dinner tonight."

Through the light of the stars and the moon I can see him shaking his head, staring at his feet. "I couldn't bring myself to be around a group of people. Just couldn't do it. I've been out here on this bench all evening; haven't eaten a bite. But you know in some unusual way it's been nice, really nice sitting here on this bench with the stars, the azaleas, and the memories."

He slips into silence again. And now we sit here, each of us alone on our bench, neither of us saying a word. I am seized with the thought that I must stand and leave, that I am disturbing the man's peace. I must rise, and I do. "I hope you find the rest of your memories. I hope you find them meaningful."

With the aid of the stars and moonlight I see the man nod. I know with so little light I shouldn't be able to see a faint smile on his face, but I think I can.

"I have a word of advice for you," he says. "When you get back to your room, hug your wife. Hug her while you still can."

I nod, but I don't say a word. I begin my trek along the brick path back to the house. Thoughts flow through my mind from all directions, the man's parting words now resonating the most, my frustration and ire toward Laura now gone; that and the overflowing thoughts of three and a half decades of shared-life, both good and bad, but shared, both of us still on the same team until we die. It is at this moment, in a flash, that I see the empty chair as it seems to stare back. The thought of the word *die* triggered it. I climb the staircase, reaching the porch on the second floor. I take a seat in a wicker loveseat to the side of the door of our room.

The *empty chair*; is it a sign? I don't believe in such things. Today, my goal was to be free. But it doesn't work that way on Earth. I'll never be free of inner-tension, not totally, will I? I'll never be free of *me*. It is the human condition. I sensed this as a child, although I couldn't articulate it. I have it at this very moment at age sixty; and it will be inside of me even if someday they say "he no longer has his mind." Somehow I believe this, although I can't touch it or see it. This is something I've lived long enough to *know*.

My thoughts and the events of this week have triggered something within me that defies the height and thickness of the wall that has surrounded me since my car wreck in college. I came quite close to tearing down that wall as I sat in the woods yesterday; and yet I did not. And today I ran, trying to escape me, attempting to push yesterday totally from my being, trying to assure that I gave no thought to it; and I have been mostly successful in not thinking of or facing what stews within me. And yet, while I blocked it from my mind, I can't from my heart. I cannot escape; I can simply evade. And this I have chosen to do. And here I sit in a wicker loveseat on the porch of an old home close to tearing down a four-decade old wall, yet not there. And what were the words of my soon to be deceased friend, Randolph Hollings? "It's always later than you think."

I rise from my chair, and enter the room through the massive antique door as quietly as I can.

"Snunkkk, snunkkk….Snunkkk."

I walk toward the bed and remove Laura's shoes, sliding the covers from underneath her, and begin to place the covers atop her when I stop. Leaning over, I wrap my arms around her, my breast against hers. For the moment she quits snoring. I squeeze her tightly.

Friday Night, March 9, 2012

Natchez, Mississippi

Dream On

"Let me help you with your chair, Ida," Laura says to Mom as she slides the chair against the wooden floor. Mom places her hands on the dining room table to steady herself as she lowers into the chair, and Laura slides her toward the table before laying one food-laden plate in front of Mom and a second at her place.

I gaze intently at the plate before Mom. It's fine china acquired as a wedding gift for Laura and me with tiny white flowers intertwined with green leaves inside a silver trim now covered with roast-lamb, twice-baked potatoes, green bean casserole, and a layered-lettuce salad. That salad is my favorite. There are two glasses in front of Mom, water and iced tea. I see this just above Laura's rounded shoulder, and to the side of the back of her head.

"Let me help you with that chair," Rob says to Celia as he slides it out and back, Celia laying her filled-plate on the placemat. Rob follows suit. *Errk.* The wooden chair scrapes on the wood floor.

It's nice to have the whole family together. We do it so seldom. I round the table and take my seat. Hey, I didn't have to slide the chair to seat myself. No scrape on the wood, no effort required, the chair already perfectly situated. Wait, there's no plate before me. Oh well, I'll arise in a moment and go to the kitchen and retrieve mine. I know the routine. We put the spread on the round-oak kitchen table that Laura and I have had since we married. You just pick up a china plate, go around the table, and serve yourself. Only unpleasant moment I can remember at that table was the night Laura found out about Summer. Squash that thought! There. Gone.

 Why, just recently at this table Laura twice "lit the candles," one time serving meatloaf, and another lasagna. Oh, with those thoughts I can feel a smile on my face. I think I'll just sit here and observe; this moment and time with my family is more important than food.

 "Rob, would you?" Laura says, as all lower their heads except for me. I continue to observe. Rob pauses. The room is devoid of sound, completely, so much so that it is deafening, if such a thing is possible.

 Why look, everybody is dressed so well. Rob wears a suit, Celia to his side in a pastel dress with flowers. Laura's wearing her favorite "Sunday dress," navy-blue, formal. She looks so nice in it. That doesn't look like a "twenty-year old dress" that Mom is wearing. It looks "fresh bought."

 "Lord. Uh…uh. Uh."

 Rob pauses again. He's never good at speaking in front of an audience. It was best that he picked the accounting field and not mine. He really has a good mind for it. I bet he'll make partner in no time. He and I must have a sit down talk soon with no one else around. I need to apologize. There's no reason to let that linger any longer. I got a feel for that at Mike Petty's funeral visitation. I should have begun the process of mending mine and Rob's fence a long time ago. I just haven't found the right time, have I? Like it's just going to conveniently happen. Maybe later today before he and Celia head home to Memphis I can get the process started. There you have it. It's a done deal. I'll do it today.

 Look at Mom, her eyes closed tight, no smile. Oh, I'm so glad she's here today.

 Is that a tear rolling down Laura's cheek? No wait, it's both cheeks. That's so unlike her. Although she's full of emotions, I've seldom seen her cry. When her father died a few years back she didn't cry until a couple of weeks later. When his death settled, her downpour was heavy, but brief. Why I bet I can count the times on both hands I've seen her cry, none of them hormonal, each time caused by a significant life-event. So what is it this time?

    Well, everybody's eating. The prayer is over and I didn't listen to a single word. Rob again said something and I didn't listen. I'll have to do better.

    I'd best go serve myself. I feel so foolish sitting here with no plate before me, so I rise, easy as one, two, three, no scraping of wood on wood from my chair. I round the table toward the kitchen to fill my plate. Right before the door I feel compelled to turn and look back, and I do, viewing the room from my vantage of a few minutes ago, peering over the top of Laura's shoulder. Mom's eating. Each minute detail is so vivid; quite so. Beyond Mom I look at the puddle of parallel lines of gold, rust, green, and white flowing against the reddish-brown grains of heart-pine floor, my eyes now looking up that curtain that drapes the French door. The puddle of the curtain against the wood floor is similar to that at Monmouth, only smaller, less magnificent. My eyes look up from the floor to the empty chair at the end of the table. I stare at it and it seems to reciprocate. It's my place at the table. It's where I sit. It's where I've always sat. It's empty. It's vacant. No one is sitting in my chair. It's empty! My chair is empty! The chair is empty! My heart's pounding as it never has before. Pounding! Pounding!

In Search of Walker Wells

Saturday, March 10, 2012

Natchez, Mississippi

    I hear myself breathing, where am I? Where am I! Oh, my chest is about to burst! Blood is flowing wildly within. Calm down, Walker; calm down. The weight of heavy covers surrounds me. Laura is next to me and I can hear her breathing lightly. I can feel her. She's wearing a dress? I'm at Monmouth, age sixty years and one day, and it's still dark, save for the red light on that digital clock that reads *5:03*. I don't sleep long; not when I have dreams like that one. I'm wide wake now; couldn't go back to sleep, even if I wanted to, which I don't. No telling what the next dream would be about. I'll get up, slip on some clothes, wrap myself in my tux coat, and sit on that wicker loveseat on the porch. I'll turn on the porch light and try to read.

    Ooh that arch and ankle hurt. I stretch it a bit. I'm crossing the Oriental rug, now onto planks of pine, the wood cool against my feet. Where's that switch to the lamp beside the table? There it is. I don't think this will awaken Laura; although she's not snoring, she's still out of it. I put on my pants, shirt, shoes, and finally the coat. Gosh, I'm still riled. Slow down, Walker. Slow your heart rate and body down. So, what do I grab, Laura's magazine that contains the answers to solving all of the earth's ills, or the liquor store version of the Bible? I grab the Bible. When I opened it the last time I didn't get what I expected, although I'm not exactly sure what I did expect. Maybe this time my motives will be purer. Last night I was looking for escape. Today I am looking for answers. I turn off the lamp, flick the switch for the porch light, open the massive door, and close it without a thud.

This wicker loveseat is far more comfortable than the concrete bench. Brr, it's chilly. The Bible goes on the wicker table to my side as I secure my hands under my armpits to keep them warm. Where did the stars go? No moon either, so that means no visible sunrise. There's a slight breeze and a cool mist in the air. My heart races. Breathe deep, Walker. One, two, three. Count slowly, take a deep breath. Now another. That's better. Slow the pulse down. There. I shift my position in the loveseat.

What a week, asleep and awake, all of it beginning with my thoughts of the day Daddy died. I've had enough happen this week to write a book. So where do I start? Why not with Daddy's death. At the time, I was a confused little boy. I couldn't wrap my arms around it all. Unlike a slow death where one can prepare himself, as well as family, Daddy's death was sudden, unexpected, no parting words of wisdom or love given to me or Mom. I've relied upon memory for these, and for the most part they were good because Daddy cared for and about me; whether he said it or not, I knew. He left a legacy of memories.

But is that all there is; memories? Memories fade and people die, and when people die, if that's all there is, the memories die as well. Unlike Daddy, Randolph Hollings, my friend who lives atop the Indian mound, a man I respect as much as any I know, has lived to old age. If he has not passed this week, he knows death is very soon. He is preparing for this; and earlier this week he sought to prepare me. Thinking back to our visit Monday, his summons to meet was more about me than him. He explained his spiritual conversion that transpired years ago, letting me know his regret for not having shared it with more people. "In a matter of weeks someone will be shoveling some of this fine Mississippi Delta dirt in my face. If that's all there is, wouldn't that be sad?" Then he said, "It's always later than you think." I can't shake those words of Randolph's.

A short time later I was holding Mike Petty in my arms. Although I didn't know he was dying, looking back, I can see it clearly. There was that look in his eyes. I can see it right now, that pleading gaze. He knew his life was within minutes of being over. What thoughts went through his mind? What thoughts would flash through my mind? Waking up that morning, I bet he had no idea; just another day of life. Three days later someone shoveled some "fine Mississippi dirt in his face."

That same day I crossed paths with that elderly black lady, Pearl, stranded with the flat tire. She was convinced that the Lord had sent me to help her; totally so. I, of course, shrugged that off, thinking I was simply glad I could help, which I was. Then within the hour, it was... What was his name? Hudson, that's it, who prayed while we waited for the ambulance to carry Mike to the hospital. A peace came over Mike as he prayed. Both he and Pearl have faith beyond themselves, and beyond some other human. Their faith seems so simple. And yet, that may not be. We humans are complex, all of us. *Human.* That word has resonated with me this week, as if each of us is special beyond comparison. That thought struck me when I looked into Randolph Hollings' eyes, as well as those of Mike Petty. It was as if I was viewing something; no, someone unique and special, a total contrast to the skeletal remains of my presumed distant cousin, the duck-billed platypus-lookalike that I once saw in a museum.

I wonder if these meetings were coincidental or were these people intentionally laid in my path? A week ago I would have never posed that question. *Never.* And although I don't have an answer for this, I do know that three people I met that day had a common thread. Randolph Hollings' conviction was real, as well as Pearl's; as well as Hudson's. With each of them, it's as though I could reach out and touch what they believe in, although I know I can't.

Brr, it's chilly. I rub my hands together to warm them. I readjust my seat, then cross my arms and place my hands back under my armpits. The mist is constant. And what is that? I'm facing east. It's the first hint of daylight.

Larry Edson, dead for nearly forty years, has been on my mind. If life has an intentional purpose, why did someone who lived the straight and narrow die so young; and why did his mother who had poured her whole-being into his life have to endure so much? Why! Just the thought of that riles me. I'm sure someone has a clean, crisp answer as to why; but does he really know? To me, my answer since that time was that the creator took one good whack and set the universe in motion, just like I once did with the tetherball, then walked away and watched it spin. He is the *ultimate spectator*.

Throughout my life all my answers have come from my intellect. But this week it has not been intellect that has unsettled me, my inward being so disturbed at times. In my dream last night I'm disturbed by an empty chair; a deceased tree that's crafted by human hands! I couldn't shake that chair during my meal. It was on my mind on the walk back to the room last night. Then I had it in my dream. This time it wasn't Daddy's death. It wasn't Larry's. It wasn't Mike's. It was me. My life was over. There was no going back. There were things I wanted to say and do, but I couldn't. So what do I do?

Well, I think that between the hint of daylight and the bulb above I can now read, so I grab the Bible. The bookmark is at the fourteenth chapter of John, so that is where I read.

In this chapter, Jesus speaks, encouraging his followers not to have troubled hearts, and that if they believe in God, that they should also believe in him. Then he talks of the "many mansions" prepared for the followers. It's strange that I thought of this in the woods the other day, of my desire to know more, my need to know the arrangement of the furniture, the location of the lamps, and the titles of the books on the shelves. I must know it all, for that's the way I am. Well, look who chimes in to interrupt Jesus. It's none other than my role model, Thomas, questioning where the path to the mansion is located, Jesus replying it is through him, that he is the path itself, as bold a statement as any ever made. Philip, another follower, interrupts to say he needs more; he needs to see God. So what was Philip saying? All he needed was to *see* the creator of the universe; that's all: the maker of the earth, and all plants and animals therein, the moon, our sun, as well as countless other suns, some of which I viewed last night, many so distant that the lights I saw may have vanished years ago, their distance so great. Have I lived under the illusion all these years that Thomas is my mentor, when in fact it has been Philip? Have I all along sought the unattainable?

    Jesus challenges Philip by saying that by seeing him he has seen God, in word, deed, and substance; and that if he can't grasp *all* of that, then look at and remember the works he has performed. In essence he is saying, "If you want to know who the creator is, then look at me." Philip could see, hear, and even touch Jesus. I don't quite have that luxury, do I? And yet, there is a promise given as I read further, a declaration of an invisible Comforter, the Spirit of truth, availing itself to me to accept or reject; my call. Yes, I am left to accept or reject a truth I cannot touch or see, although I have been granted the reading of these words, and I have seen and heard the actions of others.

    Recently I thought of another Thomas, a Mr. Thomas, my high school history teacher, a man of great wisdom who spoke of trust, in whom or what to lay one's faith. It was in class the day when we were interrupted by the news of Bobby Fortenberry's death in Vietnam that he said that one might live to a point where he might lose faith in himself. All these years I've hung my hat on me, knowing I could always count on myself; that is until this week. Is it enough to put one's sole belief in a man who sought to nourish a plastic plant with water? Is my trust in a man who broke the bond with the one he promised to love? Am I a greater fool than Philip?

    I am a man with most of the luxuries this world can afford; but the truth is I have a troubled heart to point that my chest is about to explode. Am I ready to take the step for the cure? If I took the step, would I be accepted? I cursed God. Will he forever curse me? I hear the creaking door to our room open, and Laura stands in the doorway wearing her little black cocktail dress, her hair still up, chandelier earrings still on. She looks a far cry different than she did last night when she walked out this doorway. Her eyes are puffed, quite so.

"I heard you go out this morning. I viewed you through the curtain a moment ago. Come inside, it's freezing out here," Laura says, shivering as she speaks.

I place my left hand in my right. They're both freezing. I hadn't noticed.

***

The massive door creaks and closes with a thud as I enter the room. Laura reaches the bed, laying her head on the pillow, her face still pained, same as when I just saw her in the doorway. This is a perplexing moment. A minute ago I was at life's great-crossroad, and now I stare at Laura, the person I have shared countless moments of intimacy with, emotional as well as physical. I stand before her torn between begging to return to the porch to continue the path I was on, not knowing yet my destination, or whether to open up to Laura, and reveal my internal spiritual struggle; or whether to simply deal with this present moment.

"Advil or aspirin," Laura says, her eyes squinted, she breaking my thoughts. "Either will do."

"How about some pinot grigio?" I say. This is what I do, isn't it? I deflect. It always works in shifting from the subject at hand,

"Don't be cruel."

I go to the sink and fill the glass of water, retrieving two Advil from her purse as I return. Laura plops the two Advil in her mouth and chugs the full glass.

"Need another glass?" I ask as Laura places her shaking head on the pillow.

"I'm still wearing my dress," she says, running her hands up and down her sides. "The last thing I remember is that you went to get coffee. What happened?"

"When I got back, you were asleep. So I drank both cups."

"Walker, please don't be upset. I'm sorry. I really didn't mean to pass out."

I'm hurt. Strange as it is, two minutes ago I was at perhaps the most important moment of my life. But now I feel the wound from last night, placing my fingers in it, feeling the pain. Why don't I simply say, "Okay, that's all right, I understand, maybe on my seventieth you can make it up to me." Because regardless of how tempted I am, I know that would be unwise. I remain silent.

"If you go get us some coffee, I won't go to sleep this time," Laura says before flinching.

"Okay," I say without enthusiasm. I'm hurt, although I know what happened last night was not Laura's intention. Nevertheless, right or wrong that's the way I feel. I open the massive door without commenting and walk down the staircase and across the courtyard, mist in my face, to the adjacent building. This time the coffee has already been made. I head back. I lay the tray outside our room and open the antique door. Better grab the tray and close the door quickly; Laura's outfit is not suitable for public display.

"Put that tray down and come here," she says, motioning with her index finger.

I pause to remove my shoes and tux coat, then slide on to the bed. I lay my head on the pillow facing Laura. Our eyes lock. "Come closer," she says.

She flinches.

"Are you all right?"

"Something pounded in my head," Laura says with a pained look on her face.

"We don't have to…"

"Yes, we do," Laura says forcing a smile, as she presses her body against mine, giving me a gentle kiss on my cheek. We embrace tightly. "Let me help you," Laura says backing up a space as she disrobes me.

I reciprocate. We press our bodies close, my arms around Laura's body, hers around mine. I don't want to let go. We have made love so many times. When will be the last? I've never thought this before. I shiver, then squeeze tighter.

"You're crushing me."

"Sorry."

We kiss gently. Moments later our bodies unite. Although we have done this countless times, each is different.

This time I want it to last. The desire is not physical, it's emotional. Our embrace is lengthy.

    Minutes later I stare at the ceiling.
    "Walker."
    "Yes?"
    "Your eyes."
    "My eyes?" I turn my unclothed body to face Laura.
    "When we made love you had a look in them I've never seen before. I've asked you this more than once this week; are you all right?"
    "Yeah."
    "This week a man you held in your arms later dies. As traumatic experience as that is, I sense there is something else. I've felt it for days. Do you want to talk?"
    Here we lie, neither of us clothed, "fully exposed" as some would say; and yet we are not because I choose to remain cloaked. "There is more, much more. All I'll say for now is that it doesn't involve displeasure with you. I am going through something that only I can go through. I won't conceal it from you forever. I promise."

Culpepper Webb

Saturday, March 10, 2012

The Beginning or the End

With Natchez forty miles behind, I sit behind the steering wheel listening to the sound of windshield wipers moving at a pace of just-beyond-steady, and that of rain striking metal and glass. We drive the Natchez Trace Parkway, Laura asleep at my side. This road was built in the 1930s along a trail once used as an overland route back to Nashville by men who floated their goods downstream to Natchez. The intent of "the Trace" was to follow the trail as closely as possible and to allow the land along the road to return to its natural state of the early eighteen hundreds. The timber growth, both pine tree and hardwood, of the past eighty years is stunning. There's an occasional field to break what some would call monotony, but mostly it's towering trees divided by a two-lane road. This time of year the white flowers of dogwood trees dot the forest with an occasional daffodil on its final leg on the side of the road. I am in no rush, a good thing because the speed limit is fifty. I now know because I missed that question on my driver's license exam years ago. It's strange the things one remembers.

Laura and I stayed in our room until checkout before venturing back downtown for lunch at a pasta restaurant. We then revisited a couple of shops, Laura purchasing the wedding gift she had spotted yesterday, our walk between shops today aided by the shelter of an umbrella.

As we started to leave Laura said, "Take any route you want, 'cause I'm gonna sleep the whole way." So far she has kept her promise. My inner conflict has ebbed and flowed throughout the day. This morning while Laura was in the shower I picked the Bible back up and read more scripture, hunting down the spot following Jesus' crucifixion and resurrection where Thomas said he would believe only if he could see *and* touch Jesus. During the encounter of the two, Jesus offers Thomas the opportunity to touch the aftereffects of the cross, and although it doesn't exactly state so, one can tell that Thomas does not do so, that seeing and hearing was more than enough. I made a mental note of that, just as I did of the fact today I could see the effects of the sun, although I could not see it. Some things are evident without knowing or experiencing it all.

At this very moment I am so close to abandoning my path of disbelief and lack of trust. It's…

Blummp, blummp, blummp.

"What's that?" Laura asks, startled awake.

Whoa! What is going on? The steering wheel veers to the right. I try to steer back to the left as I press the brake pedal. My heart pumps like crazy! I have a flash of Mike Petty's wreck and I think about Laura beside me.

When the car steadies and slows, I say, "I think it's a flat," to Laura, hoping to calm both of us. I guide the Explorer to the side of the road, coming to a halt on a slight incline. "I'll check it out," I say, reaching for the umbrella on the back seat, and then opening the door. The engine continues to run with the windshield wipers moving back and forth in steady motion. I circle the vehicle, rear-driver's side first, then the rear-passenger, finally viewing the "pancake" in front of Laura. I glance upward to see an eyebrows-raised Laura behind the back and forth motion of the windshield wipers, rain pelting the glass and metal.

"It's a flat," I say.

Laura cups her hand behind her ear, her facial expression saying, "I can't make out a single word you're saying."

"It's a flat!" I yell, as Laura shrugs her shoulders, followed by the raising her arms, her hands extended. The

Explorer is on an incline. Attempting to change a flat here could prove dangerous. A moment later I'm seated next to Laura, reaching over my seat, laying the umbrella on the back seat.

"What should we do?" Laura says with a look of concern on her face.

"I'm going to drive forward because we're on a slope. I don't want the vehicle to fall or to roll over on me while I'm changing the tire."

I edge the Explorer forward, the right tires rolling over the grass on the side of the road. There's a bend in the road fifty feet ahead, and I have no clue what lies beyond. We make the bend, and the road slopes downward, finally leveling about a hundred yards beyond. "Wait here until I get the jack," I say, cutting the engine. "Now that we're level, things are going to be fine," I say as I step back out into the rain and round the Explorer, opening the hatch. Let's see, I'll remove the cover to the compartment that contains what I need. There's the jack and the thingamajig that I place in to make it rise. Where's the lug wrench?? How about in a clump of johnsongrass in the Mississippi Delta. I left it there when I helped Pearl Monday.

"Sweetheart," I say.

"What?" Laura says as she turns her head, viewing me from over the top of her seat.

"I don't have a lug wrench," I say, immediately thinking that this needs to be added to the list of dumb things I've done recently, including watering a plastic plant.

"You mean this vehicle didn't come with one?"

"I changed a flat for a lady in the Delta Monday, and I left it lying on the ground."

"Walker, when are you going to quit losing things? You can't find your car keys and schedule calendar half the time."

"After I'm eighty; I hear people's awareness level improves with old age."

"What are we going to do?"

"Call 911."

"No service," Laura says immediately.
"Try mine."
"Nada. What now?"

What now? I'm not sure. "Hand me the umbrella. Somebody will happen along eventually and maybe they'll be kind enough to stop." I cut on the hazard lights.

Culpepper Webb

***

How long has it been? At least fifteen minutes with no vehicles coming or going. The rain has slowed, more a sprinkle than a splatter on the umbrella. I see an old-three-quarter-ton Ford pickup that a park ranger could pull over for going too slow rounding the bend! I move the umbrella back and forth. The truck slows, parking behind us. The driver slowly edges out of the truck.

"What we got here?" says the black man. He looks eerily familiar. His skin color is medium-brown, and he has patches of cotton scattered through his medium-length hair. He's six foot two or three, a bit taller than me, and if I had to say, he's got me by almost a decade.

"A flat tire and no lug wrench," I say, as I walk forward to meet the man, extending my right hand to shake, leaving the umbrella in my left. "Walker Wells."

"Didymus," he says as we shake. "So you're missing a lug wrench. How in the world did that happen? My Ford came with one."

Man, this guy looks familiar. Hope he doesn't think I'm staring at him. It's as though we've met before; and that name sounds familiar, like I've heard or seen it recently. "Yeah, I pulled over to help a lady with a flat earlier this week, and I left mine on the side of the road. Make sure you don't do the same."

"Sure enough; well I got a jack and lug wrench in the back of my truck. In my line of work, wood cuttin', I keep stuff like that handy all the time, 'cause you just never know. Hey, Junior. Junior! Hop out of that truck! This poor man needs some help. That grandson of mine is strong as they come. Probably don't need a jack to lift your Explorer. Only thing is, sometimes he's a little slow on motivation. Reach on back there and grab that jack and lug wrench," he says. "Yeah, that hot bath's gonna feel good tonight, that is, if Junior makes it around here before the night's over. Junior!"

In Search of Walker Wells

I turn the thingamajig to lower the tire from the underbody of the Explorer, then lift it from the ground and come around to meet Didymus and Junior at the front of the vehicle, Didymus holding the umbrella. "Hop on out, honey," I say to Laura. Didymus holds the umbrella over Laura to shield her from what has now become fine mist. "Didymus and Junior," I say. "And this is Laura."

"Pleased to meet you, ma'am," says Didymus, while Junior simply nods.

"We really appreciate you all coming along. The truth is, I was getting worried," Laura says.

Junior pumps steadily on the jack.

"I reckon the good Lord arranged this meeting," says Didymus. "Now just imagine. Me and Junior was headin' to the house, I was lookin' forward to a hot tub of water. We've been out scoutin' the woods all day, waitin' for the ground to dry enough to do some work. Headin' to the house and we round that curve and here stands a fella wavin' his umbrella back and forth. You just never know what's around the curve in life, do you?"

"No," I say, momentarily reflecting on all the turns my life has taken in the past week.

"Life's always full of surprises. You always got chances for doin' good as you go. That's the way I look at it. Me, I'm just a simple woodcutter whose never gonna be rich or famous. So I try to be the salt of the earth, just like Jesus says. Here Junior, let me hold those lug nuts," says Didymus, reaching down as Junior hands them to him while remaining silent, his face showing neither smile nor frown, my having no read as to what might be going through Junior's mind.

Didymus starts back up, "Like I was sayin', you never know what's around the bend in the road; might not want to know. Main thing is, you gotta keep your eyes open; can't go along with 'em closed. And as you go, the Lord's putting signs and people in front of you all the time. Problem is, most folks don't notice; or truth is, they don't wanta take notice. Yep, people and signs are in front of us all the time; but we gotta open our eyes and deal with what's in front of us." Didymus pauses as if to collect his next thought. He looks and sounds familiar. "Why just a few minutes ago, I had no idea that when I rounded that bend that you and the Mrs. would be out here stranded. Suddenly the need to stop for you was more important than my hot bath; although that bath sure does sound good. Yep, it was no chance that me and Junior happened along just now. It was the Lord that arranged this moment, and that's all there is to it, end of discussion. Let me hand these to you one at a time," Didymus says, as he hands Junior a lug nut.

I'm staring at Didymus again; can't help it. His face and deep-baritone voice seem so familiar, eerily so. "You sure we haven't met before?" I say, as Didymus hands Junior another lug nut.

"Can't imagine that," Didymus says, as he looks at me. "I'm out in the woods most of the time, and don't get to town often."

Junior stands, and takes the flat tire to the back of the Explorer, returning to grab the jack and lug wrench as I continue to stare at Didymus.

"Is there anything else I can do?" I say, reaching for my wallet, opening the door just in case. My desire is neither to insult, nor shortchange.

"Nope; use your right hand not your left," Didymus says, as he extends his hand to shake and we do. "We best be headin' to the house, Junior, 'cause that hot bath is callin' my name. Good to meet y'all," Didymus says to Laura and me, as he pauses to look at a clump of daffodils on their last leg, just to the side of the Explorer. "You know, won't be too much longer we'll all be pushin' up daffodils, dead and gone. We best be doin' today what we need to do today."

A moment later I'm back in the Explorer, Laura beside me. We watch the old Ford three-quarter ton slowly edge up the road, eventually losing the truck in my sight. Rather than starting the engine, I choose to catch my breath.

"Those sure were nice men, weren't they? What would we have done if they hadn't come along?" Laura asks, then pauses. "I didn't see you pay them anything. Did you?"

"No."

"Walker!"

"Didymus made it clear in his own way that he didn't want money.

"Then that makes the things he did all the more important."

"Yes it does." It really does, doesn't it? There was nothing selfish or self-serving about him. He'd been out in this mess all day, and he stopped to help rather than drive past us. I bet he'd been daydreaming since this morning about that warm tub of water, his body up to his neck in it. It's his faith that caused him to stop and help.

"Why don't you go back to sleep," I say to Laura to which she agrees as she lays her head against the passenger window. Her body is motionless within no time.

All is quiet, and for a moment my mind is blank, until I am seized by the thought of Mr. Thomas, my high school history teacher that I thought of the other day; my real-life experience on the day we learned in class of Bobby Fortenberry's death in Vietnam, the day he said that someone might live to the point in life when he no longer even believed in himself; at least totally so. For me that day is today. With the exception of formal education, Didymus is an exact replica of Mr. Thomas. Exact: his looks, his deep-baritone voice, his mannerisms, his unselfish nature, his seeking direction from God. My meeting with Didymus is now more profound than it seemed only a moment ago, as if in fact it was not a chance meeting. And what do I make of all of this? I start the engine and edge forward off the grass, the Explorer now on full pavement as I head up the road. Laura doesn't move.

So who am I? Among other things, I am a man who broke the bond with the one he promised before the creator of the universe to love, honor, and cherish until the time of one of our deaths, and in doing so caused injury to Laura, myself, and to another. Although years ago, time alone does not change that fact. This is one of my many less-than-perfect steps, that I have taken over my sixty years. If I stopped to think, rehash my life, I could go forever recalling and reliving my sins of a lifetime. I would be left in despair. And all these years my belief and trust have been in *me*, a man who earlier this week left his lug wrench on the side of the road. How am I received by the creator of the universe? I have sinned before, and I will again, whether unintentionally or willfully. My actions thus far in life have proved I lack perfection. Is it by the path of Jesus that one such as me, is allowed to enter fellowship with the creator of the universe if I remorsefully regret my actions and inactions, and seek change? I have read and heard this countless times, but I have never accepted it as true.

    I have always wanted to know *all*. I have wanted to see, to hear, to touch, even taste and smell facts before accepting them. Is a man who waters a plastic plant capable of being all-knowing? Just as with the account of Philip I read about this morning, I too have been a man who has sought, almost demanded to the see the creator of the universe. Creation itself is well beyond my comprehension. And if the universe is beyond my comprehension, would not the creator of it be even more so? Jesus' reply to Philip was that by seeing him, he had in essence seen the Father; and if that were not enough, then he should recall the signs he had observed. This week I have had signs and encounters that have gone far beyond coincidental, one within the past few minutes. So, what is enough for *me*? Am I a fool for accepting You? Or, am I a fool for not accepting You? Randolph Hollings with his blue eyes straight upon mine said, "It's always later than you think." I cannot forget his gaze or words. While on this planet I will never understand the why of everything. I know that now. My soul longs for acceptance, and I seek forgiveness, especially for my gravest sin of all. *I cursed You.* Will you forgive me? Just as I gazed into Laura's eyes many years ago and said "I do," I, at this moment, say aloud, "I do." Through your Son and his sacrifice I accept You; not until death do I part, but forever. Will You accept me?

What is that before me? Lights in all directions! I pass though beams of light with colors surrounding me. My chest pounds! I feel blood flowing through my entire body. I'm barely able to breath. Then the lights that engulfed me are gone. I look through the rearview to see light of many colors in the road, my heart still pounding. I bring the Explorer to a slow stop, trying not to wake Laura. Beautiful fields are on both sides of the road. The ground is level.

"What's going on?" Laura says. "Why are you stopping? Why are you getting out?"

"I love you," I say. "I'll be back in a minute." I face south, the direction from which I've come, the beams of light still in the road. It is the end of a rainbow, a bow that extends high into the sky before flowing downward beyond the woods to the west. Look at the sun in the west! I can see it fully now, the cloud that covered it partially has moved on leaving the fiery-orange ball fully visible, its rays bouncing off surrounding clouds. I stare a moment longer, straight on; it's bright, burning, and blinding. And now I turn my eyes away, an ache within, black and gold spots bouncing before them. I close my eyes momentarily, and then reopen them, the rainbow still covering the road right where I came through it. For some unexplained reason I'm seized with the desire to run toward it, and I take off, not at my normal gate, but a sprint, a dash with all my might, my feet arched, the balls of my feet striking pavement, my calves taunt, my thighs straining in full-motion, my breathing immediately heavy, a burn within my lungs, just as in my thoughts the other day of football practice in the seventh grade, my exertion just as intense, my speed perhaps a tad slower, but it is with all my effort. I sprint! I sprint!

I enter light and halt. I'm surrounded by rays of sunlight: red, orange, yellow, green, blue, indigo, and violet, the colors blending before my eyes, surrounding my body. I see rays before and atop me. I feel them around me.

    Collect your thoughts, Walker. What does all this mean? Is this moment to be shared with others, or kept to yourself? What was Randolph Hollings' great regret? It was that he did not share his spiritual transformation. For all these years my spiritual-wellbeing has been on Laura's mind; and for even longer on Mom's. This week I have concealed far too much from Laura; but I did so partially because my story was not complete. And although my life's story is not finished, I have a story to tell. I have a story to tell! I'll begin with Laura. I will tell Mom. I will Rob. I will tell others. And now I must pray for the Petty family, as well as for Henry David.

The End